Jade stumbled over her words and cleared her throat.

"If you'd like to come by the farm, you are welcome anytime. I'd love to show you what I'm doing with my horses, and it would be great to have another person looking out for me. My family is worried about each other, but they have their lives and I'm here alone a lot."

Declan didn't like those odds. Being alone on the farm left her open to an attack by Livia or one of her henchmen. Though the authorities had torn down the crime ring Livia had worked for over the years, they had not rooted out every person who'd been involved with Livia or who felt loyal to her. Livia was the queen of manipulation. Nothing else explained how even after all she'd done and the hundreds of people she had ruthlessly hurt, anyone would carry their loyalty to her.

Declan had loyalty to no one except Edith. Livia Colton had torn his family apart and he had sworn no one would get the better of him the way Livia had with his father.

Yet here he was, sitting in the dark with Jade Colton, Livia's flesh and blood, and thinking about how he wanted to protect her.

* * *

**The Coltons of Shadow Creek:
Only family can keep you safe...**

* * *

**If you're on Twitter, tell us what you
think of Harlequin Romantic Suspense!
#harlequinromsuspense**

Dear Reader,

Welcome back to Shadow Creek!

Jade Colton is, in many ways, an outsider in her own family. While her mother's escape from prison has brought her closer to her siblings, she has never really felt like a Colton. An abusive mother and the loss of her father in her youth has affected her in profound ways, and Jade struggles to feel safe, even in her own home in the town where she grew up.

Jade's brother's engagement to Edith brings Declan Sinclair into her life. Jade is drawn to him, but her fear of trusting another person and her professional challenges—her newly opened horse rehabilitation clinic—keep distance between them. But Declan can offer her something no one else can—closure on the past through his connection to La Bonne Vie, her mother's former residence.

As Jade revisits memories, she and Declan are drawn closer by a common enemy—Jade's mother, Livia. They will have to stand together to keep Livia from exacting revenge on the entire Colton family.

I hope you enjoy this final book in The Coltons of Shadow Creek series!

Happy reading!

C.J. Miller

CAPTURING A COLTON

C.J. Miller

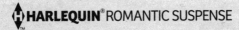

HARLEQUIN® ROMANTIC SUSPENSE

Special thanks and acknowledgment are given to C.J. Miller for her contribution to The Coltons of Shadow Creek miniseries.

ISBN-13: 978-0-373-40221-2

Capturing a Colton

Recycling programs for this product may not exist in your area.

Printed in U.S.A.

www.Harlequin.com

C.J. Miller loves to hear from her readers and can be contacted through her website, cj-miller.com. She lives in Maryland with her husband and three children. C.J. believes in first loves, second chances and happily-ever-after.

Books by C.J. Miller

Harlequin Romantic Suspense

Hiding His Witness
Shielding the Suspect
Protecting His Princess
Traitorous Attraction
Under the Sheik's Protection
Taken by the Con
Capturing the Huntsman
Delta Force Desire
Special Forces Seduction
Escorted by the Ranger

The Coltons of Shadow Creek

Capturing a Colton

The Coltons of Texas

Colton's Texas Stakeout

Conspiracy Against the Crown

The Secret King
Guarding His Royal Bride

The Coltons: Return to Wyoming

Colton Holiday Lockdown

Visit the Author Profile page at Harlequin.com, or cj-miller.com, for more titles.

To Brook. Without you, no books would be written and my muse would sleep far too often. Thank you for everything you do.

Chapter 1

Declan Sinclair was accustomed to the heat and humidity of an August night in Texas, but he was not accustomed to being this uncomfortable. If anyone other than Edith Beaulieu was getting married, Declan wouldn't willingly be within a hundred yards of a Colton—and this place was crawling with Coltons.

Despite Declan's reservations about Edith marrying the son of a criminal—a criminal who had escaped prison and was currently on the run—he had to admit that his foster sister looked happy. Her smile was bright and glowing and she seemed to almost dance as she walked. She held on to the arm of her fiancé, River Colton, as they circulated through the large gathering. The scene was something out of *A Midsummer Night's Dream*. White candles in lanterns were hung on shepherd's hooks surrounding the party. Long tables were covered in white linen cloths and the floral centerpieces provided bursts of color in pale purple, blue and pink.

Declan hadn't been involved in the planning of this soiree. This was all Colton planned. The engagement party was being held at the horse rehabilitation facility of River's sister Jade. From what Declan had been told, Jade ran the farm for off-track horses, but she also grew a few crops and had other barn animals, managing this almost by herself. The barn doors were open and lit, the glow of the light reflecting off the hay and wood, but the guests gathered outside beneath the pastel-colored paper lanterns strung together with Christmas lights. The air smelled of citronella and honeysuckle.

After Declan said hello to Edith, he could leave. Obligation fulfilled. It was a quick twenty-five-minute drive to the charming bed-and-breakfast where he was staying, where a comfortable bed awaited him. He wasn't looking forward to having a stilted conversation with River and from the way the couple was hanging on to each other, tonight they were a package deal. Though he and River had discovered that they were half brothers, neither seemed to be able to overcome the awkwardness and tension. Competition over Edith or anger over what their parents had done? He couldn't put his finger on it.

Neither he nor Edith had much biological family. Churned through the foster care system in Louisiana, they'd had each other and not much else. She'd recently connected with her uncle Mac and now Edith also had River, a fact that bothered Declan more than a little. He'd lose her to Shadow Creek and the Coltons. The thought burned through him. Wouldn't be the first time a Colton had stolen from him; wouldn't be the last.

Declan wouldn't find another friend as loyal as Edith and may never find another assistant as capable and as intelligent as she was, but as long as she was happy, he accepted her decision.

Declan was an outsider here and he wasn't working hard to become part of the scene. Sitting on a metal folding chair as far away from the party as possible, he was removed and his beer was rapidly growing warm. He had accepted the proffered drink from the bartender out of habit and social decorum, but he wasn't in the mood to drink.

His mood was dark and drinking would make it darker.

If nothing else, Declan admired Hill Country Farm for the prime piece of real estate that it was. He knew a lot about land and nothing about horses. This place would turn a profit soon, if it wasn't already. The thirty acres of pristine land, the riding ring, the stalls and the barn created the right setup for a Thoroughbred to rest and recover, and were also picturesque enough to draw donations and interest. The small touches indicated Jade took pride in her home and business: the weeded gardens, the carved wood signs with the farm's name and the manicured lawns were a giveaway that she cared.

Or it was part of the facade. When it came to the Coltons, trust couldn't be given too quickly or easily. Their mother, Livia, was the definition of evil and he didn't know how much of that had rubbed off on them. Livia had engaged in an affair with Declan's father and that affair had destroyed Declan's, his mother's and his father's lives.

Livia's escape from a maximum security prison hadn't shocked Declan; she had connections to get what she wanted and to stay on the run indefinitely. Edith's recent brush with her proved Livia still had courage in spades. Approaching people she had a score to settle with while the authorities hunted her was the ultimate in boldness.

Restless energy struck him and Declan rose to his feet. He walked the outer perimeter of the party. A dark car was parked across the street, the driver sitting in the shadows, his face hidden. Declan had noticed the car when driving into the party. The FBI was watching for Livia Colton. If she made the mistake of approaching her children, the FBI would be ready for her. She had slipped through their fingers too many times in the last five months. Working old contacts and lying had kept her hidden.

Declan watched the crowd and realized he was looking for Livia. He wanted her to show up today. With the dark sedan parked outside the party, he doubted she would be stupid enough to appear, but he had an ax to grind with her. Though ice water ran in her veins and she cared only for herself, he wanted her to look at Edith and see that she was safe and happy with River. Livia's attempts to hurt her had failed. Edith, like so many times in the past, had risen above her trials and was only stronger and better for them.

Declan took a deep, cleansing breath. This evening was about Edith and he wouldn't fixate on Livia. She had destroyed huge parts of his life and she didn't get tonight, as well. Every moment he spent thinking about Livia, was a moment of joy he was robbed of.

His eyes fell on a woman exiting the small, red-roofed cottage located on the property. The house was surrounded by tidy gardens protected by a brown wooden fence. The riding area and stables were located on the other side. She turned toward the barn, and the party, her blue dress moving around her shapely calves, her dark hair pinned back, but pieces framing her face. She was hauling a cooler.

Declan rushed to her. "Let me give you a hand."

Her brown eyes met his. She was young, mid-twenties, and her beauty and the expressiveness of her eyes knocked the breath out of him. "Thanks. I've been hauling ice all evening. It's hot tonight."

He took the cooler from her. "I'm Declan, by the way. I'm a friend of Edith's."

She brushed her hair away from her face, tucking the stray strands behind her ears. "I'm Jade. I'm River's sister. He has mentioned you."

Jade was Livia's youngest daughter. Though River was the product of an affair between Declan's father, Matthew, and Livia, Declan didn't think of him like a brother. Blood had little to do with those bonds. He considered Edith family and they weren't related. "It's complicated," Declan said. Discussing it tonight wasn't a good idea.

Declan should deliver the cooler where it needed to go and then leave the party. Interacting with any of the Coltons should repulse him. Yet, here he was, walking beside Jade Colton.

"You won't get any judgment from me. I hope you and River can work something out and be friends, but I know that might be asking too much. Just know that my brother is a good man. He's been through a lot with our mother. We all have. But he'll do right by Edith."

Her loyalty surprised him. He didn't want to discuss Livia Colton though. His anger was buried beneath his careful control and under the circumstances, and given the stressful events of late, it was ready to come roaring out. "Where do you want this?" He nodded toward the cooler.

She pointed to a table with five galvanized party tubs filled with beer and wine coolers. "On the ground there."

He set the cooler in the location she'd indicated.

A friend called to Jade and she waved in her direction. "Excuse me, please. And thank you, Declan. Thank you for coming. I know it means a lot to Edith."

He nodded to her. "You're welcome."

She rushed off to speak to her friend and Declan took the opportunity to fade back into the shadows.

* * *

Being the hostess of the party kept Jade busy and it was a role she enjoyed. Having many tasks meant she didn't get caught in small talk and avoided the complicated politics of her family. Her mother's sordid history had left scars on each of her half siblings, and Jade didn't verbally navigate problems well. Though Jade felt they had made strides recently, they were all still struggling. Until their mother was caught and returned to prison, Jade guessed it would remain the case.

Declan Sinclair, the man who had purchased her mother's crumbling estate—Edith's boss and River's half brother—was a total surprise. She had looked him up online. Young real estate mogul in his midthirties, multimillionaire. No one seemed to know why he had wanted La Bonne Vie. Seeing Declan's photo online had not prepared Jade. In person, he was almost larger than life. Dark brown hair, expensively cut, and those green, intelligent eyes. He was broad shouldered and dressed well for the occasion. Whereas she had needed her sister Claudia's help selecting an outfit for the evening, Jade guessed Declan's sense of style translated into every event.

Worldly. That was the word she wanted to describe him. The total opposite of her.

Jade had never traveled outside Texas. She had plans to one day, but between the chaos of growing up a Colton and then starting her business, she had no time or money to explore the world. Opening Hill Country Farm had put her deep in the red and it would be five years before she was turning a profit. Either that, or shutting down.

Declan likely had good business instincts. She could ask him about hers. Get his take on her plans. He likely didn't know anything about Thoroughbreds, but he might offer advice to steer her. Though no one had said it directly, Jade sensed her siblings and Mac, her father figure, thought she was too young and inexperienced to have bitten off this venture alone. Proving to herself and her family she could do this meant everything to her.

Her older sister, Leonor, had recently brought her five newly retired racehorses, whom Jade had renamed Tinker, Tots, Trace, Toy and Tiny. They were amazing specimens and Jade was enjoying working with them. Rehabilitating them and selling them would be another feather in her cap and she wanted to show her family her work had value and that she was good at what she did.

She searched for an excuse to talk to Declan again and wondered how to segue into a conversation about business. Every step of the way toward opening Hill Country had been a struggle, and her inexperience networking was showing. She couldn't ask River to help her. Declan and River's relationship was tense and complicated by Declan's relationship with Edith, who spoke only good things about her boss, but others seemed to believe Declan was cold and harsh. Having met him and spoken with him for a few minutes, Jade sided with Edith's opinion.

Jade looked around for Declan. He may have left. The idea disappointed her immensely.

Taking a deep breath, Jade took in the scene around her. River and Edith were only recently engaged and they were planning to marry quickly. It hadn't given the other Coltons much time to plan the wedding festivities. Edith looked beautiful in a blue dress. Claudia had a hand in selecting her outfit as well as the shoes she was wearing. The dress fell just above her knee and was the right amount of sweet and sexy. Jade admired her ability to pull it off.

Her brothers and sisters were there, surrounded by spouses and boyfriends or girlfriends or fiancés, and everyone seemed so happy. Jade felt a twinge of loneliness and tried to brush it away. Feeling alone while surrounded by her family and friends made no sense.

The party could go on for several more hours and the idea exhausted her. Offering to host had been her attempt to further her connection with her siblings. With the exception of her relationship with Knox, the Coltons had not been close after Livia was arrested and it was a fact Jade regretted. Since Livia had escaped prison, it had gotten better between the siblings as they united against their mother. Jade wouldn't ask anyone to leave, but she had to get an early start in the morning. Her animals needed her and as a new business owner, she didn't have extra funds to hire many hands for around the farm. She kept pigs, chickens and goats and, of course, her horses. With the extra noise of the party, Jade needed to check on them to be sure they weren't riled up.

First she looked in on her barn animals. Feeling secure that they weren't upset by the party sounds, she walked around the back of the barn, cutting behind her house and into the stables. Her path was deliberate. Though her siblings were friendly and warm toward her, while she couldn't put her finger on it, she didn't fit in. Trying in her own way hadn't taken her far.

Her thoughts turned again to Declan and she swatted them away. He was trouble for her. River's relationship with his new half brother had overarching complexities Jade didn't fully understand. More than that, Declan was La Bonne Vie's owner and as far as Jade could tell, that place brought nothing except problems, including becoming a hideout for their mother last month. Having lived through Livia's lifetime of crimes, Jade wasn't naive and sheltered, but Declan had a polish and sophistication she didn't. Getting caught up with a man more mature and experienced would land her in trouble. Being in over her head in business was something she could handle, but not in her personal life.

Assigning blame wouldn't help, but Jade believed her mother had a hand in her daughter's inability to fit in. With the exception of Mac, father to Jade's half brother Thorne and the man who had taken Jade and Claudia in after Livia's arrest, Jade hadn't had a guiding hand growing up. She hadn't been close with her siblings and Jade hadn't confided in them when she had problems at school. Same as it was now, except she didn't make mistakes in school, it was her life and her business that took the hit.

Jade unlocked the stable door and entered. Her horses were all retired Thoroughbreds in need of rehabilitation. Most were three to five years old and had either retired from racing or had never competed because they weren't fast enough, strong enough or had the wrong dispositions. When the horses no longer required her stable's services, she would place them for sale. Since opening Hill Country Farm as an equine rehabilitation center two years ago, she had rehabbed, retrained and had found homes for three horses. In her long-term plans, she wanted to work with more horses at one time.

Rehabbing horses, depending on the condition in which she received them, required dedication and commitment. The horse showing the most problems was Tinker, a bay mare. She was nowhere near ready to be rehabbed or retrained. After receiving arthroscopic surgery to repair a leg fracture, Tinker had spent the last month in the pasture during the day and needed to relax and grow accustomed to the changes in her life. Lower protein, higher carbohydrate diet, easy, lazy time spent grazing.

When Jade entered the stable, she sensed the tension rolling off the mare. She spoke to Tinker quietly and calmly, same as she did every time she was near her.

Tinker had a faraway look in her eyes. Though Jade rarely received the complete history of a horse's life, and no owner admitted to drugging or abusing the animals, she had the sense that Tinker had not been treated well. To date, she might be the most difficult horse she'd taken on, but Jade would not give up. Hill Country Farm would be a place known for sticking it out even when the times were tough.

Claudia had mentioned that some animals, as with people, were beyond repair. Jade heard her meaning, but she wouldn't accept it. Their mother was a monster. Jade had written her off. But these horses deserved a better life.

Jade sensed someone watching her. If Livia had crept onto her farm to corner her, Jade was ready. Her adrenaline fired and her muscles were tight. Rational thought struggled against her fears. It couldn't be Livia. Showing up tonight would be audacious, even for Livia. Jade whirled and her eyes landed on Declan.

"Excuse me, I didn't mean to stare."

Excitement and happiness danced inside her at the sight of him.

Tinker whinnied, as if sensing the energy in the air, and Jade reached to soothe her. Her heart thundered against her rib cage. "You surprised me. I thought I was alone." Taking in a measured breath, she kept her cool for her animals. If she got too rattled, they would sense it and act out. Part of her therapy was teaching her horses that calm was okay. They didn't need to be ready to perform at a moment's notice anymore.

"You were talking to that horse in a way I've never seen before," Declan said.

"You're from Texas," Jade said. Most of the people she knew loved horses: Mac and Thorne and her nephew, Cody, especially.

An uninterpretable emotion passed over Declan's face. "I was born here. But I spent a good portion of my life in Louisiana."

Jade mentally kicked herself. She had heard from Edith that Declan had been in foster care in New Orleans. Not knowing him well enough to pry, she didn't ask how he had come to be in another state. She didn't appreciate when people asked her invasive questions. Much of her childhood was filled with dark, twisted memories she hated recalling. "I love all my horses." Stick to a topic she was comfortable with.

"How many do you have?" he asked, taking a couple of steps toward her.

She would give anything to have something more to do with her hands, to keep busy. "Eight. Which is max capacity for us. I just sold a horse last month." Nine had been near impossible; only with Flint so close to finishing his rehabilitation had it been possible.

Declan tucked his hands in his pockets. He looked at the rows of stalls. "More room than for eight."

Talking about her big plans made her nervous, almost as if admitting her pie-in-the-sky dream would get her laughed at. Her mother had laughed at her. Her teachers had expected her to fail. After her father died, only Mac had believed in her. Without him, she wouldn't have had the courage to open Hill Country Farm. "I have room to grow, but I need additional staff to make that possible. Right now, I'm the only full-time employee. My brother, nephew and Mac pitch in from time to time, and I have a few part-time employees and volunteers, but the horses rely almost solely on me." She was babbling. He didn't need to know every detail of her business. Asking for his advice would be harder if he thought she was spacey.

"I've heard good things about this place," Declan said.

A pleasant surprise and her pride touched up a notch. "People are talking about Hill Country?" Or maybe Edith or River had mentioned something.

"Shadow Creek is a small town. Doesn't everyone talk about everyone else?" Declan asked.

He grinned and his smile felled her. Gorgeous and charming, he was sweeping her off her feet without lifting a finger. They had known each other a short time, yet she was drawn to him. "No one seems to know much about you," Jade said. She regretted the implication that she had been asking around about him. She wasn't exactly, only about La Bonne Vie. But she was curious about him now. She was hungry for more knowledge about the mysterious Declan Sinclair.

"There's not much to know," Declan said.

"I doubt that very much," Jade said. In addition to his interesting real estate purchase, he was wealthy and good-looking and likely had experiences and interests to share.

"I can tell you my big secret," Declan said.

Interest brought her a few steps closer. Confiding in her during their first real conversation, he must feel the pull too. "I'm a great secret keeper." An understatement. Desperate to be brought into his confidence, she waited.

"I'm married to my job. My calendar is booked and I'm rarely sitting around, but it's almost all related to work. So while I know there have been rumors about me and what I do and where I go, it's all about my job."

"All real estate, all the time?" she asked, not truly believing that was the whole story and wondering how La Bonne Vie fit into his plans.

He nodded. "The most interesting thing to happen to me today was meeting you and talking with you. I've seen you around town, but tonight you look especially beautiful. Maybe it's how you look when you talk to your horses. There's something so entrancing about it," Declan said.

The reflection of her love for her horses must radiate from her every pore. She lived and breathed her work, much like he did. "Then I guess that's something we have in common. My work is my everything too."

But Jade did feel beautiful as Declan looked at her, and it had been a long time since she had felt this giddy with a man. She was happy she had taken the time to have her hair styled at Marie's Salon and

Spa and she had worn the dress Claudia had helped her select. Declan's attention was flattering and the admiration she saw in his eyes as he looked at her stables made her proud.

The stables had been her design. Each stall was intended to be safe and comfortable. The wood was a lighter color, sanded and polished with materials safe for the horses. She had a place for the hay and food to be stored and prevented from rotting. Overhead, the loft held additional supplies. She had extra chaps, protective helmets and riding boots close to the hose bib for easier cleaning. Bibs and saddles, blanket bags, feeders, measuring scoops, extra water buckets and brushes had their places in an alcove of bins and hooks. Muck carts and cleaning buckets were ready; the ones she had used that morning were clean and drying across the way.

"You sound like me. All work and no play," Declan said.

A man who looked and dressed like Declan, with those smoldering eyes and fit physique, had to date society women. He likely had his pick of companions when he wanted one. But maybe that was what he was telling her; he was only interested in brief affairs. Jade shook off the thought. She was overanalyzing, a bad habit she had picked up from trying to read her mother's moods to know when to avoid her.

Jade kept her tone carefully casual. "Anytime you want to get away from your job and spend time here, you're welcome. There's plenty to do."

Declan studied her and Jade found herself loving

how he looked at her. Attention from men sometimes confused her and she wasn't sure what they wanted from her. She wished she hadn't had a totally manipulative psychopath as a mother. Though Livia had been great at tricking men into doing what she wanted, Jade wasn't eager to use those methods and follow in her footsteps. She often wondered if she would unintentionally do just that, so she was careful not to coerce people. It had become almost instinct to speak what she wanted plainly and honestly.

"I may do that. This is a great place and the work you're doing is good for the community. A positive endeavor," Declan said.

Unlike her mother's "endeavors," which had been dark and twisted. "You'd have to dress differently."

He glanced down at his suit. "You're wearing a dress. Is a suit that much more overdressed?"

She laughed. "I don't wear dresses most workdays."

"You could start a new trend and look great doing it," Declan said.

His compliment brought color to her cheeks. "If it fetched money to the cause, I'd do anything," Jade said. Almost anything shy of illegal dealings to raise funds. Jade hadn't meant to mention money, but it was on her mind. Working with charitable organizations to fund the horses' care and veterinary bills were her top priority. Without it, she couldn't keep Hill Country open. She didn't make enough from the sale of her crops and horses to cover her costs.

"Consider it as a way to get your name out there."

"My name is out there plenty," Jade said with a helpless shrug.

Declan smiled. "Lead with the name of your cause. I saw a post on the table toppers in Big Jim's for Honeysuckle Road. I had never heard of it, but while I'm not their target demographic, it got my attention. A picture of you with your horses with the cause would show people what a special place this is."

Honeysuckle Road was Claudia's boutique. Given his business success, Jade tucked the idea away for the future. "I'm devoted to making my farm succeed. My father was a great horseman. I inherited his love of horses." The sadness and grief at her father's passing never left her. It had been almost two decades since he had died and she still missed him every day. "He passed away when I was seven."

It was something she rarely talked about with anyone, and she was surprised she mentioned it to Declan. When Jade was a child, Livia had made her feel bad for being sad about her father and had forbidden her from talking about it, even though her mother was responsible for her father's death. Though she had gotten a few sympathetic looks from Claudia whenever it came up, the rest of her siblings had kept their heads down and their lips sealed. It was as if they knew Livia had done something wrong and they were too scared to say anything. That left Jade on her own. Growing up with a house filled with siblings, she had been utterly lonely.

Her father had been kicked by a horse, but the secret cause of his demise was one that Jade had kept for years. She had been terrified of her mother then and she was afraid of her now. Livia Colton was capable of true acts of evil. "Mac loves horses too, so I feel comfortable around them." Better to keep the conversation light.

Jade hadn't before had a friend who she could confide in about her family. To some extent, she could talk to her half siblings about their mother, but with varying degrees of success. Some didn't want to speak of her; others seemed to turn a blind eye to the whole truth. Though her siblings' feelings on their mother had changed in the last five months since Livia had escaped prison and began showing up in their lives, bringing more ugly truths to light, Jade hadn't developed an open rapport with her family yet. But to have someone, anyone, in her life who she could speak to about Livia and about her childhood, would be therapeutic beyond measure. To open up to someone and not worry about them turning away from her would be a first.

Cheering and whistling from the party floated through the air. "We should get back to the party," Jade said. Except she didn't want to return. Talking to Declan had been the highlight of the night for her. He was open and easy to talk with.

Declan extended his elbow to her. "May I escort you back?"

She took his arm. "I'd like that, thank you." When her hand set on the crook of his arm, she felt heat and a twinge of excitement.

* * *

Declan prided himself on having good instincts about people, business deals and properties. He had walked away from million-dollar deals because he didn't trust someone's motives. Since he'd been in Shadow Creek, seeing the Coltons around town was usually accompanied by the impulse to avoid them. The rule of thumb was that they could not be trusted: proceed with extreme caution.

That response presented a problem when it came to River. Edith wanted them to be friends and since Declan cared about Edith, he felt the obligation to try to get to know him better. Edith had strong opinions on the matter and, true to form, she wasn't shy about telling Declan what she thought. Knowing their history, she thought they could move forward in a positive direction. Optimistic Edith.

Jade was the sole Colton who gave him no pause. Her beauty was undeniable, but it was more than that. He witnessed her caring for her family in the manner she worked the party and she was warm and kind to her horses. Yet he sensed she wasn't on the inside circle of the Colton clan.

Declan shook off his strengthening emotions for Jade. His entire adult life, he'd held people at arm's length. The engagement party was getting to him, his affection for Edith coloring the entire situation. He wanted to believe that the Coltons weren't rotten to the core and that desire was influencing how he viewed Jade.

"There you are!"

At the sound of Edith's voice, Declan turned, forcing a smile. Her happiness was of the upmost importance to him and tonight was special for her and River. Though he had reservations about how fast they were moving, he understood Edith's unmet desire for a family. She wanted to belong to something and the Coltons had embraced her. If nothing else, Declan gave them credit for that.

Edith's eyes sparkled with joy and excitement. River was standing next to her, decidedly more stoic. A few minutes before, he had been smiling when talking to his family. With Declan, he was serious and seemed almost wary. They had talked about what had transpired between their parents, but the brothers had not moved fully past the awkwardness. It took a long time for a lifetime of hurt and betrayal to cool.

"Congratulations, both of you," Declan said. He reached into his pocket and withdrew the card he had brought for the occasion. Extending her hand, Edith took it. "Thanks, Declan. It was nice of you to come tonight." She knew this wasn't where he wanted to be.

He'd picked out a card and bought her a gift certificate for a spa she liked in Austin. His obligation was fulfilled. "For you, I'd go anywhere." Having survived a rough part of his life with Edith's help, Declan wouldn't forget her strength and how it had kept him going. Her optimism had pulled him through then, and he relied on it now.

"I have an awkward question," Edith said. "Since

you're the closest person I have to a brother, and you're River's brother—"

"Half," he and River said at the same time.

Edith shot her fiancé a disapproving look. "Since you're River's half brother, would you give a toast?"

"No" was on the tip of his tongue. This night was to celebrate Edith and River. Declan had made his peace with the fact that they were getting married. But to stand up in front of the Coltons and give his blessing was asking him to dig deep for acceptance he didn't have. "What would you like me to say?"

Edith touched her chest. "Speak from the heart."

The pleading in her eyes got to him. Lying to a crowd of strangers wasn't beyond him, but he wouldn't do that to Edith. Already mentally composing what he would say, he nodded. "I can say something."

Edith smiled at him and River nodded his appreciation. They would bond over their mutual affection for Edith.

Declan grabbed a glass of champagne from the bar. In the crowd, his eyes fell on Jade. She watched him and he read the burn of interest in her eyes. His interest had to be reflecting back to her.

Declan raised his voice. "Excuse me, if I could have your attention for a moment."

Sixty pairs of eyes turned toward him and the conversation dulled to quiet.

"I'm Declan Sinclair, Edith's brother. I want to say a few words about Edith and River." Unexpected emotion swamped him and Declan marshaled his control. Harboring anger and resentment for the Coltons, he had not anticipated any warm emotions regarding this marriage, but here they were. Edith was marrying a Colton, the family of his enemy. Though River loved Edith without question, Declan worried about Edith's future and her happiness because he himself had learned at a young age it could be taken quickly. Even the best homes could be ripped apart. The greatest love could be destroyed by devious schemes and manipulation.

Declan cleared his throat and pushed away the sentimentality of the moment. "I've had the honor of knowing Edith since we were children. There is not a more honest, generous or talented woman in the South. She is the epitome of class and style and I am so happy for her that she has found someone to spend the rest of her life with. And while I've only known River a short time, it's clear he makes Edith happy and for that he has my appreciation. I wish them both a lifetime of happiness. Cheers." He raised his glass and the crowd echoed "Cheers."

No lies. All truths. He felt good about that.

Edith came to him, hugging him tight. "Thank you, Declan. This has been the perfect night. Please make sure you get some cake. The baker is the same one we're using for the wedding and I want your opinion."

Cake was cake to him, but Declan walked to the table where pieces were set out on white plates with clear plastic forks. A white napkin was tucked beneath each. The napkin had a wedding bell on it and Edith's and River's names. The more he thought of Edith and River together, the more he saw their names together, the easier it became, like callousing himself to the inevitable.

Declan saw Allison Colton, Jade's sister-in-law, who was doing some work for him at La Bonne Vie. She ran a construction company and had completed several projects in town, including renovating a boutique along Main Street for one of the Coltons. He raised his hand in greeting and she did the same.

At the end of a long table, Jade was sitting alone. Declan grabbed a second fork and sat beside her. He extended it to her. "Cake?"

She accepted the utensil. "Sure, thanks. That was a nice toast."

"It's easy to say nice things about Edith," Declan said.

"What about River?" Jade asked.

Most people weren't so blunt. He liked that she was honest about her thoughts. "He's growing on me," Declan said.

"You haven't known him as long as I have, but I promise you, he is a good man," Jade said. She took a bite of cake and then looked around.

"Looking for someone?" he asked.

Jade met his eyes and the haunted look startled him. She licked a small dot of pink icing from her lip.

"Did I say something wrong?" he asked.

Jade patted her hair. "I know this is paranoid thinking, but I feel like my mother is watching me."

Every instinct to protect and fight roared to life.

Anger followed quick on its heels. When it came to Livia Colton, he carried only rage and resentment. Ruining this day or attempting to hurt Edith again would be met with a swift and severe response. His business acumen took over and he hid his reaction. "Why would you think that?"

Jade shivered despite the warmth and humidity of the evening. "Nothing logical, and I haven't seen her. I just feel it. Maybe because she's tried to make contact with my other siblings and not with me. I wonder if she's waiting."

"Waiting for what?" Declan asked. If Jade had some sliver of knowledge that her mother was lurking around Shadow Creek, he wanted to know it. How he would use the information, he wasn't sure. After the crimes Livia Colton had committed and after her escape from Red Peak Maximum Security Prison, she deserved to be punished.

"I guess my mother has become my personal boogeyman," Jade said. "I don't want to see her or talk to her, and sometimes I think I'm crazy believing she's coming for me."

Since Livia had been in Shadow Creek recently, it wasn't crazy. She had reached out to each of her children and not in ways that were pleasant and warm, nothing about a mother wanting to reconnect with her children. She was looking to settle some scores.

Jade took another bite of cake. "I want to protect myself and my siblings from any further interaction with her, but I don't know how. Mother always did what she wanted. Heeding someone else's words wasn't one of her abilities."

Declan had spent far too many hours thinking about Livia Colton and trying to understand her. The ultimate narcissist, sociopath and driven solely by her own needs, she defied understanding. Prison hadn't changed Livia or made her see the error of her ways. From what Declan could tell, she was the same self-serving, hateful woman she'd been all her life.

Livia had been thought to be in Mexico, but she'd been spotted in Shadow Creek and murdered a man. Then she'd killed a man in Dallas who'd threatened Jade's half sister Leonor. Livia had been spotted in Florida and was using old allies, look-alikes, prison guards, a judge and a Texas senator, to keep the authorities guessing as to her whereabouts. As quick as the authorities arrested and shut down her accomplices, the more people she found to help her.

"If you're worried about your mother, I could check in on you." If the expression on Jade's face was any indication, she was as surprised by the offer as he was. His motives were a blend of wanting to find Livia and bring her to justice and wanting to see Jade again. When it came to women, he wasn't usually this impulsive.

Jade stumbled over her words and then cleared her throat. "If you'd like to come by the farm, you are welcome anytime. I'd love to show you what I'm doing with my horses, and it would be great to have another person looking out for me. My family is worried about each other, but they have their lives and I'm here alone a lot. It's a big place and I'm one small person."

Declan didn't like those odds. Being alone on the farm left her open to an attack by Livia or one of her henchmen. Though the authorities were disassembling the crime ring Livia had worked for over the years, they had not rooted out every person who'd been involved with Livia or who felt loyal to her. Livia was the queen of manipulation. Nothing else explained how, even after all she'd done and the hundreds of people she had ruthlessly hurt, anyone would carry their loyalty to her. Human and drug trafficking, smuggling and money laundering were among her convicted crimes.

Declan had loyalty to no one except Edith. Livia Colton had torn his family apart and he had sworn no one would get the better of him the way Livia had with his father.

Yet here he was, sitting in the dark with Jade Colton, Livia's flesh and blood, and thinking about how he wanted to protect her.

Chapter 2

Jade hadn't had a crush on a man in months. She'd been too busy.

Too busy working on Hill Country. Taking pride in every inch of her land, she spent hours weeding, working the soil, maintaining her stables and barn, and caring for her animals.

That left little time for herself. Her personal life was the occasional outing with her half siblings, but even those had dwindled as each of them had found romantic relationships. Teenage sweethearts Knox and Allison Rafferty had been reunited and with their son, Cody, they were the sweetest family. Joshua Howard and Leonor had gotten together. Thorne and Maggie Lowell were married and had a baby on the way. Claudia and Hawk Huntley were crazy about each other. Of course River and Edith were the latest to fall in love. Even Mac and one of Claudia's new employees, Evelyn, seemed to have started dating in a very adorable, old-fashioned courtship. But Jade? Her last relationship had ended in a crappy breakup. Had it been important to her, Jade would have made time for socializing.

But she hadn't and she was booked solid seven days a week. While her work was a joy, it was a constant in her life and there were times she wished she could sleep in or stay up late to watch a movie without regretting it the next day. Some nights, she barely made it through dinner before she collapsed into her bed and fell asleep. After working every day for years, she hadn't thought of taking a break until recently. Very recently. Like when she had spoken with the charming and charismatic Declan Sinclair and she'd started to wonder what it would be like to go on a date. On a date with him, specifically. What it would be like to have a weekend away from work, the two of them taking off in her car on a road trip to somewhere quiet and relaxing.

She was getting way, way ahead of herself. Declan had mentioned he would stop by the farm to check on her, but that could mean anything and it certainly wasn't a promise. His words weren't the reason she had spent an extra few minutes that morning getting ready for work, ensuring her jeans were clean and her boots polished, her hair brushed neatly into a braid. She had stopped shy of putting on makeup, which would melt off in minutes under the sun.

Plenty of reasons to avoid Declan. River's half brother. River had issues, like all of Jade's siblings. Some of those problems were related to Livia, others of their own making. But his biological ties to Declan and their ongoing effort to form some type of relationship were awkward. He was Edith's boss. Edith would be her sister-in-law and if Jade was dating Declan, that could put her in the middle of something. But evaluating the complexities wasn't enough to put her off from the idea.

Nothing in Jade's life flowed easily. By virtue of the fact that she was Livia Colton's daughter, she was destined to struggle at every turn. The fear of Livia returning and hurting her or her horses or even outright killing her was her constant companion. Meeting new people was dicey; Jade didn't know if they would make the connection to her mother and what they would say or do if they did.

As she was walking across the training circle toward the stables, a terrible memory speared into her brain. Jade standing behind the split rail fence, watching her father, Fabrizio, train one of his horses. Livia stormed toward him, her fists balled, already yelling. Her mother always seemed to be yelling. At Fabrizio. At her. At Claudia. At the housekeeper. At the chef.

Fabrizio turned toward Livia, calm and cool. He was the only person who didn't seem to get visibly upset when Livia threw a tantrum.

Jade couldn't recall what they were saying or why Livia had been shouting. Jade's hands hurt and she

scrunched behind the post, trying to hide and turning her face away. After more shouting and several
loud noises, curiosity got the best of her and she
peeked around the fence. Her father suddenly lying
on the ground, tan dust blowing around his unmoving body. His horse, his most favorite horse, pranced
nervously near him.

Livia had raised her fists and lowered them on
her father's head. Again. And again.

Jade hid behind that post and squeezed her eyes
shut and cupped her hands over her ears. The ambulance had come. Livia had screamed and wailed in
grief. A police officer had found Jade. He had taken
her to the EMT.

The police had questioned her while Livia
watched with her eyes narrowed.

Jade had lied. She had said she hadn't seen anything. She had come running when she heard the
ambulances. She didn't know what had happened.
She wanted to know how her father was.

Livia had been the one to tell her that her father
was dead, kicked to death by his beloved horse. Then
her mother had embraced her and Jade had wanted
to kick her. But even at the young age of seven, she
had recognized that Livia was not to be trifled with.
Jade kept her mouth shut about what she had seen.

When her father's horse disappeared, Jade
mourned that too as another loss.

"Jade? Jade, are you okay? I'm calling for an ambulance."

Jade opened her eyes. She was kneeling by the

training circle, her head in her hands. The bright Texas morning sun hurt her eyes. Looking up, she could make out the shadow of a huge man, broad shoulders and crisp slacks, shiny polished shoes.

"Jade? What happened?" Declan knelt beside her, his strong hand on her shoulder.

It took several deep breaths for her to clear her head and focus. That memory of her parents pulsed through her like a bad hangover, the horror and the grief fresh every time. It had been years since her father had died and she had never told anyone except Mac and the federal agents he had put her in touch with. Even after Livia had been arrested, tried and jailed, Jade didn't believe it was safe to tell anyone else what she knew about her mother's crimes. Livia's reach was too long and Jade had been right to be afraid. In prison, *forever* hadn't meant that for Livia.

Her mother had escaped. Though she had never said anything, she had seen Jade that day in the training circle. It was part of the reason for the grieving wife performance and why she had pretended to care so much about Jade in front of the police and paramedics. When she had delivered the news about Fabrizio, Jade remembered the look of vicious joy in her eyes.

"I'm sorry, I had a sudden headache," Jade said.

She rose slowly to her feet and Declan did, as well. "Let's get a glass of water. Is there medication you need? Pain pills? Maybe an ice pack?"

His caring attention was almost too much for her and the wave of emotion brought the threat of tears.

"I'm okay. I have a lot of work today." Her animals, first and foremost, needed their breakfast.

"Jade, if there's something that needs to be done, I'll take care of it. After I take care of you."

Her nerves were still rattled and she hadn't cleared the fog left by the memory yet. Declan led her toward the house. He held open the screen door and she unlocked it. The kitchen was in the front of the house. Taking a seat at the wood kitchen table, Jade watched Declan. He got her a glass of water. "Headache meds anywhere?" he asked.

She pointed to the cabinet next to the black refrigerator. Her coffeepot was still half-filled, her mug and plate from breakfast in the farmhouse apron double sink.

Handing her the pills, he took a seat across from her. "Tell me what you need."

Tossing the orange pills in her mouth, she swallowed them with water. "You are sweet to care, but I'm doing okay."

"Then give me the farm to-do list and I'll handle it until you're feeling better."

She reached across the table and covered his hands with hers. Meaning the gesture to get his attention, it did more than that. Heat vibrated between them and Jade felt desire blossoming inside her. Her crush on him was growing deeper. "I'm really okay. I wasn't feeling well and I should have slowed down. You aren't dressed for farm work."

"The list," he said. He stood and started unbuttoning his shirt.

"I don't have an actual list." And now that he was taking his shirt off, her mouth went dry.

In just a white T, he was something to look at. He frowned. "Then I'll accompany you."

Sensing he wouldn't give up, she stood, too tired to fight and wondering why chasing him away was important. His willingness to help should be accepted with open arms. "You may find it interesting."

"I find a lot about this farm interesting." The look he gave her seared her to the core.

Her. He found her interesting and that was an exhilarating experience.

After spending the morning with Jade at Hill Country, Declan's shoulders were tight. He had respect for what she did every day. He'd needed to stay to be sure she was fine. It had scared him to see her crouched in the dusty training ring and she hadn't exactly explained what had happened.

Though he was behind on his own work, spending the morning with her had been eye-opening. Her work was tough and endless, and her devotion was admirable.

Declan showered and changed into fresh clothes and shoes and then headed to La Bonne Vie, his most recent acquisition. He had plans for the run-down mansion and the valuable land it sat on. Edith had come to Shadow Creek first to look at La Bonne Vie to fix up the house and make it inhabitable. Buying the old estate had brought Declan no satisfaction. The house was dark and haunted by the evil that had gone on there. He had tried to stay there, but nothing could fix the damage to that property; it was beyond repair. His new plan was to start paving the way with the local government toward rezoning the land into developments.

Residential neighborhoods or a commercial property would be well suited to the area. Shadow Creek was a small town, located about one hour south of Austin in the great Texas Hill Country. The perfect place to raise cattle, with rolling hills and green land, it was comprised of a central town and surrounded by cattle ranches. From Declan's experience, it had room for growth and that meant development opportunities.

The small-town atmosphere would attract people looking for a less hurried way of life. The shops along Main Street and local businesses were quaint and welcoming. Burnout from big-city living would send people to Shadow Creek if Declan provided them the right place to live. The local schools were underpopulated, so there was room for plenty more families to settle on La Bonne Vie's three hundred acres of land. The natural spring running through it provided the best source of water for local ranchers and was another selling point. He was already thinking of neighborhood names that brought to mind the type of living he wanted to sell: Spring Overlook, Well Wood Spring, Springcrest or Bishop's Spring. Packaging the houses with the implication that the homes would be luxurious and the neighborhood would be elite would allow him at least a fifty percent markup on every option sold.

Though he wondered if he would catch flak from Joseph "Mac" Mackenzie, owner of the Mackenzie Ranch that bordered La Bonne Vie, Declan would overcome it. Mac was Thorne Colton's father, the result of an affair with Livia Colton while she had been married to her third husband, Wes Kingston. Livia had deflected gossip about her and Mac by concocting lies about Wes, claiming he'd mistreated her, working to ruin his reputation. Wes divorced her and left his land behind in a settlement that gave Livia full custody of both River and Thorne. Until recently, when a DNA test had proved otherwise, River had believed Wes was his father.

From what Declan knew of Mac, his affair with Livia had been out of character for him. Mac had worked as a foreman on Livia's property. Livia hadn't been willing to raise cattle because their noise bothered her, so Declan wondered what exactly Mac had done at La Bonne Vie.

La Bonne Vie being run-down didn't bother him; he had seen worse properties and had made a fortune renovating them. The main house, built in a French country style, sat on top of a hill with a long drive and a fountain in front. The grand staircase inside the foyer, the seven bathrooms and eight baths, heated pools and beautiful barn: all spoke to the lifestyle Livia had led.

But the stigma La Bonne Vie carried because of what had gone on inside the house wouldn't be scrubbed from local memory anytime soon. No one wanted to live there. It was haunted by the people whose lives Livia had destroyed. Quite a fall from grace for Livia, to move from the mansion to prison. Declan delighted in knowing the drastic change had to have been terrible for Livia. She deserved every ounce of suffering she had withstood over the last ten years.

Seeing La Bonne Vie in its current state made it easier to tear it down. Declan was removing anything that remained in the house that he could sell. Though the state had taken most obvious items of value, Declan knew how to squeeze every last penny from a property. The house had items to be sold and Declan had them taken to a nearby auction house each week, where they wouldn't be recognized as Livia's. When he was finished stripping the house, the structure would come down, the wreckage hauled away, and he would start new.

A new beginning for the property and perhaps, a fresh start for Declan. He hadn't managed to outrun the ghosts of the past, but this effort was for revenge and closure.

The big fountain, thanks to the local spring on the property, was still spouting water into the algae infested bottom. The sight disgusted him, not only because of the grime, but because it represented everything Livia had been. An air of grace from a distance, but dirty and rotten close up. Livia had built everything on the backs of the people she had hurt and used. The house was dilapidated and smelled terrible from years of being vacant. The decor was outdated and water leaked in every bathroom and in the kitchen. The roof had been blown off in parts and several windows were broken. Even the work that Edith and River had done on it could not address the massive renovations needed. Those would take years. And while he didn't have a problem putting time into a property, being in that place depressed him. His home awaited him in Louisiana and Declan couldn't wait to return to it.

The one part of the property that had stood the test of time was the ostentatious red barn that Fabrizio, Jade's father, had built before he'd died. It contained twelve stalls, a tack room, indoor corral, a feed room and a storage room. Aside from the indoor corral, it reminded Declan of a large version of Jade's stable.

Declan hated being inside the house. Not a paranoid man, he was sure they would find a dead body somewhere. The police had brought out cadaver dogs when they were investigating Livia ten years before, but the land had a series of underground tunnels that had not been fully explored. No one knew exactly where those tunnels led, but Declan took great pleasure in dynamiting them closed. Livia had recently been hiding inside La Bonne Vie's underground tunnels and run off the land. Declan would not give her an opportunity to return.

Shutting down each entrance to La Bonne Vie was like tying off a part of the past, closing that section of the town's history. And it needed to be closed. There was nothing good about it.

Behind the house on the crumbling back porch, the construction crew had laid out items they had found.

Today's items were a silver photo album, a gold bell and several dusty books. Declan picked them up. They might fetch a small amount of money at auction. Flipping open the photo album, he found pictures of Livia. How narcissistic. Livia with Fabrizio, her most recent late husband. In every picture, he was looking at her adoringly. Declan couldn't imagine how Fabrizio had married her. Not even her money or beauty could hide how ugly she was inside.

Allison Rafferty Colton joined him on the covered porch. Declan had hired Rafferty Construction to help with the teardown of La Bonne Vie. He liked the pretty blonde. She was no-nonsense and direct. From what he had heard, she was married to, and shared a child with, Knox Colton. Declan didn't hold that against her. At least, not for now. It hadn't become a problem and it seemed in Shadow Creek, the Coltons were everywhere and into everything.

"It's been a productive morning. We've removed some copper wiring from the second floor. We'll take that to be recycled. The crew has been enjoying these treasure hunts. That's what they call them. Person who finds the coolest trinket for the day wins."

"What do they win?" Declan asked.

"I buy them their first round at happy hour," Allison said.

Declan was pleased to hear the crew were at least somewhat enjoying the task. They'd work harder and get the job done faster. "Interesting collection today. Those wine bottles and racks you found sold great at auction."

Allison glanced at the table. "I keep expecting we'll find another secret room and it will be filled with treasure. I've taken the measurements of the outside of the house and of each room inside, and we could find small spaces stacked with goodies."

"I was over at Hill Country Farm this morning." Off topic and not what he'd intended to say. The words had popped out.

Allison nodded. "I thought I saw something between you and Jade at River and Edith's engagement party."

The statement made him feel defensive. "There isn't anything between us. We just met. It was nice of her to host the engagement party."

"Why were you at Hill Country today? Looking to buy a horse?" Allison asked.

He didn't have time for a horse and he couldn't read if she was being sarcastic. "I told Jade I would check in with her. Livia is still out there and seeing this done to her house has to piss her off." Livia knew exactly what he was doing to La Bonne Vie.

Allison looked back at the house. "I figured that was part of the reason we were doing it. Knox will like seeing this place taken off the face of the earth. Nothing but heartache here."

It was one of the first times Allison had mentioned her Colton husband. "The town doesn't want it here. I wouldn't have torn it down otherwise." Not exactly true, but it helped that most of the town was happy to see it gone.

Before the town had known about the criminal enterprise Livia had helped run from La Bonne Vie, it had celebrated her and her children. They had been local celebrities. Livia had donated money to build Shadow Creek Memorial Hospital. Her name had been on the chapel inside the hospital, which had been renamed after her conviction. Her generosity had been the veil covering the truth of Livia Colton's life.

She was a liar, murderer and a thief and used people like disposable lives.

"I'll let you know if we find anything of major interest," Allison said. She returned to the house and Declan was left alone with his thoughts.

The finality of destroying La Bonne Vie would be the jewel in the crown of Livia being found and arrested. Staying away from her home was impossible; she had just stayed there for weeks. When she was caught, Declan would campaign for her to be transferred to the most secure prison in the South.

Livia Colton wouldn't see the light of day again.

Declan's nerves were tight. Another conference call with SinCo's lawyers and another week had gone by since Tim DeVega, SinCo's former accountant, had taken off with over two hundred thousand dollars, embezzling the money and then disappearing. Declan refused to let DeVega go without pursuit. The authorities hadn't found him, but Declan wouldn't give up. He had hired private investigators to track DeVega down.

The money was important, but it was more than that. It had cost Declan a deal in progress when he hadn't had the cash on hand to close. He was heavily invested in his real estate company. After acquiring one property and finalizing the development plans, he was quick to move forward with another property. Each sale netted him more money, and the more properties he turned over, the better.

He had his eye on three burned-out apartment buildings in Killeen, located in central Texas. The structures had been built in the twenties, renovated over a dozen times, each time cutting a few corners, until a fire had demolished all three. The violated building codes had made the apartments a hazard. Declan wanted to buy the destroyed buildings cheaply, tear them down and construct a luxury condo community with a view of the nearby lake.

Leaving the B and B in Shadow Creek, he stopped at the Cozy Diner. He ordered two meals to go. Though he wasn't obligated to, he wanted to check in on Jade. Her concerns about her mother were well-founded. Recently, in an absolutely terrifying ordeal, Livia had kidnapped Edith and had almost killed her. Understanding Livia's motives were impossible, except to say they were selfish.

When he had seen Jade kneeling on the ground, head in her hands, he had been scared and worried, borderline panicked. That reaction was a surprise to him. Caring for someone he knew so little about wasn't like him. He kept people at a distance for a reason. His father had betrayed their family, his mother had left, and during almost every other experience he'd had in foster care and in the business world, he'd had to watch his back. Keeping a cool distance from others was in his comfort zone.

Carrying the handled plain brown bag from the Cozy Diner, Declan stepped out of the car. He'd parked in front of Jade's house, which seemed to be the heart of the farm. Across the street was parked a dark sedan with tinted windows. It might have been the same one from the night of Edith's engagement party. Not very subtle. The FBI couldn't know how much the Colton children were involved with Livia, and Livia could show up any place, any time. Her connections and access to funds made her hard to catch.

Jade was in the round pen with a horse. She was wearing tan boots and tight khaki pants. Her white collared shirt fit her curves, giving her a casual and sexy appearance. In her hand was a long rope attached to the horse's halter, and she turned as the horse moved. Watching her, he was captivated again by her intensity and focus. He approached the five-foot-high slatted fence. Not wanting to break her concentration, he waited.

After a few seconds, she turned to him and waved. The smile on her face socked him in the gut. She was beautiful. He motioned for her to come over. She said something to her horse and then approached.

"Hey, stranger," she said. "Two days in a row. How did I get so lucky?"

"I told you I would come by. I know you're anxious about what's been going on around Shadow Creek."

Jade looked over her shoulder. "I've called Shadow Creek home all my life and I love the wide-open spaces. But I've been starting to wish I wasn't as isolated out here. It gets creepy."

"Do you have time to take a break?" He held up the bag. Not mentioning the incident from the day before, it crossed his mind a filling meal would help her through the day.

"Let me take Tiny to graze. Then yes, thank you—that sounds great."

As Jade took care of her horse, Declan looked to where he had seen the dark sedan. It was gone. Many Coltons in the region meant the authorities had to split their time. Couldn't sit on Jade's farm around the clock. Though Declan liked the idea of them being close in case Livia approached her daughter, from what Declan knew of the local authorities, led by Sheriff Bud Jeffries, he couldn't count on them to keep the Coltons safe. Bud didn't hide his blatant dislike for the Coltons. Bud Jeffries wasn't an idiot, but he was inept and stubborn. He wanted to run the sheriff's office in his own way and he didn't like anyone telling him what to do.

Jade appeared again. She walked with a swagger and the sway of her hips captivated him. Declan was lost. She was everything a Texas woman should be, except that she was the daughter of his enemy.

"We can eat under the acacia tree," she said, pointing a distance away from the house.

He followed her and then sat in the grass beneath the tree, enjoying the shade. Declan set out the food, letting Jade pick first. She selected the club sandwich: turkey, black forest ham and roast beef, cucumbers, tomatoes and lettuce on a fresh sub roll. Declan unwrapped his cold cut with ham, salami and bologna on a wheat roll with mayonnaise and tomato.

"I asked the waitress at the Cozy Diner for the two best sellers," Declan said.

"Good choice. They're both great picks," Jade said, taking a bite of sandwich. She closed her eyes and leaned her head back against the tree.

They ate in comfortable silence.

"I appreciate this, Declan," Jade said. "I sometimes forget to take breaks and it catches up to me."

"Is that what happened yesterday?" he asked.

After a thoughtful moment, she shook her head. "That was just a bunch of problems and worries catching up to me. My farm hasn't been open long and while I love the work, there's so much of it. It will be years before I'm out from under the paperwork and the financial pressures. I run this place on donations and the occassional horse sale, and I try hard not to dip too often into my salary, but it's hard. I want to do all I can for the animals and it's never enough. I've been giving riding lessons when I have time for extra money, but not all my horses are amenable or able to do that, and it takes away from working with the horses that need the most attention."

Declan didn't like to talk about money outside a business setting. When he had been younger and had none, he hadn't felt like enough. When he had finally made his fortune, he had learned that friends weren't necessarily happy that his hard work had paid off. A few even resented his fortune. Some expected he would give them money when they needed it, even when their definition of need—a brand-new car, a trip to a tropical island, a coveted piece of jewelry— didn't align with his. Some criticized presents as not being extravagant enough. It was the ugly side of having money and people knowing it.

Jade took a sip from one of the water bottles he'd bought at the Cozy Diner. "One of my biggest costs is the veterinary bills. The horses come to me in various states of bad health. If I were a veterinarian, I could treat my horses without that expense. Don't get me wrong. I have a great vet who doesn't charge me nearly what she could. But it's a big part of the budget."

Becoming a veterinarian to treat her horses didn't seem like the most time- or cost-effective option. Raising the money herself or finding a marketable product to supplement her income would be easier. Jade had a great place and he could think of several moneymaking opportunities. "Do you plan to go to vet school?"

Jade sighed. "I can't. Every penny I have is wrapped up in this place. I wouldn't have the time and I can't afford to hire anyone to run the farm. And as much as I'm ashamed to admit this, I don't even know if I could get into veterinary school. My grades in high school were bad and I haven't gone to college."

"Yet you've figured out how to purchase land and set up this elaborate horse rehabilitation business. You must have a knack for animals and numbers. If you were interested, you could go to school for business, learn ways to grow your farm."

Jade stretched her legs out in front of her. "You think I could do that?"

"I know your time is limited, but you could manage." She could find a way if she were resourceful.

"Wow, thanks, Declan. I appreciate the vote of support. I can't say that formal school appealed to me before opening the farm. I had a complicated childhood and that led to a confusing adolescence where I looked for attention in the wrong places. If it wasn't for Mac, I would have gone way, way off the skids. Probably would be working some dead-end job that paid nothing and counting down to the end of the shift. At least with the farm, I love what I do. The hours pass quickly. There are days when I don't have enough hours to finish. I'm never bored here."

Declan knew of Mac and had heard good things about the older man from Edith. He had been involved with Livia and managed to leave her without being killed. He owned a ranch in the area and, since reuniting with Edith, had been good to her. "That's great that you had someone to help you."

He hadn't had anyone who'd cared for him in that way. Not a single foster parent took an interest in him. He was a paycheck to them and while he wasn't ever mistreated, he had never felt the consuming love of family. Edith was the only person in his life who had shared his triumphs and failures.

Jade's eyes were bright when she looked at him. "For all my misfortune being a Colton, I've been blessed."

Declan wasn't sure what to make of Jade and that statement. His attraction to her defied explanation and while he had expected someone cold and hard, the warm and generous woman in front of him was a pleasant surprise.

"Can I be blunt with you?" Jade asked.

"I appreciate honesty," Declan said. He anticipated a question about Edith or River, or maybe his father. He wasn't quick to talk about any of those subjects, but he was curious what was on Jade's mind.

"Why did you buy La Bonne Vie?" Jade asked.

Without getting into the emotional reasons for his decision, he could lay out his plan. "It's a valuable property. The house poses a problem, but I'm tearing that down. I'll divide up the land and use it for commercial or residential properties."

Jade frowned. If she had sentimental attachment to her childhood home, he was sorry about that. He hadn't meant to speak bluntly about the house, but when he spoke of business, he left emotion out of it.

Jade set her sandwich on the wrapper. "Do you think I could visit?"

"The house?" he asked. It was being taken apart by Rafferty Construction. Given Jade's connection to Allison, she had to know that. Having anyone walk around in the middle of the teardown was dangerous.

"Yes. This might sound strange to you because my mother did bad things in that house, but I've had nightmares about that place for years. I've never visited, even when the state owned it, because it holds terrible memories and I wasn't ready to confront them. But I'm ready now." She lifted her chin.

He admired her courage. He knew all about the ghosts of the past and how they seemed to howl when they were needed the least. "Are you sure you want to see it? You could wait until it's torn down." Might give her a sense of peace to know that it was gone.

"No, I need to see it. As it is. I remember the house being huge and grand and I remember my mother moving through hallways like a queen. I want to watch it burn."

Chapter 3

Like still photographs in her mind, Jade pictured La Bonne Vie. It meant "the good life," in French, but for her, it was anything but.

Her father being struck in the head by Livia. His body unmoving on the ground. Hurt and pain. Livia flirting with men, touching their chests with her fingertips, leaning close, rubbing against them. Confusion and anger. Livia flying into a rage because something had happened or she'd perceived a slight. Fear. Livia calling to her children, asking them to line up along the grand staircase, looking them over for imperfections, like a hair out of place or not wearing the complete outfit she had purchased for them. As if wearing the wrong-colored socks would distort the image of the Coltons as the perfect family.

Resentment and more confusion why they only mattered when other people were watching.

Livia striking her so hard across the face, she had fallen down the stairs. Sadness and hurt. When her father had asked her what had happened, she had lied and said she had slipped. Fear and desperation.

Memories that Jade had never made sense of until after her mother had been arrested: men coming to the house late at night with packages and people. Those packages and people being nowhere in the house the next day.

When Jade was older and bolder, she had found some of her mother's secret rooms, hidden behind wainscoting and panels and some leading to a complex serious of tunnels under the property around La Bonne Vie. She had also found a book of passwords.

"Are you doing okay? If you've changed your mind, I can drive you back to the farm," Declan said.

Jade had been wringing her hands and she stilled them on her lap. It wasn't a long drive to La Bonne Vie, but the memories hammered at her so viciously, she wished she could scream out loud. The tension in her chest was nearly unbearable. By confronting the past, she could put it behind her. After La Bonne Vie was torn down, she wouldn't have the opportunity to gain that closure.

"I'm fine. This is hard for me. There's a lot about my childhood that still haunts me," she said.

Declan reached across the car and set his hand over hers. "I'll be with you. I called and Allison is on-site too. Is there anyone else you'd like to be with you?"

His compassion and warmth struck her and she felt a kinship with him. "I can do this. Maybe I can even help."

"Help?" he asked.

"I'm sure you've found some of the secret passageways tucked around the main house and the other buildings," Jade said.

"Edith and River found some. The construction team has since done a thorough search. They've found and closed a number of them," Declan said.

"I can show you ones they may have missed," Jade said.

"Only if you want to," Declan said.

As he turned his sporty car into the driveway leading to La Bonne Vie, Jade's breath caught in her throat. The house was different than she remembered. It wasn't as big as it was in her childhood memories. It looked broken, like she and her siblings were, like anyone who was involved with Livia Colton eventually became.

Construction noises rose around her. Her mother wouldn't have allowed banging and sawing on the premises when she was in residence. Renovations and additions to the house had been completed when her mother was traveling.

Declan parked his car a good distance away from the house.

Jade stepped out. Taking several deep breaths, she reminded herself she was an adult. Livia had no hold over her. Livia didn't have power over Jade and her siblings the way she had when they were children.

"She can't hurt me," Jade said.

"What?" Declan asked.

Jade shook loose the thought of her mother. Thinking about Livia never brought anything positive. Getting sucked into a spiral of negative thoughts wasn't something Jade could do anymore. She needed her energy to run Hill Country and she needed to overcome her fear of La Bonne Vie.

"Is it safe to enter anywhere?" Jade asked.

"Yes. Your choice," Declan said.

Jade walked to the front of the house. She didn't want to enter from the back as if she were sneaking inside. Piles of broken bricks and debris were stacked outside the house. Large Dumpsters were filled with wood, drywall and trash.

The front porch was crumbling, paint peeling from around the double-door frame. The window to the left was cracked and the window to the right was covered with cardboard. Jade stepped across the threshold.

The grand staircase had once gleamed in the ornate chandelier fixture that had hung from the center of the two-story foyer. Now, the wood was scuffed, the bannister missing on one side and the chandelier gone, nothing hanging in its place. Livia had loved using the stairs to make a grand entrance to parties. She would gather her guests in the entryway, serve them champagne and cocktails and, when enough people had arrived and the band was playing one of her favorite songs, she would sweep out into the limelight in her couture gown, her hair arranged artfully, and she would descend the stairs as if she were royalty greeting her subjects.

How the people in Shadow Creek had put up with that, Jade had no idea. It had struck her as odd then, and now she wondered if they didn't fear Livia, the same way her children had. Jade didn't realize she had walked up the stairs until she was halfway to the first floor. Her mother's bedroom had been off-limits. Jade shuddered to think what had gone on in that room.

Her mother had cheated on all her husbands. She hadn't been faithful to another human being once in her life. Her words were cruel and her mouth spewed lies, deceit and hate.

When the details had emerged of Livia's crimes, Jade had been disgusted and horrified that she had lived in a house where organized crime, human trafficking and drug deals took place. Jade walked to her room first.

She hated everything about it. For her ninth birthday, Livia had offered to remodel her bedroom and Jade had been excited at the prospect. Seeing her siblings' rooms, she had thought about colors and curtains. An interior designer had met with her and had sketched a room perfectly suited to Jade. Her anticipation at seeing the final product had been immense; she had slept in Claudia's room while the work was completed on hers. After three days, she had entered her room and had been met with disappointment.

The colors and styles she had discussed with the designer were nowhere to be seen. She had turned to her mother, sight blurry through her disappointed tears, and her mother had looked at her through narrowed eyes. "Stop crying."

"This isn't…"

"This isn't what? What you wanted? I made it better. What you picked was ridiculous. Horses in a room? Horses stink. They are dirty and they make the people around them filthy. Are you a common stable girl? What do you want to do with your life? To clean up horse crap? I thought you were smarter than that. This room is what I wanted."

Jade had felt utter defeat, as if Livia's comments about horses were another insult to her father. She had wiped at her tears and had sat quietly in her bedroom alone until bedtime. When she had been called for dinner, she had pretended to be asleep in her new bed, underneath the purple-and-green bedspread that she'd hated.

"I wish I could burn this room down," she said.

Declan was standing in the doorway. "Some dark things happened in this house."

Jade turned, surprised at how much being here was affecting her and bringing to mind memories she had thought were buried. "Everything my mother did or said or touched turned to pain."

Declan walked into the hallway and returned with a sledgehammer and a pair of goggles. "I can't let you burn the place down. Too dangerous. But you can smash whatever you want."

Jade slid the goggles over her eyes and took the sledgehammer from his hand. "Really? You'll let me smash holes in the wall?"

He shrugged. "Sure. Go ahead. If it gives you an ounce of therapeutic value, then it's worth it. Just be careful around the window. I don't want you hit with flying glass."

Jade walked to the corner of the room, lifted the tool over her shoulder and swung it at the wall. It was an intensely satisfying sensation and sound. Then she lifted the heavy hammer and swung again. The more that wall crumbled, the better she felt. Her mother flirting with other men and acting smug when her father asked her about it. Another bash to the wall. Fabrizio being hit in the head by Livia. Crashing and banging. Hiding in her bedroom beneath the covers, wishing she couldn't hear her parents fighting. The sledgehammer tore apart the wall and every loud noise was utterly satisfying.

When she was finished, she stood in the middle of the room, surveying the damage. "This place looks better." She was panting and hot, but felt good.

"Was there something about this room that offended you in particular or just the whole setup in general?" Declan asked.

He didn't seem fazed by her destruction of the room, his posture calm, his voice neutral.

"My mother decorated this room against my wishes. It was another of the hundred ways that she disrespected me. Nothing I said mattered and nothing I did had any value."

Declan came closer and brushed debris off her shoulders. "I can't imagine what it must have been like for you to grow up with Livia Colton as your mother. She hurt many people, and perhaps most appallingly, her children. You're doing good work at Hill Country. Living in a way that contradicts everything she stood for. You care for your horses. You're part of the community. I heard two mothers at the Cozy Diner talking about something they do there called Farm Fridays and they seemed excited. You're doing great work. Whatever your mother did, it doesn't shadow your life now."

Declan knew what a monster her mother was. Livia had tried to kidnap Edith, but the younger woman had been rescued before any real harm could be done. When River had told her the story, Jade had been, and still was, appalled, but not surprised by the attack. It was not beyond her imagination to picture her mother doing any manner of evil. If it suited some end goal, her mother would do it without a care in the world.

Jade rested her head against Declan's chest. The outpouring of emotion inside this room had whipped through her. The anger had been exhausted. Now what remained was sadness.

Some of her friends had complained about their mothers growing up. A few were even jealous of Jade, with her big house and swimming pools and adoration of the town. No one had known her secret. Witnessing her mother kill her father had destroyed her. Money and fame didn't cover up that deep hurt.

Sliding her arms around his waist, she felt the stillness of the room settle around her. "My mother was an evil woman."

"I'm sorry she hurt you," Declan said.

"Me and everyone she came into contact with," Jade said.

Declan's stronger arms banded around her. The heat in the room and smell of broken drywall had Jade's nose itching. She took a step back from Declan, wondering if she had been inappropriate. He was watching her with that cool stare.

"Hey, guys." Allison was standing in the doorway, her smile bright. "What happened in here?"

"This was my room," Jade said.

Allison held up her hands. "Say no more. I think given the opportunity, Knox would do the same thing to his. And if I ever see Livia, I'll do the same thing to her."

Livia had kept Knox and Allison apart in high school by offering Allison a college scholarship. They had grown apart, but a visit to Shadow Creek and a one-night stand had left Allison pregnant with Cody. Allison had kept Cody a secret until Knox found out about him; then the boy had been kidnapped. Livia had been a prime suspect. Though it hadn't been easy, Jade was glad her brother and Allison had worked things out and were now a family with Cody.

"I had no idea this house could still affect me," Jade said.

"I didn't even grow up here and the house affects me. I catch myself thinking about what went on here and I feel betrayed. Disgusted. Angry," Allison said. "Pile on what she did to Cody and Knox. I hope the authorities find Livia first. Because if not, she'll face me."

Guilt plucked at Jade. She'd had nothing to do with Cody's disappearance, and she had been devastated that he had been taken and it was hard to distance herself from her mother. People lumped the Coltons together—as if, by being related to Livia, they were all tainted. Jade wished she could have done something to Livia, said something to her, to change the course of their family history. Maybe help her to see that riches weren't the only end goal. Life had many other joyous prospects that were worth pursuing.

Allison's phone buzzed and she glanced at it. "We're working on taking down the pool and filling it in. But the authorities have asked us to be careful."

"Because of the electrical lines?" Jade asked.

Allison paled slightly. "Because there could be bodies. Drugs. Anything out there." She answered her phone and stepped into the hall. Her voice grew more distant.

"I can show you a couple of the places where my mother used to hide things," Jade said.

Declan gestured ahead of him. "Lead the way."

With every step, Jade reassured herself she was strong now. She was not a child anymore. It was daylight and she was surrounded by dozens of people. Her mother wouldn't come at her in this space. She entered Leonor's bathroom. Leonor had been her mother's favorite. They were closer than Jade had been to her mother, and that was something Jade had never understood. She chalked it up to Leonor's inheritance from her biological father, CEO Richard Hartman, and Livia's love of money.

Many of the fixtures had been removed. She knelt in front of the cabinet beneath the white marble sink, dusty with age. Reaching behind the plumbing, she pulled a wood knob to the side. A door behind the cabinet swung open.

She couldn't get inside now, but as a child she and Claudia had discovered it. Peering inside, it looked empty. Dust and dirt and cobwebs.

"What is that?" Declan asked.

"A secret area of the house. I only found something once. My mother had placed nesting dolls inside. I thought they were cool and maybe she was hiding them for my birthday. When I didn't get one, I asked her about them. She pretended not to know what I was talking about. I checked that night and they were gone. I didn't know when she'd moved them or what they actually were, but I suspect she was smuggling something inside them."

Jade left the secret door open. She went into Thorne's room. Thorne hadn't cared about his bedroom. He had spent as much time as Livia would allow with Mac. Given that the Coltons had been raised by nannies and Livia rarely made an appearance outside public functions, that had meant that Thorne could be with his father often.

Jade knelt on the floor and ran her hand over the wood boards. When she found the small notch, she lifted up. Once the first board came free, she could lift the flap built into the floor. It was heavy with the floorboard on top of it.

A ladder led down into a secret room on the main floor that could only be accessed from Thorne's room. That then led to another room, which led beneath the house.

The electricity might not be working down there. The darkness that awaited her at the bottom of the metal rung ladder scared her. This tunnel led out to Fabrizio's barn, meaning people and items could be moved between the two buildings without the knowledge of anyone watching.

Could Livia be waiting in those secret, underground tunnels? She had been chased off and it would be ridiculous for Livia to still be lurking around La Bonne Vie. The authorities were looking for her. While the manhunt for Livia Colton immediately following her prison escape from Red Peak Maximum Security Prison in Gatesville, Texas, had been intense, she was a dangerous woman with connections and contingency plans and the smarts to stay one step ahead of the authorities. Thousands of volunteers had combed the woods and hidden areas for Livia and had come up empty.

"Do you want me to check it out?" Declan asked, pointing to the ladder.

Jade shook her head. "It leads to the barn. Part of the tunnel could have collapsed. It could be unstable or dangerous, especially with the construction outside."

"I'll get a hard hat and a flashlight and check it out," Declan said.

Jade didn't like the idea, but it was his property. She couldn't stop him. After grabbing the equipment, he handed her an orange hard hat. He put one on too and went down the ladder. She joined him on the main floor. The walls were drywall. Jade gave a small kick. If she could puncture it, it would be like unveiling another of Livia's secrets, which felt like she was getting back at her mother.

Declan set his hand on her shoulder. "Allow me." He lifted his knee and kicked through the wall.

Once the drywall had been pierced, it was easy to remove the rest, leaving the wood two-by-fours. They were standing in the secret area in the formal dining room. The dining room was empty; curtains and light fixtures had been removed. Jade had recalled the room being flooded with light during one of Livia's soirees. Now it seemed dim and ugly, the gold floor tile brown with age and grime. The wallpaper was peeling off the walls, hanging in limp sections.

"This room looks terrible," Jade said.

"We haven't done any demo here," Declan said.

"It feels empty and cold." She didn't want to explore that emotion too deeply. "Let's keep going."

Another ladder led deeper.

Declan shined the flashlight down. "I don't see anything. It smells like wet earth."

Jade was curious. She checked her hard hat. If she was going to do this, if she wanted to purge her bad memories and overcome her fears, she had to face them head-on. She knelt on the floor and started down the ladder. Her legs quaked and her hands felt weak. When she reached the bottom, she looked around.

Declan jumped off the ladder and landed next to her. "We can do this together." He extended his hand to her.

Jade took his hand and was happy he was beside her. Moving aside a large plywood sheet that was sunk in the mud was a two-person job and then a tunnel was revealed. It was constructed like a mine shaft, wood beams holding out the walls with rocks along the floor. The walls were packed mud and she tried not to think about them caving in.

Jade let out the breath she hadn't realized she was holding. Her mother wasn't in the small space. Her mother wouldn't be waiting in the dark on the off chance Jade visited La Bonne Vie and decided to spill a family secret.

Jade envisioned her mother as two people: the graceful and wonderful woman she pretended to be when someone was watching, and the person she morphed into when she was upset. Though Livia could maintain a cold facade regardless of the circumstances, even a husband's death, when it came to her children, she was often more cruel than indifferent.

The tunnel was dark. Declan flipped on his flashlight. "If you want to turn back, let me know. Parts of the tunnel might be caved in. We can see how far we get." Declan had to bend his knees to enter the space.

Jade walked behind him, keeping her hand on his back. The strength in his body was a reassurance. The confidence in his steps kept her going. Only the flashlight illuminated the small space. Her boots stuck in the mud and Jade shivered in the cold, damp air.

"I remember it being light down here," Jade said. They turned a corner and lost the little light from the entry. Though the walls were two feet apart, claustrophobia began to creep at her. The tunnel could collapse and they could be stuck under the ground. Each step felt like effort.

When they reached another plywood board, Declan pushed it to the side. They were inside another room. This one was lined with wood on the floor and sides, creating a box, like an unmoving elevator. Declan scaled the ladder and pushed at the top. "I can't open it."

Panic flared, but Jade tamped it down, reminding herself they could go back through the tunnel if they had to get out. But she wanted fresh air. The humid room was musty and stale. Her imagination took flight, thinking of the people and drugs and items that had been moved between the house and barn using this tunnel.

It felt dirty and wrong. "Let me help you push."

Declan moved to the side of the ladder and tucked the flashlight in his belt. Jade held on to the other side and they pushed at the ceiling. Their bodies pressed together on the narrow ladder.

"Count of three, big push," Declan said. "One, two, three."

Shoving the wood as hard as they could, the hatch flew open and Jade shielded her eyes from the light. For a flash, she imagined it was Livia standing over them.

As her vision adjusted, Jade realized she was clinging to the ladder with both arms wrapped around the metal bars. Declan was helping her out, guiding her up the last few rungs.

They were standing in Fabrizio's barn. Unexpected emotion wrapped around her. Her father's barn. Jade hadn't realized how much she had remembered until she stood in the far corner, recalling everything in its place. The feed, the medicines, the saddles. Her shoes next to her father's when they would change into riding boots.

Her father had put love and care into its construction, wanting a place for his horses, thinking about every detail, overseeing the construction himself. He had wanted a certain type of wood, and the layout was based on the one his family had in Argentina.

During the time he'd known Livia, had Fabrizio questioned how she had so much money? Jade was too young to remember, though her father had told her stories about his work in Argentina and how he had moved to America to be with Livia, leaving his family, including his five brothers. Livia had worked to ensure that Fabrizio lost communication with his family and Jade had been too timid to reach out to them, feeling they would reject her for her father leaving and for the crimes Livia had committed.

Allison entered the barn. "You made it. I was about to send in a search party after you." She glanced at her phone. "I'll be back in a bit. Much to do. My customer is very demanding." She winked at Declan.

"The barn is still lovely," Jade said. Unlike the house, it seemed fresh and bright and welcoming.

Declan looked around. "I haven't decided what to do with the barn."

He sounded casual, but the words rattled her. Tearing down her mother's home—and in Jade's thinking, that giant mansion was her mother's alone—was okay with her. Demolishing that horrible place off the face of the earth would be better for everyone— her siblings, the town and Livia's victims.

But the barn. Her father's barn. Jade had memories tied to this space. Jade walked to the back. Her footsteps echoed across the emptiness, which brought a sense of sadness. At one point, every stall had been filled, hay was stacked high and the whinnies of happy horses echoed when Fabrizio would let them out to roam. Along the back wall, her father had a small desk where he had written notes about his horses. He had made notches in the wood to show her growth. Small lines with the dates written beside them.

They were still there.

Jade ran her fingers over the notches and a lump

formed in her throat. Her father had doted on her, showering her with his time and love. After he'd died, Mac had done what he could, but there was no replacing her dad.

"Your father made those for you," Declan said.

Jade spun around. Declan was standing five feet away, watching. His head was inclined and his green eyes shone with compassion. "Yes." Jade looked up to the second-story loft. She had hidden up in that loft. It had been rare for Livia to care where she was or what she was doing. The loft had been filled with horse supplies that had reminded her of her father.

Only a few weeks after Fabrizio had died, someone had come to take the horses away. Livia had gotten rid of most of her stock. On the heels of losing her father, Jade had lost her horses too.

Jade had hidden. Hid in the loft with a book and whatever food she could swipe from the kitchen. She hadn't announced her hiding spot to her siblings, either. Long afternoons of being alone with her thoughts had helped her grieve for her father and everything she had lost when he'd died. Gone with him were also her sense of peace, genuine affection, love and warmth. The horses, happy days spent with her father and her innocence stamped to death by Livia.

"Maybe you'd like time alone in the barn," Declan said.

Jade shook her head, answered a question he hadn't asked. "I don't want you to tear it down."

Declan lifted his eyebrows. "What do you want me to do with it?"

Options came to mind, but the most realistic was to sell it to Mac. "My stepfather would make good use of it and the land around it." The barn was a good place for supplies or more horses.

Declan rubbed his jawline. "I know you feel strongly about this. I can see it in your eyes. I'll think about it." Though he was being reasonable and he owed her nothing—he owed the Coltons nothing, especially after what Livia had done to Edith and his parents—his response angered her. It was as if he didn't understand how much the barn meant to her. While she couldn't expect him to fully get it, she needed him to know. "I need you to promise me that before you tear the barn down, you'll give me a chance to buy it and the land it sits on."

Declan set his hands over hers. She hadn't realized she had crossed to him and her hands were fisted in the cotton fabric of his shirt.

"I thought you were invested in Hill Country."

She had no money. Not even a few hundred dollars to spare for the application to a loan that would be denied. "I am," she said. Frustration plucked at her. Every dime she had was tied up in her farm. Her lines of credit were fully extended. She could beg her siblings to help her buy the plot that contained the barn, but would they help her? They had their own demons when it came to La Bonne Vie. Knox, Leonor, Thorne, River and Claudia had admitted at various times over the years that Fabrizio had been a good stepfather. But Jade knew none of them carried the same deep connection she had with him.

They might not be willing to do anything to keep the barn standing.

Declan touched her shoulders. "I am working with the state and the county on getting the permits to use the land in different ways. Before I move forward with anything, I will check in with you. I will tell you my plans and give you a chance to buy the plots this barn sits on."

It was a small concession, but given her financially weak position, she would have to take it. They hadn't known each other long enough to call on favors.

"That's a promise?" she asked.

"Are you asking me to give my word?"

She nodded, needing him to give a firm commitment.

"My word is my bond. I will come to you with the plans and you'll have the right of first refusal to buy the barn."

"Thank you, Declan." She was overcome with gratitude and reached up on her tiptoes; intending to kiss his cheek, she had pressed her lips against his.

Electricity fired between her and Declan as long slumbering desire awakened. Falling back to flat feet, she touched her lips. That kiss could have turned into something amazing. She had liked him from the first time she had laid eyes on him, and now that feeling had grown stronger. They kept finding time and ways to see each other and Jade knew without asking that it wasn't one-sided. He liked her too. Maybe not enough to promise her the barn, but enough to care how it affected her.

Stopping the kiss was the right decision. This day had been filled with emotions and letting those spiral into a sexual relationship was a mistake. Because it wouldn't just be about a kiss. More was tied into her feelings for Declan.

Searching for a way to segue this into another topic, any topic, Jade grasped for words. "I was the one who gave the FBI my mother's bank account passwords."

Declan's eyebrows lifted. "Your mother's bank account passwords?"

The story had weighed on her and she had never told her siblings what she had done. She had trusted Mac enough to confide in him. Telling Declan felt safe. When she had chosen to give the authorities her mother's passwords, knowing they would help build a case against her, Jade had worried about Livia finding out and seeking retribution. She was concerned about her siblings learning what she had done. Hard to feel like family mattered given how their mother had treated them, but Livia had liked to pretend she was loyal, and Jade had liked the idea of it. "My mother kept a logbook with passwords. I found it in one of her hiding places. I memorized some of them. Not hard. They were our names, middle names and her husbands' names and birthdays." Telling the FBI, she had felt simultaneously like a rat for turning in her mother and justified because Livia had killed Fabrizio.

"That was brave of you," Declan said. "You should be proud that you did the right thing under difficult circumstances."

"Not sure *proud* is the right word," Jade said.

Livia's reach was long and she was hateful and vengeful. Her father had believed that Livia was a decent person and he had told Livia on many occasions, often after a particularly vicious fight, that she was a good woman who could do better. The belief that Livia had good inside her was misplaced. There was nothing good about Livia Colton.

Declan was seeing a side of Jade he hadn't expected her to be honest about so soon. The Colton children were Livia's victims, as well, but now, seeing the riotous emotions plaguing Jade, Declan had underestimated her anger for her mother.

More than that, Declan had believed the Colton children would be loyal to Livia and defend her actions. But the opposite was true. Jade had provided evidence against her mother. Though she clearly struggled with that decision, she had done what was right, and as a young woman. That had taken courage and strength. He admired her and that kiss had emotionally rattled him. The last few months had been trying for her and her family and she deserved his support and respect.

"My mother didn't like the barn. I'm surprised she didn't burn it to the ground after my father died," Jade said.

Livia wouldn't have done that—it would have cut

off a useful location in her complex system of underground tunnels. "She needed the barn as another route from the house."

Declan could see nothing of Livia in the barn. It was very different from the grand house in style and function. The elements of the barn were utilitarian.

La Bonne Vie had been her place of business, a part of the carefully crafted lie she pretended about her family. It wasn't her home. Livia didn't care for it as a place to raise and nurture her children. The parties she had thrown and the image she had tried to convey were attempts to hide the ugly truths in her life.

"Does your mother know that you spoke to the authorities?" Declan asked.

Jade rubbed her forehead. "I don't know. I suspect she may know one of us betrayed her. It's part of the reason I worry about her coming after me. She's come after my siblings."

"I'll keep you safe." Declan hadn't considered every aspect of that statement, but he meant it. Livia had a long reach, but not long enough to get past him and his resources.

"I can't ask you to trail me around town or come by the farm every day. You have a job," Jade said.

He could be flexible about his work. "I'll speak to Sheriff Jeffries. See if he's heard anything about Livia's whereabouts."

"I'm sure Hawk would tell me if Livia had been seen around town," Jade said.

PI Hawk Huntley was involved with Jade's sister Claudia. "It can't hurt to ask some questions. I've seen a dark sedan parked outside Hill Country a couple of times. I wrote down the license plate. If the authorities are watching you, that could mean they have information about Livia. Maybe they expect her to show up in Shadow Creek again." If they did, they wouldn't necessarily clue the Coltons in on that. From what Declan had heard, no one knew the specifics of who had been involved in Livia's jailbreak. Jade's older sister Leonor was wealthy. Knox was a former Texas Ranger who would have inside knowledge of the penal system. Though it was hard to imagine, and no evidence suggested it, any of them could have been involved.

"If she does, this time, I'll be ready to face her," Jade said.

Chapter 4

Declan parked on Main Street. It was a short walk to the sheriff's office. Posted in some local business windows were "Knox Colton for Sheriff" signs in dark blue background, white lettering and underlined in red. Knox's bid for local office might prove successful. Bud Jeffries was inept and Declan had heard that the town wanted him voted out in the upcoming election. Though the town wasn't sold on Knox Colton, either, given his ties to a criminal mastermind, he was a former Texas Ranger and that carried weight. Despite the embarrassment that Livia caused him, he wasn't turning away from the opportunity to enforce the law in Shadow Creek. It took courage to step up and not let his mother define his life.

The sheriff's station was located next to the

Shadow Creek Mercantile. Declan strolled inside the quiet office. With the exception of Livia Colton's crime spree and the events of late related to it, Shadow Creek was a slow town. The receptionist was seated at a scarred wood desk, surfing the internet on a desktop computer. The office needed updates that weren't in the budget for a small town. The peeling white paint, the tile floor in a black-and-red checkerboard pattern and the dusty miniblinds, half of them closed, made the office feel dingy.

Four metal desks were set in the main room behind the receptionist's area. Bud Jeffries's office was in the back. Bud was on the phone, his feet propped on his desk and a can of diet cola in his hand.

Declan tapped on the door and Bud motioned for him to come in. Bud had a stain on the front of his tan work shirt and the buttons were straining. Losing five pounds or wearing a properly fitting shirt would go a long way to make him look the part of sheriff. He wasn't Declan's favorite person, but he had information Declan wanted. Being a visitor, Declan had no pull with the sheriff. He'd need to be polite.

Bud finished his conversation and hung up the phone.

"Sheriff Jeffries, how are you today?" Declan asked, taking a seat in the wood chair across from the older, heavier man.

"Good, Declan. What can I do for you?"

Declan hadn't had much time to get to know the other man. Though winning over local law enforcement could help with his plans at La Bonne Vie and gain the support of the community to parcel up the land. Declan hadn't gotten the impression that Bud Jeffries held much sway in Shadow Creek. He suspected that Knox would have an easy time being elected. Knox, or anyone who wanted the position.

"The manhunt for Livia Colton. How's that coming?" Declan asked.

Bud set his cola on his desk and swung his feet to the ground. "We haven't found her."

Obviously. "Leads?"

"Nothing that I've been clued into. Why? Do you have something? If she's around and watching, she can't like that you're tearing down her place. I figure she'll show up again spitting mad."

"I haven't seen her," Declan said. If he had, he would have called the authorities immediately.

Declan thought of the slip of paper where he had written the license plate for the sedan outside Jade's farm. If Bud expected Livia to show up, he'd have deputies posted and on the lookout. "You have someone watching Hill Country?"

Bud shook his head. "Should I be? Jade up to no good?"

Before Declan could answer, Bud leaned forward and shook his finger at Declan. "I never liked those Coltons. Bad seeds, all of them."

Declan's defensiveness rose. He shouldn't take what Bud was saying personally. Jade was a good person. Lumping her in with her mother was unfair. "Jade isn't involved with her mother." Knowing her for a short time, he was certain of it.

Bud knew nothing. If he was involved with the case, he was either pretending to be ignorant or willfully choosing to be.

"I've seen a car hanging around the Coltons'," Declan said.

"At La Bonne Vie?" Bud asked, scratching his head.

The Coltons didn't live at La Bonne Vie. Declan tamped down his irritation. Bud wasn't really listening because he didn't care. "Nope. At Jade's farm," Declan said.

"I don't know about that. Could be someone from that support group," Bud said.

"What support group?"

"They have those flyers all over town. The Victims of Livia Colton support group. I checked them out. Seems legit. They have a website and meetings, get together and talk about Livia Colton and what she did to them. A little bit whiny if you ask me. It happened decades ago. But if that's what they need, then okay. They aren't breaking any laws."

Declan hadn't heard of such a group. "Are they new to town?"

Bud shrugged. "Don't know. Just saw the flyers last week. I figured it was a long time coming. The Coltons ruined this town. Brought their lies and crimes and bad vibes. I'm surprised they haven't been run out of town yet with torches and pitchforks."

Declan's irritation prickled. "The Colton children are Livia's victims too."

Bud snorted. "Maybe. Maybe not. I wouldn't be surprised if one of them knew where that criminal is hiding. And all that money she made? Where exactly is it? One of those kids had to have taken a cut."

Declan wasn't getting anywhere with Bud. He stood. "I'm just looking out for my investment. Doesn't help me if Livia Colton shows up anywhere near my property."

"Call me if you see her," Bud said.

He sounded bored, like he didn't care either way and he certainly had no intention of getting up off his rear end and looking for her. Declan kept cool. Shooting off at the mouth to protect Jade would get him in trouble down the line. Bud could have influence over the local government and Declan didn't need the hassle.

"Pass the pretzels," Maggie said, reaching across the ottoman between her and Jade for the open bag on the coffee table.

Jade handed her the bag. If Maggie was going to keep helping Jade with her accounting for her farm, the least Jade could do is provide her pregnant friend, and now her sister-in-law, with good treats.

"I don't know, Jade. This doesn't seem so bad," Maggie said, turning the page on the spreadsheet where Jade had painstakingly laid out her expenses and income how Maggie had showed her.

Maggie was trying to be positive. The truth of the matter was that running a nonprofit seemed to mean no profit for the owner. While Jade was happy to give everything she had to help her horses, she needed a salary, enough to cover her basic expenses. She had known it wouldn't be easy when she'd come up with the idea of running the farm to rehabilitate retired racehorses. But some of the bigger, longer running farms that did similar work had more volunteers to handle fund-raising and promotion and help with the horses.

Maybe it was a good thing she didn't have much of a personal life. Her last one had ended a few months after Livia had escaped from prison. Dumped because of her mother. It didn't bother Jade much; in her life, Livia had disappointed her and ruined so many precious things, another broken relationship was par for the course. For someone to walk away when she needed him most meant she was better off without him.

A good man would stay by her no matter what. The right man would care for her, regardless of who her mother was or what her family had done. Declan came to mind. Jade thought of him, about his visits and bringing her lunch and allowing her to go to La Bonne Vie. Being in her old house had been good for her.

"What's that face mean?" Maggie asked. She removed her reading glasses and narrowed her eyes.

"No face," Jade said. "Just thinking."

"Worrying about this stuff? Because maybe there's some way we could help you."

Jade appreciated Maggie's offer, but she was about to have a baby. She and Thorne would be incredibly busy, too busy to help around the farm. From a financial perspective, they needed their money. Figuring out how to run her business was her challenge. "I'll be okay. I'll figure something out. You should be resting while you have time."

"Thorne makes sure I rest plenty. We have everything we need for the baby."

That wasn't entirely true. Leonor was planning a baby shower at the end of the month. Jade had purchased the bassinet from Thorne and Maggie's registry and stored it in her guest bedroom closet. It was more than she could afford, but the beautiful white bassinet with storage for diapers and wipes and onesies and the soft bedding with tiny ivy printed on it had struck her as something her future niece or nephew needed.

"We could run an online fund-raiser," Maggie said. "Or do a walk or run to benefit the farm. Host an open house so prospective donors could see the horses and the work you do."

Jade had put together a website for the farm and had included profiles of her horses. "No open house. The horses might get skittish around too many people and if they act out, I'll look like I don't know what I'm doing."

"Good point," Maggie said, dipping her pretzel in honey mustard sauce.

Jade liked the idea of a digital campaign with the right hook, but also thought of Leonor's experience with *Everything's Blogger in Texas*, a wildly popular gossip blog that had run stories about the

Colton children. Unbeknownst to Leonor, her former boyfriend David had gotten information from her and sold it to the site. When the site went live with the information, it had hurt the Colton children for many reasons: among them, being associated with their mother and having their family trashed all over again in the media was working at scars that had never healed properly. To expose her farm to more scrutiny was something she couldn't handle. Opening the doors to her farm would mean some folks would feel it was perfectly acceptable to verbally assault her, as well.

"With my mother's prison escape, I don't know that many people would be willing to donate. The Colton name is associated with scams and lies and fraud. I don't know how to convince donors that I'm using the money for the horses," Jade said. She had tried posting pictures and explaining her horses' weekly improvements, but it was another task in a list of endless to-dos. And it didn't seem like it was helping.

Maggie sat up and rubbed her belly. "You could hire a CPA to review your accounts and have her write something confirming where the money is going. Or what about asking Declan for the money?"

Jade's initial reaction was complete disagreement. She didn't want to ask him for money. If he wanted to donate to the farm, he would. Asking him would change their relationship, and she liked where it was and where it might be going. "Maybe the CPA idea. But it's a firm no about Declan. I can't do that."

"Why not? He's rich and he's in town doing who-knows-what at La Bonne Vie. He's investing in the community. That includes your farm."

Jade tried to see it from another point of view. While she would like to spend her days working with her horses, she understood running the business had an office component and a financial obligation. "I feel like he would see it as a personal request and not just me pitching him on a local nonprofit."

Maggie inclined her head. "Back up. Personal request? Since when are you and Declan Sinclair personal?"

Jade wouldn't lie to her friend. It would make its way through the family grapevine eventually anyway, since now Allison knew about her and Declan after their visit to La Bonne Vie. Jade explained about talking to him at Edith and River's engagement party and then about the interactions they'd had since. "It makes me think he likes me, but I don't know how to best handle it. Or even if he wants something. He's from Louisiana. He'll go back there when he's finished with La Bonne Vie."

"Edith isn't going back to Louisiana."

Jade had heard that. "I don't know what her situation is there. She's a great enough employee and Declan might let her telecommute from Austin."

"I'm just saying that you shouldn't get too worried about the future this soon in your relationship."

"I don't even know if it's a relationship."

Maggie laughed. "From what you said, it's at least an attraction. Just because you haven't slept with him doesn't mean it's not real. Wait, you didn't sleep with him, did you?"

"Of course not. We barely know each other," Jade said.

"Hang in there. Things have a way of working themselves out."

"Are you thinking of Thorne when you say that?" Jade asked, seeing something in Maggie's expression.

"Thorne and the baby, yes," Maggie said, her eyes sparking with joy. Maggie set Jade's accounting log on the ottoman. She stood. "I need to stretch my back and my legs. Let's go for a walk. I want to hear more about this romance with Declan."

"I didn't call it a romance," Jade said.

"That's what it is though? Right?" Maggie asked.

Jade liked Declan. He made her feel safe and happy. The idea of him showing up at the farm brought tingles of excitement. "I hope so."

They walked out onto the front porch. The sight of her farm made her happy. At the end of her driveway, a black sedan was parked. "I need to call the sheriff about that. That car has been there every day and I know everyone is looking for Livia, but it's starting to creep me out."

Maggie glanced in the car's direction. "You want to call Sheriff Jeffries about an actual problem? You'd have more luck reporting it to Hawk or Josh. I haven't seen any cars hanging around Mac or Thorne's."

A few months ago, Maggie's car had exploded in

an act of violence against her, and Sheriff Jeffries had begun with the assumption that Maggie had set off the blast herself. No goodwill existed between Bud and Maggie. Lately, Bud didn't seem to be impressing anyone. "Another reason why I hope Knox wins the election. But I should call it in. It's getting weird. If it's an FBI agent, they're making it known that they're watching, but whenever I approach to talk to them, the car speeds away."

"That is weird. Let's go back inside and call the guys. I don't like the sound of this and after what's been going on around here the last five months, it would be wise to be overly cautious."

Twenty minutes later, Mac and Thorne arrived at Hill Country. Thorne and Maggie embraced as if they hadn't seen each other in years. Jade tried not to be jealous that her brother had found such all-consuming love. He and Maggie deserved it.

Mac slung his arm around Jade's shoulder.

"You doing okay? I didn't see the car you were talking about," Mac said. He helped when he could, and he was a stable and loving parent figure when Jade had most needed one.

"It was there," Maggie said. "Watching her. Strange and creepy."

Thorne kissed his wife's temple. "Maybe until things settle down, you stay close to me."

Maggie shot him a look. "I'm fine. I know how to protect myself and this little one." She rubbed her belly.

"I called Josh. He said he was planning to be in Shadow Creek tomorrow for another assignment for his security firm. He'll keep an eye out and ask a few questions," Mac said.

"We could hire Hawk to do some digging into the car's owner," Maggie said.

"No money for that," Jade said.

Three pairs of eyes turned in her direction. Though Maggie was aware of Jade's financial constraints, Jade hadn't told Mac or Thorne about the issues her farm was having.

"Are you having problems with the farm?" Mac asked, concern bringing wrinkles to the corners of his eyes.

He and Thorne had been there too. Lean years and tough times. It was part of starting a new farm, being entrepreneurs in a new venture. "Not problems. Just trying to work a few things out. Forget I mentioned it. Let's just focus on why someone is watching me," Jade said.

"The FBI thinks we're in touch with Livia," Thorne said. "At least, they believe one of us is. For her to hide this long and evade them, she probably has help."

"Help in the form of her former contacts and whatever she squirreled away over the years. Not help in the form of her children." Jade would bet her farm that her siblings and Mac weren't helping to harbor Livia.

"It doesn't help that rumors keep circulating that we've helped her escape prison. Every time I think the community realizes we wouldn't do that, I over-hear someone whisper the name Livia and then give me a sideways look," Mac said.

Mac deserved better than what Livia had done to him and what he had been through after she'd had Thorne. "Until she's caught, that's something we'll need to face," Jade said.

"Livia planned a dozen steps ahead. She has contingency plans and plenty of hidey holes to disappear into," Mac said. His history with Livia was cloudy. Though his affair with her had been a mark on his honor, it had resulted in Thorne, a bright spot in Mac's life. Despite his shady past with Livia, Mac had stepped up to help the Colton children when Livia was in legal trouble.

"Then let's hope the FBI knows more of those places and catch her soon before she slips away for good," Thorne said.

Sunday afternoons were quiet in Shadow Creek. Declan enjoyed the chance to work with minimal interruptions.

Edith had scouted a few real estate opportunities. Declan liked to have four or five projects at SinCo in various stages at any given time: analyzing the potential of a given space, deciding to purchase and arranging financing, acquiring the property and then moving through the phases of development. When he'd first started his career, he had worked one property at a time, learning the technique, mastering the ins and outs of tax codes and legalities. Now that he was more experienced and his cash flow was significantly higher, he could juggle multiple projects and he enjoyed it. To date, he only purchased and sold real estate in Louisiana, Texas, Arkansas and Mississippi. He wanted to be able to fly, or in some unfortunate instances, to drive to those locations when the need arose.

All seven properties Edith had drafted portfolios for were in Texas. Spoke plainly enough about where her heart was. Staying close to Austin was important to her, doubly important as a newlywed starting a life with a man who had some deep issues: his mother and his own. Edith and Declan's relationship would change after she married River. Declan worried about losing her, both in the workplace and as his friend. He wouldn't be her first or only confidante. They had become brother and sister through their shared experiences. After Edith became a Colton and if she started a family of her own, Declan didn't see how he would fit in.

Already, after she had connected with Mac, she had found family. After Edith's mother, Merrilee, had been admitted to an inpatient psychiatric hospital, Edith had been in foster care. Mac felt guilty for losing touch with his sister, but he was doing his best to make it right with Edith and being as supporting and loving as he could.

Declan didn't like the Coltons. Couldn't trust them. What would he do at holidays? Sit around a table and pretend he was part of their family? They wouldn't accept him any more than he could open his heart to them.

The ties were there, of course, to the Colton clan. Being River's paternal half brother was a connection. But Declan didn't know how to forge a relationship with River. He had been through some tough stuff on the heels of leaving the marines. River hadn't left willingly. An explosion had caused the loss of his right eye. Declan felt like they'd had a brotherly moment when they had been focused on finding and rescuing Edith, but even now, Declan didn't know if he had imagined the connection or if their bond had been over mutual concern for Edith. When Edith and River were together, Declan felt like the third wheel and most definitely not part of their family.

Thinking about it hurt more than it should. Declan's mother had left him in Louisiana after his father betrayed the family and it all fell apart. His father had killed himself and his mother had abandoned him. His foster homes had been temporary stopovers and Edith was the one good thing to come out of them. Being alone wasn't something Declan enjoyed, but he hadn't been lucky enough to be born into a tight-knit family.

Declan read through the information Edith had gathered. The properties were the type he most liked to buy. She knew him well and by working together, she had honed her business senses. The last dozen properties they had purchased had been wild financial successes. Though Edith was technically his assistant, she was more like a partner and he paid her as such.

Declan wondered if their property winning streak would end with La Bonne Vie.

That house had been cursed from before he'd bought it. The ghosts of the people Livia had killed and harmed haunted the grounds. Declan had been trying to make a point to himself, and maybe to Livia Colton, that he was in charge. He was powerful and he could have what Livia couldn't.

Now that sentiment felt stupid.

Declan didn't want to be in Shadow Creek. There was nothing here for him. While the spring on the property made it a prime piece of real estate, the costs associated with tearing down La Bonne Vie were substantial. Making that money back in the acreage would be tough. Jade had suggested he sell to Mac and Thorne. Not out of the realm of possibility, and he would avoid zoning issues, but certainly he wouldn't recoup his investment selling it as farmland.

Saying no to Jade was tough. She was an intelligent and warm woman. Feisty and passionate. Though his work schedule was too intense for some, he guessed hers was similar. From what she had indicated, she did a lot of the heavy lifting around the farm herself.

He wasn't getting work done. His thoughts circled on Jade Colton. Leaving the B and B, Declan climbed into his black car. He hadn't fully thought out his plan until he was driving to Hill Country Farm.

The white fence around her property had the ability to close across the main driveway, but they were open. He guessed she didn't often close them, a practical matter since they weren't automated. Declan parked next to the training ring and went in search of Jade.

She was easy to find. First place he looked. She was in her stables, cleaning them.

"Need a hand?" he asked.

She looked up, gloves to her elbows, rake in hand and laughed. "This is one of the most unpleasant jobs on the farm. I can't ask you to help."

"That's okay. I don't mind. And you didn't ask. I'm offering."

Jade leaned on her rake. "I'm almost finished. But if you're staying, I have more things to do. You're welcome to help."

Spending the afternoon with her was infinitely more appealing than reviewing property proposals. "I'd like that." He was glad he was wearing casual clothes. A T-shirt and shorts would keep him cool.

They talked easily while Jade finished the last stall.

Declan heard noise outside the stable. He and Jade exchanged looks. "Stay here. I'll see what the ruckus is about," he said.

It sounded like chanting, almost like a protest was taking place. If it was Livia, odd to announce herself loudly. Declan would love to face off against the woman.

It wasn't Livia Colton. At the end of the driveway, walking back and forth between the open fence posts, was a group of eight people, holding fluorescent yellow and pink colored posters. They were chanting, "Coltons not wanted. Leave our town."

Declan walked closer. They were standing at the foot of the driveway on the road. Not technically on Hill Country property. Jade didn't need this stress. It was Sunday. Didn't people take a day off from complaining? Sheriff Jeffries had mentioned a support group at work in the town. Was this them or another one formed to make the lives of the Coltons harder? Declan walked down the driveway, contemplating getting his car, gunning the engine for show and forcing them to flee. "Excuse me." When he reached the edge of the property, he folded his arms across his chest.

The chanters glanced in his direction, but continued yelling.

The farm closest to Jade wouldn't hear them. This was a wasted effort if they thought they could run Jade out of town. "I assume you are here to make a point. Your point has been made. Now go."

The protesters ignored him. Declan had dealt with a similar situation involving a property he had purchased a few years ago. The group opposing his ideas hadn't stopped development, but they had been annoying and had brought unfavorable media coverage.

The chanting grew louder and two of the women in the group turned and shouted.

Declan looked over his shoulder. Standing in the driveway, rake still in hand, was Jade Colton.

The expression on her face conveyed her devastation. Her hair was piled on her head, pieces escaping down the side. Her jean shorts and T-shirt were caked with mud.

Declan walked toward her, wanting to give her support. He slipped his arm around her waist. He wanted her to know he would support her regardless of what a bunch of angry people near her driveway said. "Let's go back to the barn. They'll get tired and leave."

"They want me to leave town?" Jade asked.

Declan should have known it wouldn't have been that easy for Jade to let it go. It was unsettling to know a group of people, especially people who didn't know her personally, were out on a Sunday to scream negativity at her. "That seems to be their point, yes."

"Who are they?" Jade asked.

Declan had read about the support group online after Sheriff Jeffries had mentioned it. It had formed after Livia Colton's crimes were brought to light. She had psychologically damaged people, torn apart families and ruined lives. "This has nothing to do with you. It's your mother."

Speaking the words, he heard the truth in them. At some point since meeting her, Declan had stopped lumping Jade and the Coltons into one big group. Seeing Jade as a woman separate from her mother and siblings was a huge step for him. She was different from Livia, warm and genuine, unassuming and kind. Having her in his life had bettered it.

"I didn't leave Shadow Creek because this is my

home. I know people in town think badly of me and my siblings. But I haven't done anything wrong."

Her hands trembled and she looked back over her shoulder at the people carrying signs. Their words were harder to make out from a distance. "We can call the sheriff if you want."

Jade shook her head. "He won't help. They aren't on my property and the sheriff hates the Coltons anyway."

Declan didn't deny it. Sheriff Jeffries had a chip on his shoulder about the Coltons. Whether it was because of the trouble Livia had brought to town or that Knox was running against him for sheriff, Jade had the right idea. She had to cope with this on her own. Unless the protesters openly threatened her, she had to ignore it the best she could.

They returned to the stables. Declan took the rake from her hand. He continued what she had been doing, mimicking her actions.

Jade seemed distracted and Declan didn't blame her. While they went through her chores, she half explained them, half spoke about her life as a Colton. None of it was good. Living in a big house and having money didn't make up for their mom's emotional negligence or the impact of her criminal life. From what Jade explained, she had never felt comfortable or safe in La Bonne Vie. Livia's behavior was hard to predict and she could be volatile and angry.

By early evening, Declan had to sit down. His back was aching and his legs were sore. He'd worked out with a personal trainer in Louisiana, but working on the farm for hours was much harder, using muscles he didn't know he had. "You may have miles to go, but what do you say we take a break and I treat you to a dinner at El Torero's?" About now, the local Mexican restaurant was sounding amazing. Declan could taste the nachos supreme and cold beer.

Jade looked at the sky. "I'm sorry, Declan. I've kept you all day. I didn't mean to chatter. I should treat you to dinner."

Wasn't going to happen. Talking about her life had seemed to help her calm down. He was glad this had helped her. "I enjoyed talking with you. And you've taught me about running a farm. Namely, it's not for the weak."

Jade laughed. "My farm is much simpler than a lot of farms and ranches around here. There's so much to do and not enough time."

It wasn't the first time she had mentioned being short-staffed. He wondered if she preferred to work alone. A strange paradox; she might not want help in the sense that working alone gave her complete control, but she might want help to give herself time off.

"You work hard. I've seen that clearly," Declan said.

"But it's enough for now. I skipped lunch."

Declan wished she would slow down. He understood her urgency. He had been like that when he'd started his business. But she would burn out or hurt herself if she didn't relax now and then. "I can't stop thinking about spicy enchiladas and lime rice and beans," Declan said. In every town where he had worked on a real estate project, he visited local restaurants. It was one of the upsides of traveling: food experiences and meeting the locals. El Torero's was one of his favorites in Shadow Creek.

"Now I'm thinking of tacos too," Jade said. "Let me lock up and grab my keys. We'll have to make it fast though. I need to feed my animals before dark."

Fifteen minutes into her meal with Declan at El Torero's, Jade realized that she might be on a date.

She had washed her hands and changed her clothes, but hadn't done anything with her hair or taken a shower. Self-consciousness crept over her. It hadn't dawned on her to dress up. She had been thinking about her horses and had been relieved that the protesters had moved on before she'd left the house.

Looking at them and having them screaming hurtful words was too much. Though Jade had come to terms with her mother's true nature years before, it seemed to follow her. She couldn't escape it. Leaving Shadow Creek would put distance between her and some of the problems, but Jade didn't want to abandon her siblings, and she shouldn't have to run away because of what her mother had done.

If she moved, it would be because she wanted to. Because of a good opportunity. Not because she was trying to escape the past.

El Torero's was like other Mexican restaurants with a dark interior and the smell of onions and peppers heavy in the air. On the walls were painted murals that needed touching up. Jade had been to the restaurant dozens of times and eating here had never felt special. Until tonight.

The votive candle in the yellow glass with brass etching seemed romantic. The white linen tablecloths were pressed and clean. Even the waiters in their black outfits moved like a dance, darting to tables and taking orders quickly and efficiently. Being with Declan put an entirely different spin on the drudgery that was life in a small town.

Jade wished she had mentioned something to Maggie, Leonor, Allison or Claudia. Even a quick text and they would have mentioned a shower. Rookie mistake, not thinking ahead. Declan didn't seem bothered by her appearance. Maybe it wasn't that bad.

Sitting across from Declan, she took a minute to drink him in. He was so handsome and sweet, it was hard not to fall for him in that instant. She caught herself and tried to derail that train of thought. Until she knew what he wanted from her or how long he would be in Shadow Creek, she would be smart to guard her heart.

Jade looked away from Declan, realizing she was staring. She spotted Allison and Knox at a table in the back of the restaurant. "My brother and Allison are here. Do you mind if I say hi?" Walking away for a minute would give her time to think. Maybe she could even ask Allison if this was a date. Jade should know, but she wasn't sure. Her mishaps in romance came to mind. Misreading a situation was her forte.

"Sure. I'll go with you," Declan said. He leaned back in his chair and looked so casual and confident.

Asking Allison about Declan in front of him wouldn't work. Jade threaded through the tables and around booths and arrived at Knox and Allison's table. She felt Declan behind her and she was self-conscious all over again about her messy hair.

"Hey, guys," Jade said.

"What are you doing here?" Knox asked. He glanced over Jade's shoulder and he straightened. "Declan."

"Good evening. I hope we're not disturbing your meal," Declan said.

Knox and Allison each had a margarita in front of them and a plate of nachos between them.

Allison smiled warmly. "You're not disturbing us. Mac and Evelyn are hanging out with Cody. He was asking Mac a thousand questions about the horses and Mac offered to keep him for a few hours so Knox and I could be alone."

"I just wanted to say hi," Jade said.

Allison pointed between Jade and Declan. "I thought I saw something the other day at La Bonne Vie between you two."

Jade tensed. "This isn't a date." She felt almost like she had to defend herself or explain the situation. This couldn't be a date. It was a letdown to think her first official date with Declan, who she was crushing on big-time, was happening while her shoes were covered in mud and she was dirty and sweaty from a day of work.

"I wasn't…" Allison glanced at Knox as if to say, *help*.

Knox cleared his throat. "It's just unusual for Jade to be out with a man."

Allison gave him an exasperated look and Jade felt her cheeks heating.

"What Knox means is that we didn't expect to see you here."

Jade shifted on her feet, wishing she had stayed at her and Declan's table.

"We won't keep you. I'll see you at work tomorrow, Allison," Declan said.

Then he set his hand on Jade's hip in a decidedly date-like way. He steered her toward their table.

Declan didn't bring up her comment about this being a date and she let it pass. Maybe he hadn't heard her.

After talking for a few minutes, Jade relaxed again and forgot about her brother and the mud on her shoes and her hair. She lost herself in Declan's green eyes and bright smile.

When they arrived back at the farm, Jade was nervous. She felt like she had flubbed their first date. Declan had been acting boyfriend-like. Long glances, listening intently and sitting close to her. When he looked at her, she felt like the only woman in the world.

As she climbed out of Declan's car, her legs felt weak. A date ended with a kiss. He might kiss her. She wanted him to. If he didn't, she would chalk it up to tonight's trip to El Torero's being a casual meal between friends.

They had lingered at the restaurant longer than she had expected. The conversation had flowed and when she had stopped being nervous, she had enjoyed Declan's company more than she had enjoyed anyone's in a long time.

Running to the stable to check her horses or dashing to the barn to feed her animals and busying herself would avoid the situation. Nerves were getting the best of her. Jade waited on her side of the car. She took a deep breath.

Declan circled around toward the stable and she stayed at his side. Disappointment streamed through her. Just a goodbye. He wasn't planning to stick around after a day of gritty work or acting like he wanted to kiss her. His strong stride and his confidence were magnetic.

"I hope I didn't keep you out too long," Declan said. "I thought it would be a quick meal."

Jade unlocked the stable door, focusing on that and trying to hide the disappointment that had to be clear on her face. "I had fun. I have the last feeding and then I'll hit the showers."

Declan plucked the front of his shirt. "I must smell like hay."

She shook her head. "Nope. You somehow managed to work all day here and you smell and look terrific."

Sliding open the doors, she entered the stable.

"Need help?" Declan asked.

She shook her head and walked backward while speaking to him. "I got it from here. Thank you though. For helping with the farm and for dinner." The incident with the protesters earlier in the day ran through her mind, but she beat it back.

"I could wait until you're inside," Declan said.

He must have sensed her unease, but he couldn't be her shadow around the clock. If she wasn't safe in her home and on her farm, she wouldn't truly feel safe anywhere. "I'm okay." Now that she was back on familiar territory, she was thinking too much about how she wished she would have handled the night and scrutinizing it.

"Good night, then," Declan said. He turned to leave.

Jade leaned against one of the stalls, feeling like there wasn't enough oxygen in the room. A few deep breaths, finish the day and then wine and a shower. Declan was being friendly and she had built up his intentions in her head. She had constructed a romance between them, but it was one-sided. Thankfully, he didn't know what she had been thinking or he would believe she was ridiculous.

The next time a man showed interest, Jade would make more of an effort. Do something to get and keep his attention. Claudia and Maggie would have to give her some advice.

"I changed my mind."

Jade started at the sound of Declan's voice, deep and animalistic. Declan was striding into the barn. Before she could ask about what, he was standing in front of her, six foot something of raw masculine energy and power. His arm went around her waist and he lowered his mouth to hers.

The kiss was like from a movie. Passion and heat, sending excitement and emotion spiraling through her body. Her world was shaken and shattered and pulled back together by Declan, irrevocably changed. Their mouths pressed together created a firestorm. The man could kiss. The right amount of pressure and softness, and she tasted a hint of lime. Her body slumped against his. His hand spread open on her lower back and he deepened the kiss.

She was falling for him, tumbling head over heels, going into a complete emotional free fall. Declan was suave and sexy, with only a hint of arrogance, which might be well deserved. He was class and style and sophistication and still warm and sweet to her.

His other hand moved into her hair and tilted her head back. Every nerve ending in her body reacted to the way he touched her.

She would have stripped naked in the stable if he'd asked her to. One kiss and he had control.

Too soon, he broke away, brushed his lips to hers and relaxed his arms around her. Staying close, she set her hands on his chest.

"You came back to do that?" Jade asked.

"Didn't even make it to the car," Declan said. He was slightly out of breath and it was a bump to her self-esteem that she had a hand in that.

"Why did you hesitate?"

Declan's green eyes studied her face. "You have a lot going on. I have a lot going on. Together, that makes it complicated."

"It doesn't need to be complicated. It can just be two people spending time together, having fun. And mucking out a horse stall now and then."

He tossed her a boyish grin. "You're game for that?"

For having fun? Sure. After a simple kiss, she couldn't ask him for commitment and forever. "I like spending time with you."

"What about your family? What about River?"

Her family would be fine with him. "I'm not worried about River or what he might think." Her family had plenty of issues. Accepting that long ago, she tried to focus on her life as an individual and not her life as a Colton.

"We'll see where this leads," Declan said. He brushed his thumb down her cheek.

An unspoken connection had been formed. Crossing from friends into more-than-friends was a scary step, but Jade was confident that Declan would be good for her. In some way, he would be who she needed, at least for now.

He helped her feed the horses and her barn animals and then walked her to her front door. Setting one hand on the doorjamb and the other at his side, he kissed her. This time was quicker, but as intense. It was on the tip of her tongue to invite him inside, but she thought better of it. Moving too fast would get her in trouble. Her heart was already running away with ideas and she had to protect herself.

"Good night, Jade," Declan said.

"Night, Declan."

Chapter 5

Big Jim's had the best burgers in Shadow Creek. Though the floor seemed to be perpetually slick with grease and the desserts in the display case were too old to be appealing, no one came to Big Jim's for the ambiance. The white-tiled walls were too sterile looking and Jade wouldn't have been surprised to learn they hosed the place down with bleach every month to keep the grease and germs in check.

Jade ordered her mushroom Swiss burger with extra mushrooms, extra ketchup and fries on the side. She sat across from Maggie, who had ordered a much healthier option, a hamburger on wheat and loaded with romaine lettuce, Roma tomatos, red onions and sweet peppers.

"If I squint, this almost looks like a salad," Maggie said.

"You don't need to worry about eating salad. You're pregnant. That's the green light for great food. You have to feed the baby's cravings."

Maggie laughed. "Good point. I might regret this after I have him, but the baby is hungry. I've been waking up in the middle of the night starving. Thorne caught me the other night eating apple pie directly from the pie tin."

"I've done that and I'm not pregnant," Jade said.

"He didn't say anything, but I felt judged. But then I soothed myself by eating a piece of chocolate cake."

Jade laughed.

"Now that I'm this big, I spend more time eating and sleeping than I do with Thorne. I feel bad."

"I'm sure he understands," Jade said.

"He's good about it. I've been moody too, but he doesn't get riled up when I pick a fight."

"Thorne is a good man," Jade said.

"He is. The best. And what about you? I heard a family rumor from Knox and Allison that you and Declan had dinner the other night."

Jade was planning on telling Maggie about her "date" with Declan. "He'd come by earlier in the day to help me."

"Help you do what?" Maggie asked.

"Do chores around the farm."

Maggie swiped a french fry from Jade's plate. "He isn't a farmer. Or a rancher. He's a real estate mogul. What's he doing poking around the farm?"

Jade couldn't explain that fully. "He offered to check in on me."

Maggie's eyebrows lifted. "Because he has a crush on you?"

Jade wanted to believe he did. "He's been by a few times. I am not sure how he feels about me."

"Tell me about the date."

"I was wearing my work clothes. I think because I didn't realize it was a date until we were at the restaurant. Even then I wasn't really sure."

"Then he just suggested it casually," Maggie said.

"Yes. But this is the part that makes me think it was a date and I should have at least showered. At the end of the night, he kissed me."

Maggie leaned forward and set her hands on her belly. "Tell me that part. You should have started with that. That's the really good part."

It was the most amazing part of the story. "It was the best kiss I've ever had."

"Then you're interested in Declan? You want to be in a relationship with him? Is it serious?"

Jade held up her hands. "Of course I'm interested in him. He's a great guy. He's sweet and smart and sexy."

"He is all those things, but he also bought your mother's house and land and he hasn't explained why. Allison has tried to bring it up in conversation, but he avoids answering her."

"He's a real estate developer. He thinks the land is useful for something."

"Did he say that? Because Edith has been tight-lipped about La Bonne Vie too," Maggie said.

"He wants to tear down La Bonne Vie. He invited me to tour the house, which was a therapeutic experience. I needed to walk through and chase the demons from that house. There's so much that went on. I have memories from living there and I'm not sure if they're real, or if they were dreams or some type of mixed-up memory or an exaggeration of what actually happened."

Maggie inclined her head. "Like what?"

"My mother did strange things. Leaving the house in the middle of the night and returning in the early morning hours. Whispered conversations on the porch. Meeting strangers at the house or in the barn. She must have been conducting her business and trying to keep me and my siblings from knowing anything." But Jade had caught on to problems and stress. Even as the youngest, she had heard hushed whispers, phone calls in the middle of the night, large truck deliveries in the early morning. Jade was a big reason the authorities were able to nail Livia Colton with evidence of her crimes.

Jade snapped back to reality. A woman in a pale pink T-shirt stood in front of their table. She set her hand on her hip; her stringy, blond hair with three-inch brunette roots was in need of a washing and a dye job. Her nose ring glinted in the lights overhead. Her square glasses had thick brown frames and she had a beauty mark on her cheek close to her mouth. "You're Coltons."

Jade imagined she would describe rotting filth in the same tone of voice.

"I'm Jade Colton." Jade stood up and wedged herself between Maggie and the woman in the pink top. Maggie was Thorne's wife and the mother of his child. If this woman wanted to confront someone, she would need to get through Jade first. Maggie didn't need stress right now.

Jade felt Maggie's hand at her hip, nudging her to move, but Jade didn't budge.

"Can I help you with something?" She recalled the protesters outside her farm, but didn't remember if this woman had been one of them.

"Coltons aren't wanted in Shadow Creek."

Jade stared at her, never breaking eye contact. "It's not your business where I choose to live."

Pink Shirt folded her arms across her chest and leaned forward. "Everyone hates you."

The words stung more than Jade had expected. "Everyone" was an exaggeration, but the point hit on insecurities Jade had carried since Livia had been arrested. It seemed to have gotten worse since Livia was discovered hiding at La Bonne Vie. No one wanted her around; it added fear and anger into the community.

"I'm not leaving Shadow Creek," Jade said.

The woman glared at Jade as she walked away.

Jade was proud of herself that she hadn't slapped her. She turned to Maggie. "Are you okay?"

"Except that I was wedged between the wall and

you and couldn't get up to scream in her face, I'm fine."

"She was ignorant and rude," Jade said. "There's not much we can say to combat that." Her attempts to blow off the woman's words weren't working. They had struck a chord.

Jade noticed other patrons were looking in her direction. Were Pink Shirt's words drawing attention or were people in the shop whispering and talking about her? It shouldn't matter. She was a grown woman. Gossip and malice should roll off her. Except they hit her and stuck.

"We should go," Maggie said.

"You didn't finish eating," Jade said.

"I've lost my appetite. That's saying a lot."

Jade and Maggie left money on the table. They walked to Claudia's store, Honeysuckle Road. Claudia's clothing targeted all types of women, including those who loved their curves. From the number of women in the store, business must be good. Leonor had been kind enough to invest in Claudia's venture. Leonor had recognized Claudia's fashion expertise gained from working in New York, which gave her a unique perspective that was fresh and fun for Shadow Creek, Texas. As an art museum curator, Leonor had an eye for beautiful things and she was right to spot Claudia's design genius. Claudia had been responsible for a number of outfits the family had worn over the last several months.

Claudia raised her hand in greeting from behind the checkout counter and indicated she would be with them in a minute. Jade admired the clothing. Claudia had moved some of her summer items to the back of the store and the front displays were in fall colors of red, orange, yellow and browns.

Claudia finished with a customer and sauntered over. "Hey, Maggie. Hey, Jade. What a pleasant surprise."

"I'm glad it's a pleasant surprise for you because we just had the most unpleasant lunch," Jade said. She filled Claudia in on the details.

"Those awful people have said things to me too," Claudia said in a hushed tone. "The first time it happened, I was so shocked, I didn't know what to say in response. The next time, Hawk was with me. They shouted garbage at me and he looked at them. Just looked. And they went silent." She laughed. "They're trolls. Don't let them get to you."

Evelyn joined them, setting her hand on Maggie's back and hugging her. "What am I missing? Are we having a gossip session?"

She smiled at the women whom she treated like her children. Evelyn had been widowed and had two grown daughters and since the Coltons had known her, she had been warm and kind. "Jade and Maggie had a run-in with the local anti-Colton group," Claudia said.

Evelyn set her hand on her hip. A petite woman, she was fierce and few people messed with her. Though Mac towered over Evelyn at five-eleven, their mutual respect and admiration for each other kept their relationship balanced and even. "Those nasty harpies. They put a flyer on my car for their group, asking me to join them. I took that flyer over to the sheriff. Littering. That's what those are. Bud acted as if I was the one overreacting, but that group is bad for the town."

"What is their group all about?" Jade asked, curious about this group causing problems in Shadow Creek. If the local law enforcement wouldn't step up, she would need to do some investigation and see that she was protected from their antics. The Coltons had been through enough in the last six months. They didn't need this too.

"They're a support group for victims of Livia Colton. But they don't seem to be fixated on healing. They seem bent on harassing her children," Claudia said.

Jade was momentarily jealous of Claudia because she wasn't Livia's biological daughter. Though the town treated her the same as the others, Claudia was another of Livia's victims. Jade felt like being unrelated to her gave Claudia more freedom from the responsibility of the crimes Livia had committed. Not everyone knew the story about Claudia being a Krupid and many considered her a Colton.

"Excuse me," Evelyn said, leaving their group to assist a customer who was checking out with an armful of clothing.

The door to the shop opened again and Jade held her breath, expecting to see another angry protester.

Hawk Huntley strode through the door. Claudia's eyes lit and she ran to greet him. Hawk was protective of Claudia. His late wife had been killed by a murderer who hadn't been brought to justice. Hawk had also dropped a big bomb on Claudia, whom many considered Livia's most beautiful daughter: Claudia wasn't Livia's daughter at all. Hawk had reunited her with her biological family. Claudia had been shocked at first, but since reuniting with her biological family, seemed to take it in stride.

"I'm heading out to meet a client in Austin, but I heard some ruckus about protesters and the Coltons. I wanted to be sure you were okay." Hawk looked at Claudia, taking her hands in his.

Jade glanced away, feeling like she was interrupting a private moment.

Claudia leaned on Hawk's shoulder. "I'm fine. It was Jade who had to face it today. Maggie was with her."

Hawk's gaze swerved to Jade. "Are you okay? What did they say to you?"

Jade explained and Hawk crossed his arms over his chest, listening intently. He had a way of getting people to talk more than they should. When she finished, she waited. Maggie had wandered off and was looking at fall sweaters.

Hawk rubbed his jaw in thought. "I'm looking into the possibility of getting a lawyer to handle this. Their harassment has to stop. It can't be legal to confront people this way. Shadow Creek is a good place to live. There are decent, hardworking people here."

Except Shadow Creek hadn't always been a good place to live. Livia's crimes had been hidden beneath a guise of warmth and affection for the community, and she had done horrible things.

It boggled Jade's mind that Livia had been able to fool so many people for so long about the true nature of her business.

"Good, hardworking people who want the Coltons gone," Jade said. Her horses needed her. They didn't judge. She liked that about them.

Hawk folded his arms. "Claudia has the shop. Thorne has the ranch. You have the farm. You aren't going anywhere and I'll stand up to anyone who says otherwise."

Declan didn't know what to say to River. He wanted to say something to his half brother. Words that would undo some of the awkwardness, that would make it easier on Edith to be married to River while working for Declan. Their paths would cross and it would be less stressful if they could dissipate some of the tension between them.

If she had to choose, Edith would choose River, and Declan didn't want her to feel like she had to make that decision. Declan had only met a few people who he couldn't get along with. He had to make it work with his brother.

Declan reread the email he had been composing and then hit Send. The sun was higher in the sky now and it was too hot to work outside. When he had started at five in the morning, it had been cool, but humid. He liked to sit at the wrought iron table beneath one of the balconies. The shade kept him cooler and the view was spectacular. The bed-and-breakfast had put considerable time into landscaping their outdoor property into a thick garden with a walking trail lined with redbrick paving stones. Birdhouses hung from an oak tree.

Two men in suits rounded the corner of the bed-and-breakfast's entrance. Declan stood. There had been enough going on around Shadow Creek that strangers were a cause for concern. Declan didn't recognize the men as being from the sheriff's office, although they walked like they were cops. Their tan-colored suits were unusual and the pastel shirts a different choice. They looked like twin toddlers getting ready for church.

"Declan Sinclair?" the one in the pale yellow shirt asked.

"How can I help you?" Declan closed his laptop.

The men flashed badges at him.

"FBI Special Agents Monroe and Fielder. We have a few questions for you." Yellow Shirt, Special Agent Monroe, spoke again. Green Shirt was silent, standing a few steps back, hands at his sides, one resting on his gun.

Declan had thought the authorities were watching the Colton children for signs that Livia would show. Perhaps it was a private investigator whom Declan had seen. Livia had made plenty of enemies who might want to know her whereabouts. Declan also wondered if Livia had someone working for her, possibly gathering information around town.

Declan didn't volunteer information. He had his

reasons for being in Shadow Creek and wasn't interested in talking about them with the FBI.

"Have you seen Livia Colton in Shadow Creek in the last two weeks?" Monroe asked.

Declan shook his head. "Haven't heard from her since she tried to kidnap my assistant, Edith. I'm sure you have my statement about that incident."

The agents exchanged glances. Declan didn't know what that meant.

"You've been spending time with Jade Colton," Special Agent Monroe said.

It wasn't a secret, but it wasn't something he was announcing around town. The FBI must be watching Jade.

Declan didn't want them poking into his relationship with Jade. He wanted that part of his life as separate from Livia as possible. "Hard to throw a rock and not hit a Colton around Shadow Creek."

Special Agent Monroe removed his suit jacket. The yellow shirt was short-sleeved and his white tank top showed through the fabric.

"You've been following the Colton children," Declan said. It wasn't a question.

"We're looking for Livia Colton and following every lead possible," Special Agent Fielder said.

"Have you seen any signs that she has returned to La Bonne Vie?" Special Agent Monroe asked.

"You could check with my construction foreman, Allison Colton of Rafferty Construction. She's overseeing the teardown. Her team is on-site every day and they would have more information about whether or not they've seen signs that Livia has returned. Allison would contact me if she saw her, but I don't know if they've been looking."

"The Coltons are thick as thieves. They might be harboring Livia on one of their properties," Agent Monroe said.

It sounded like an accusation. "I don't know them well enough to say." Jade wouldn't do that, but Declan couldn't speak for the others.

"We're investigating if they had a hand in helping Livia hide at La Bonne Vie," Monroe said.

If they were dropping bait to see if he'd rise to it, they were mistaken. He had a score to settle with Livia, but the closer he got to Jade, the less interest he had in seeing it through. Though Jade was angry with her mother, it would raise some complex issues between them if he inserted himself into the investigation.

"I hope you find her," Declan said.

Special Agent Monroe handed him his business card. "Call me immediately if you see anything."

"Will do." Declan wouldn't hide Livia. He had no loyalty to her and from what he had seen from Jade and her siblings, they weren't interested in protecting their mother.

He watched the agents leave. Edith should arrive soon. They were planning to drive to Austin today to look at a condominium property that had gone bankrupt three-quarters of the way through building. Declan wanted to see if it was worth the investment to finish it.

It was five minutes past eight thirty. Edith came onto the patio from the bed-and-breakfast. "What was that about? I was eavesdropping inside, but I couldn't hear everything."

"What every problem in Shadow Creek circles back to."

Edith's mouth tightened. Her ordeal with Livia had been terrifying. Enough time hadn't passed for her to feel completely safe. Until Livia was back in custody, she might not ever. "That hateful woman. She's been ruining lives for decades. Karma has to catch up with her."

Declan felt his anger rising. Edith had been through enough in her life and this latest trauma would leave scars. "Did you call the therapist I suggested?" He was a big believer in getting help when it was needed and after what Edith had lived through, it was needed.

Edith sat in the chair across from him. "I did. I have an appointment this week."

"She might help you put it behind you," Declan said.

"River is doing that. He is going with me to the appointment to be supportive. He has no loyalty to his mother and he's been there for me every tear, nightmare and breakdown. Dealing with Livia isn't the hardest thing I've ever done, but recently, it has been smoother sailing. I'm an adult making my choices and I had been making pretty good ones."

"I never should have sent you to La Bonne Vie alone. I should have gone with you," Declan said. By sending Edith to Livia's house, he wondered if he'd inadvertently painted a target on her chest.

"Livia is to blame. Not you. Speaking of her, I had a flyer on my car this morning and there were pamphlets on the coffee table in the parlor. The Victims of Livia Colton support group is gathering people to join them."

After the incident with the protesters at Jade's farm, Declan was aware of the group. Given how much some of the Colton children had invested in their businesses, Declan didn't see leaving as a feasible option for Jade, Claudia, Knox or Thorne. "I've seen a few things around town I find disturbing. But unless it escalates beyond words, I'm going to see if it flames itself out."

"They seem to be amping up their effort. Maybe Livia's escape from prison stirred up a lot of emotions. Knox wants to be sheriff. He's not going to give that up over a few loudmouths, but the open protests and the campaign against the Coltons might hurt his chances," Edith said.

"Colton or not, Knox has to be a better sheriff than Bud."

Edith touched her chest. "I would be a better sheriff than Bud."

Though the idea of Edith as law enforcement didn't resonate, she was right. "Let me grab my notes and we'll head to Austin."

Edith broke into a smile. Declan guessed it had something to do with River. "I'm planning to meet River for lunch," Edith said.

There it was. Even work trips involved River now. Declan tried not to let it bother him. Territoriality over Edith, worry for her safety and his unresolved issues with River amounted to uneasiness. "That's fine."

"I hope you'll join us," Edith said.

She wanted her boss and friend to get along with her future husband. Declan understood that. But he and River just had awkwardness between them that they couldn't move past. Lunch together might help. "Okay, I will join you."

Edith's bright smile was worth the concession.

Jade's pocket vibrated. She hoped it was a phone call or message from Declan.

An unknown number appeared on the display and she hesitated. Her imagination and fears played together: her mother calling with a threat, the authorities delivering the news that one of her siblings had been hurt or killed. The terror she carried for Livia Colton was alive and well inside her. Reminding herself she wasn't a child and her mother didn't wield the same power she once did, Jade answered.

"I'm trying to get in touch with the owner of Hill Country horse rehab about a horse."

"This is Jade. How may I help you?" Her breath came out in a whoosh.

"I bought an off-track Thoroughbred. I had read about them and I thought I could handle him. But it's been three months and I've gotten nowhere. The horse still freaks at loud sounds. The Fourth of July was a nightmare. I've been to four veterinarians and no one knows what to do. Morning Glory isn't my first horse. He's not even my twentieth. But I can't handle him. I heard your name from a friend in Shadow Creek and I wondered if you'd come out and do a consultation and maybe even take him to your place until he's a little better."

She had a to-do list a mile long and knew that a quick look-over might not give her the information she needed. Each horse she added to her stables was additional work and a large financial commitment by the owner. Jade didn't have the capacity to care for more horses that didn't also come with monetary support. Food, vet and supply bills were rolling in faster than donations. But the idea of a horse suffering bothered her. The man sounded desperate. If he felt his options were limited, he could put the animal down or send it to another farm and without the proper care, it would be hard for the horse. "I can come take a look at Morning Glory," she found herself saying. Adding more to her plate wasn't a great idea. Her love of horses had gotten the better of her.

"I'd be eternally grateful," the man said.

After getting his name and address of the farm, Jade climbed in her white pickup truck and headed to a farm located ten miles west of Shadow Creek.

She parked in the driveway and walked to the light blue clapboard house. The house was well maintained, with tidy rows of white, purple and pink flowers in the front surrounded with a six-inch mini picket fence. The white front porch wrapped around the house. On the side of the house was a navy ship wheel, a unique decoration for a farm. She wondered if the owner had ties to the navy. Lining the porch was an eclectic mix of rockers, wicker and wood, in white, brown, tan and black.

Jade knocked on the door. There was no answer. She walked down the four steps and circled the house. The man who had called her might be in the barn. Taking the dirt path, Jade admired the farm. Crops spread across the land as far as she could see. The barn was the same color as the house.

"Jade?" She recognized the man's voice from the phone. Phil Siefert was a balding man in his late thirties with round spectacles and a warm smile.

"Yes, hello." She extended her hand in greeting.

A woman in her thirties with red, tightly curled hair was sitting on the back porch, wearing a yellow dress and white apron around her waist.

The man shook her hand and gestured to the barn. "Come meet Morning Glory."

"Was that his racing name?" Jade asked. She was politely digging into the horse's history. Though not all horses could be saved, she believed most could.

"Naw. I changed it. Didn't want him reacting to those verbal cues. He's been difficult since the first day. He had a leg fracture, which the vet repaired. But the horse thinks he's still meant to run. Takes off any chance he gets. If he sees bright colors or sees a small group, he wants to perform," Phil said.

"I've seen that before," Jade said.

They entered the stable and Jade knew immediately which horse was Morning Glory. The horse was restless, his nervous energy pulsing off him in waves. He wouldn't want her to touch him.

"Tried letting him in the pasture. He lost it. Got aggressive with my other horses," Phil said.

Jade watched the horse, the way he tensed when she drew closer to him. Taking a few steps back, she watched. Morning Glory would know she hadn't left, but she didn't want to crowd him.

"Phil?" The woman from the porch was standing in the entryway.

"Excuse me," Phil said to Jade and walked to his wife.

Jade focused on the horse, but in the stillness of the barn, she couldn't help overhearing. The woman hadn't said anything to her, but her mannerisms were hostile and she pointed at Jade several times.

Then Jade heard the words, "Livia 'Black Heart' Colton."

It was like a boom had been lowered on her head. Jade felt dizzy and nervous and sad at once. Though she hadn't mentioned she was Livia's daughter, as it wasn't something she was proud of, her mother's legacy followed her children everywhere.

Phil walked back to her and his wife left.

"I'm sorry, miss, but we're going to explore other options."

Because she was a Colton. Phil had to have known that when he'd called her. Or maybe he had been hoping she wasn't one of *those* Coltons. Jade was embarrassed and angry. She wasn't here to hurt anyone and she was different from her mother. "I have a busy schedule. I came out here to help Morning Glory. I know he seems difficult, but difficult horses are my specialty. I could help him. But you won't give me the chance because of who my mother is." Though she didn't like addressing the issue so directly, she had hit her limit.

Phil's face grew red. "Your mother ruined Shadow Creek. She brought criminals and evil to Texas. Everything she touched turned vile."

Jade's mouth went dry. No illusions about what her mother had done, the words spoken to her face felt harsh. "She did wrong. I know that. But I am not her."

Jade stalked away, wishing she could take Morning Glory, but knowing his owner wouldn't give him to her.

Being a Colton in this part of Texas was the same as having a scarlet letter on her chest.

As Jade pulled up to her farm, dread washed over her. The protesters were back. They must not have jobs or lives to keep them busy, if they wanted to spend their time bothering her. On the heels of her experience with Morning Glory, she wanted to scream at them.

Except yelling would make her look like the monster they believed her to be. A profanity-laced tirade would have them nodding their heads as if she was proving them right.

This afternoon, two girls from the high school

were coming to help feed and care for the animals. The school bus dropped them off and their parents picked them up. Jade didn't want them to walk through the picket line.

Jade pulled into her driveway and stopped the car. Still reeling from the treatment she had received at Phil's farm, she stepped out. Anger and resentment bubbled up inside her.

One deep breath and every ounce of effort to control her tone and stay calm. "This is my place of business. This is a place where I take care of horses that need me. I've taken animals that no one else will. But you're fixated on what my mother did. Do any of you really believe that I don't know what a monster she is?"

She waited and no one spoke. They were holding their signs and staring at her like she was a two-headed snake.

"I don't know why I'm bothering to speak. You don't care who you hurt. You aren't interested in a conversation or in mending fences. This is fair warning. I'm calling the sheriff."

Doubtful that he would do anything to help her, but it was worth the call. She climbed back into her car and drove slowly to the front of her house. Parking, she took out her cell phone. After filing her complaint with the sheriff's office with a totally unsympathetic deputy, she called Declan, needing a boost.

"What are you up to today?" she asked.

"I had lunch with your brother," he said.

"River?"

"I'm wrapping up business in Austin. Edith and I had work to attend to. Talk about being a third wheel," Declan said.

"I'm sure it wasn't like that," Jade said. River and Edith seemed to want Declan to have a relationship with his brother and Declan was resistive. Was it because of whatever had happened with their father and Livia? Or did it have more to do with Declan's relationship with Edith?

"I get along with Edith, no issues. But I don't know how to talk to River," Declan said.

"Because of his injury?" Jade asked. Her brother had lost an eye while serving in the marines overseas.

"Because of our history. We have the same father, but those circumstances are unpleasant."

Jade knew most of the story of how Declan and River shared a father. Livia Colton wasn't known for her chastity or for being monogamous. "You guys should come here for a slice of pie and I'll keep the conversation going. Good practice."

"How all-American. If you're there, I think it would be less third wheel and more double date," Declan said.

At the mention of a date, a thrill of delight moved through her. "But until I have pie and can make arrangements, why don't you stop by for a glass of wine? I had a hellish day and I could use some company."

"Only if you'll let me bring dinner," Declan said.

"Gladly."

"It will be a couple of hours before I can leave."

"No problem. I have work to finish up here. If it's dark, try to avoid hitting the protesters in the driveway," Jade said.

He groaned. "They're back? Wow, that's really upsetting. I'm sorry, Jade."

"I can deal with it. It's not the worst thing I've been through, but it's working on my nerves."

"I'll see if I can cheer you up tonight," Declan said.

After saying goodbye, Jade went about the rest of her work with a spring in her step. The protesters moved on after another thirty minutes of shouting. After they left, her nerves calmed down and her help arrived in the form of two dedicated students. They had been working with her for so long, they knew the horses and the routine. Her trust in their abilities was absolute and she felt great when she could teach them about horses or the farm.

By the time her student help was leaving, Jade had at least thirty minutes to shower and change before Declan arrived.

She peeled off her sweaty, muddy clothes and stuffed them in the hamper. Turning on the shower, she waited for steam to rise from the stall and stepped in. The ritual was cleansing and renewing.

This was a date. No question about it. She would put forth the effort because she wanted this with Declan.

After getting out of the shower and opening the

door to her closet, she turned her attention to the left side, where she had nonwork clothes. It was the smallest part of her closet, taking up only about eight inches of space. Slim pickings, but she would make do. The yellow dress with the ruffle at the top would give her a more shapely appearance. A dress might be too fancy for dinner and wine at home, but after completely skipping any pretense of preparation for a date the last time she went out with Declan, she wasn't taking chances.

Slipping the dress on, she dried her hair, leaving it loose around her shoulders. Then she went to the kitchen to make sure she had two clean glasses. The doorbell rang and Jade walked to it. She opened her door and air backed up in her lungs.

Declan was on the porch, carrying dinner in a handled brown paper bag in one hand and a bouquet of wildflowers in another. He was wearing gray trousers and a light blue dress shirt, sleeves rolled to the elbow.

The top two buttons of the shirt were undone. He nailed the look.

"Thanks for inviting me over," he said. "These are for you."

Jade accepted the flowers, the oranges, pinks, yellows and purples bright and beautiful. "Come in. Please."

Striding to the kitchen, she felt Declan's gaze at her back and she was pleased she had chosen to wear the yellow dress instead of something more casual. She pulled out a decorative pitcher that Maggie had given her and filled it with water. Setting the flowers in them, she tried to hide the shaking of her hands.

"Is something wrong?" Declan asked.

He was standing behind her, closer than she had realized. Turning, she met his eyes. "I'm nervous."

His hands were free. Dinner was on the table, beckoning to her with the delightful smells of basil and cilantro. But even though she hadn't eaten since lunch, Declan had her full attention and her appetite was nonexistent.

"Nervous about me?" he asked. "Why?"

Needing something to do, she handed him the corkscrew and the bottle of wine.

"I feel like something is going to happen," she said. "Something between us. I've felt it since I first met you. It's complicated because you're Edith's boss and River's brother and you bought La Bonne Vie, but I feel this connection to you." The honest statement helped her nerves settle.

"I feel a connection to you, as well. I didn't expect that," Declan said.

Jade set out two plates, wineglasses and utensils, and Declan popped the cork on the wine. He poured them each a glass.

Accepting the proffered drink, she drank deeply. The wine went to her head, warmth spreading through her body. Her shoulders relaxed and she stepped toward Declan.

"Then if you think something is going to happen, why aren't you worried?" Jade asked.

"Why would I be worried?" he asked.

"I'm a Colton. That worries people." The protesters in town, the sheriff, most of Livia's victims and associates and most recently Phil Siefert's wife.

"That doesn't bother me. You're a kind woman with a good heart. I've seen that time and again."

She wanted to be those things. Jade wanted to throw off the hurtful legacy her mother had left and embrace the life she wanted. Her farm would be successful because of the love and attention and work she put into it. When she walked into town, it would not be with whispers chasing her and sideways looks tossed in her direction. She would wave to the people she knew and smile at friends. After a while, her mother's crimes would be forgotten because of the good deeds Jade was doing. Wishful thinking, perhaps. "Thank you. I'm trying to change what the name Colton means in this town."

"I can tell. There's nothing about you that makes me think of the crimes Livia committed."

If Jade were taller, she could kiss Declan. She could wrap her hand around his neck and pull his mouth to hers.

Declan took a sip of his drink. "This is good."

She didn't want to talk about wine. Going for it, she pulled his mouth to hers. He didn't resist. She kissed him long and slow. His lips tasted sweet.

Declan had his hands on her shoulders. He deepened the kiss and his hands moved to her back. Jade arched into him, wishing they didn't have clothes between them. Being skin to skin with him would be amazing. Underneath his business attire, she imagined he was built strong. Her hands verified the thought, her fingers digging into the tight muscles of his shoulders.

Her heart was pounding with excitement, urging her forward.

His hands slid to her hips and then to her rear. He lifted her and she wrapped her legs around his waist. Carrying her to the counter, he set her down, remaining between her thighs.

"Don't you want to eat?" he asked.

She took his face in her hands. "No. I don't care about that."

Declan kissed her again. Tongues dueled. Hands explored. Hearts pounded. She forgot about dinner and focused only on Declan.

Chapter 6

When Declan broke away, he ran a hand through his ruffled hair. "Wow." Every other time Jade had seen Declan, he'd looked put together. Now he looked disheveled and she liked that. "We should slow down. Have some dinner."

Her pride took a beating. If he could break away that easily, was he not into her? He helped her off the counter and they sat at the table. Declan spread out the food, a wide range of dishes from a gourmet restaurant in Austin.

They ate and after a couple awkward moments, conversation flowed, along with the wine. He looked at her and touched her casually in a way that made her feel special and wanted. A brush of his hand, his foot resting beside hers underneath the table. Like slow and deliberate foreplay that did nothing to clear the daze of excitement from her thoughts.

Jade was out of her element. Declan was tough to read. His plate was clear, but he was sipping his wine. She made a move to clarify her intentions. She stood and pushed his chair away from the table. Sitting in his lap, she threaded her hands around the back of his neck. "Are you finished with dinner?"

"What's the plan?" he asked, setting his wineglass on the table.

"To take it easy tonight." She pressed a kiss to his lips.

With the right amount of firmness, their chemistry sizzling, he returned the kiss. His hands wrapped around her back and Jade let herself fall into the dizzying sensation of being in his arms.

Three hours after they finished their dinner, Declan left Jade's place. If he didn't leave, their relationship would escalate and move into her bedroom and he sensed neither of them was ready for that. Being on the same page physically wasn't the same as being in the right place as a couple. Declan liked Jade enough to wait until it was right before moving forward with their relationship. Advancing too fast would torpedo an otherwise good thing.

Their attraction was off the charts, but she was still Livia Colton's daughter and that presented challenges.

Edith knew the truth about his and River's father, but it was a sad, twisted story and Declan hated talking about it. He hated admitting that Livia Colton had torn his family apart almost easily. Livia's affair with his father, Matthew, had broken Declan's mother's heart. The result of that affair was River, and Declan wasn't clear if his father had known he'd had another son.

Matthew had been obsessed with Livia. Obsessed to the point that nothing mattered except being with her. When that wasn't possible, Matthew had lost it. He had committed suicide and Declan's mother had abandoned him.

Declan's clothes were rumpled but, miraculously, still on. They hadn't left his body during the course of the evening. Though Jade had explored almost everything over his clothes, under them, his body was humming.

The dark sedan Declan had seen several times lingering around the Coltons was parked on the street. Special Agents Monroe and Fielder? Declan strode to the car and tapped on the window.

Not the FBI agents he had spoken to earlier that week and no one he recognized from the sheriff's office. Surprise registered in the driver's face. He must not have seen Declan approaching.

"Can I help you with something?" Declan asked.

The man rolled the window down a few inches. "Mind your business."

Declan didn't care for that comment. "Jade Colton is my business."

The man sighed. "I'm a reporter. I'm tracking Livia Colton."

Declan's intuition pinged that something was wrong, though he couldn't put his finger on what. "Jade is not harboring a fugitive. If she saw Livia, she would call the sheriff."

The reporter narrowed his eyes. "I'm not looking for trouble. I want to find Livia, get the story of her escape and collect the reward money for helping to bring her to justice."

Livia wouldn't share her story without something in return. "Why don't you believe me and move on? Livia Colton is not here."

The reporter shrugged and started the engine of the car. "We'll see about that." He drove away from the farm, tires squealing as he turned out of the driveway.

Declan watched him leave. His bullcrap meter was squawking. The man was not a reporter. No recording equipment and no paper. An odd sense of unease passed over Declan.

He had left Jade in her house and had waited for the bolt to lock before he had left. But she was out here alone. Like most of the farms and ranches in Shadow Creek, the wide spreads of land meant most were isolated. It took the sheriff time to respond to calls, and given Bud's history with the Coltons, he might take his sweet time responding, if at all.

Turning around, Declan walked to Jade's front door and knocked.

Jade peeked through the curtain before opening it. "Forget something?" The yellow dress she had worn tonight had the most enticing straps. Pushing them over her shoulders would be easy and he had been tempted several times.

"Besides you?" Declan asked.

She smiled up at him.

He hated to break her smile. "There was a man in the driveway. He said he was a reporter."

Jade looked around Declan and folded her arms. "Was it a reporter for *Everything's Blogger in Texas*?"

Declan knew the Coltons had had some trouble with that particular website in the past. He had read it, but had lost interest in it. "He didn't say which media outlet he was with, but I think he was lying."

Worry crossed her face and Jade waved him into the house. He stepped over the threshold. She closed and locked the door behind them.

"Who do you think he was?" Jade asked, a tremble in her voice.

He hadn't meant to upset her, but she needed to be informed. More than that, Declan wanted a plan that would help her feel safe. "I don't know. I should have snapped his picture and asked River or Hawk to look into it."

"River? You'd hire River for the job?" Jade asked.

Though he hadn't progressed much with his relationship with the man, when it came to Jade, they had her best interests at heart. "He's working for Joshua at the security company, isn't he?"

"He is, but I'm surprised you mentioned him."

It wasn't the point of the story he wanted her to think about. "I'm staying here tonight. On the couch.

I don't like the idea of people watching the house. Between the guy in the sedan and the protesters, it's better if I stick around."

"You don't have to do that. I'm not alone here. I have my animals," Jade said.

"The animals won't protect you if someone comes after you," Declan said.

"You don't have to sleep on the couch. I have a guest bedroom. From time to time, I have help stay with me when I have a big job that requires an early start."

The tension in the air was thick. Declan couldn't interpret if the reason was the sedan and the unsettling feeling it had left or because they were spending the night together in her home. Being in close proximity accented several emotions, like his desire for her and the slow progression of their relationship that, at least on a physical level, they both wanted to kick up a notch. But Declan had control and he would wait. His return to her house had everything to do with keeping her safe.

The spare bedroom was at the rear of the house, and a door led onto the back porch. Together, they made the bed in the guest bedroom with fresh sheets the color of the inside of an avocado. The room was simple, with two single beds and a small table between them, a white lamp and a black-and-red alarm clock positioned in the middle. The walls were painted tan and the hardwood floor was polished and clean. The curtains over the window were frilly and reached from the ceiling to the floor.

"I should say good-night now," Jade said. "My day starts in a few hours."

"We've already said good-night once," Declan said. He needed his self-control to part ways with her again in the same evening. Her bedroom was across the hallway, a fact that would play on his mind all night.

Jade rose on her toes and kissed his cheek. "Night, Declan."

Jade retreated to her bedroom and he heard the door shut. Thank God she had set the boundary. Having that clear made him sure he wouldn't cross it.

Declan cleaned up in the bathroom and then laid on the cool sheets in his boxers. He should talk to Jade about his father and Livia. She might have heard it from River's point of view, but it was the most painful piece of his past and sharing it with her felt important.

Realistically, and from a business perspective, after Declan was finished with La Bonne Vie, he was finished with Shadow Creek. He had no reason to return unless it was to see Edith. This place was filled with signs of Livia Colton and with that brought fresh waves of grief. To tell Jade about his mother abandoning him after his father's death wouldn't make her feel better.

On a personal level, there was a very important person who would make him stay in Shadow Creek: Jade. If someone had told him a year ago a Colton would change his plans, he would have laughed in their face.

Declan turned off the light and closed his eyes.

The creaking of floorboards had him bolting up-right. He flipped on the light. Jade stood in the door-way of the room, wearing a pale blue tank top and printed shorts.

"Everything okay?" he asked.

Jade walked to him on the balls of her feet. Nudg-ing him over with her knee, she lay beside him on the bed. "Nothing will happen tonight, but I need you. I need someone. I just don't want to be alone."

He shifted to give her more room and then closed his eyes again. Her even breathing was calm and his arm over her hip rose and fell with her chest.

When Jade woke, she realized first that she wasn't in her bed and second that she was in bed with De-clan.

She had spent the night with Declan. Except her clothes were on. There was intimacy and trust in that act, sleeping beside him.

Not wanting to wake him, she slipped from the bed and to her shower. Her animals needed to eat. Though lying in bed late would be great, her work schedule didn't allow it. After brushing her teeth and taking a quick shower, she put on a T-shirt and shorts. Opening her bathroom door, she smelled cof-fee.

Declan was awake. Deep breath. They had spent the night together. She could speak to him now. It wouldn't be awkward unless she let it.

"I made you coffee," he said, pointing to the cup

on the counter. He was wearing a white T-shirt and his dress pants. Hung over the back of her kitchen chair were his dress shirt and tie.

"Thank you," she said. She took a sip. The right strength and heat. Perfect. She added that attribute to the list of things she liked about him: he made good coffee.

"Are you eating breakfast?" he asked.

She shook her head. "I'll feed my animals first and then get breakfast."

"I can cook breakfast for you," Declan said.

Jade pointed to her refrigerator. "You won't find much to work with."

Declan laughed. "Understood. I've got a few calls to make. I'll come back with a late breakfast in a couple of hours."

He was being kind and attentive, but she was taking advantage of his generosity. "That's okay. I don't know if I'll have time to take a break today." None of her part-time help was coming.

Declan set his mug in the sink. He kissed the top of her head. "Everyone needs to eat. Be back soon."

After grabbing his shirt and tie off the back of the chair, he strode out of the house. Jade watched him leave, a mix of curious and nervous. She hadn't been looking for a relationship, but it seemed like one had found her.

Declan showered and shaved at the bed-and-breakfast and almost missed a call from SinCo's lawyer.

"Glad I caught you this morning," Ricardo said. Ricardo had been with Declan from the beginning. An expert in property law, he'd reached out to some colleagues to consult on the criminal issues with the embezzlement.

"What's the word?" Declan asked. SinCo's former employee's misappropriation of company funds bothered him, but since coming to Shadow Creek, it had become less important. It wasn't on his mind all the time and when it was, it was easy enough to find a distraction. He wouldn't see that money again and he had ensured that his other employees hadn't been impacted, using his personal funds to cover any amount missing.

But it had shaken his trust. Tim DeVega must have seen a giant dollar sign stamped on his forehead. Declan had been a boy when Livia was in her prime as a general in a crime organization, but he imagined the town had viewed her the same way, as a source of money. They had turned a blind eye to her illegal activities. The hospital she had built and the 4-H club events she had sponsored, the elaborate holiday barbecues and allowing the ranchers in the area to use her water: these were the actions of a woman who cared about her community and the other stuff was ignored.

Every picture Declan had seen of the Colton family showed Livia surrounded by her children, her face in an expression of admiration and joy, as if being with her family was fulfilling and wonderful. Lies. Acting. Livia's soul was black. She had fooled people, the town, the men who had married her, the men who she'd had affairs with; they were all pawns in her game.

Declan had contemplated her reasons for marrying so many men and having children with some of them. He wouldn't believe for a minute that the intention was love or respect or commitment. Whatever had happened to her in her life, she must have enjoyed the attention she received from men who dated her and from people when she was pregnant. The children were traps for wealthy men to ensure Livia received payments, either during a divorce or in child support.

Some of those behaviors had to have trickled down to her sons and daughters. While Jade's siblings seemed to be in stable relationships, Declan wondered what went on with the Colton children behind closed doors.

As he got to know Jade, he kept waiting to catch her doing something deceitful or cruel. But every experience with her was refreshingly enjoyable. Declan didn't know how much longer that could last. Jade seemed so different from her mother. Her work was selfless, except for the satisfaction she derived from doing it. Though she didn't seem especially close with her siblings, she was kind to them.

If she was going to behave like her mother, Declan would have expected it when the protesters had showed up at her house. But though Jade had been rattled, he hadn't detected rage in her response.

Jade was different from her mother. Could he and

Jade create enough distance from their parents that their issues didn't pass to the next generation?

When Leonor had called earlier in the day to ask Jade to attend the opening of a new exhibit in the art museum where she worked, Jade had wanted to say no. By the end of the day, she was exhausted and driving an hour to Austin to look at artwork she didn't understand sounded boring and a waste of her time.

But then she had thought about asking Declan to come with her and the idea became infinitely more appealing.

Claudia had helped Jade select a blue dress with a white lace overlay. Jade had driven with Claudia and Hawk to the museum. Declan had business in Austin and had promised to meet her there.

Jade stood in front of the wide windows, adjusting her shawl around her arms. She clasped a white clutch and tried not to look nervous. Obsessively checking her phone would be bad. Instead, she watched couples entering the museum. Leonor had done great publicity for the museum to draw so many people to see the new exhibit.

Jade sensed him watching her before she saw him. She turned. Declan was sauntering down the street, wearing a gray suit with a pressed white shirt. He smiled in greeting and when he was close enough, he took her elbows and kissed her cheeks.

"I didn't know that sculptures were your thing," Declan said.

"They aren't really. I'm here for Leonor."

Declan set his hand on Jade's lower back and steered her toward the front door. "I don't think we should linger on the street."

"Joshua is helping with security for the event. We're safe," Jade said.

"I'd still feel better inside," Declan said.

He held open the black door and she entered. Leonor had done a good job with the exhibit. The walls were white and the floor light-colored hardwood, but the paintings and murals and sculptures were arranged tastefully. Near the front of the museum were two large, ten-foot walls set about eight feet from the windows that provided privacy. In front of them were displays of the current exhibit to draw interested parties inside. Strolling behind the walls, Leonor had set up a welcoming atmosphere. Music played softly and a black lacquered bar was set in the corner of the room with drinks for the opening night of the exhibit. Sculptures were arranged under bright lights and the volume in the room was conversational without being too loud.

"I half expect Livia to show up, half expect she would be a fool to come here. We're all looking for her," Jade said. She scanned the crowd just in case.

"Who else from your family is attending?" Declan asked.

"Claudia and Hawk gave me a ride here. Maggie and Thorne are planning to come. Allison and Knox have a parent-teacher meeting at Cody's school, so they couldn't make it. Mac and Evelyn were planning to be here. Edith and River said they have an appointment with the DJ for their wedding," Jade said. She surprised herself by knowing where her siblings were. Six months ago, Jade had been rarely in touch with them.

Part of it was that she was consumed by ideas for her business, but the other part was that she felt like an outsider, even among her brothers and sisters. That had changed somewhat as they banded together over their mother's escape from prison. It was an emotionally trying event for all of them.

They'd put aside their differences and come together as a family. Though Thorne and Leonor had gone through their share of fights, most of them about their mother, he had forgiven her blindness in regards to their mother's schemes and actions when he had learned that Leonor had bailed Mac out of a tough spot a few years ago. The more they talked, the more from the past was brought to light and old grievances and hurts cleared. At least those in relation to each other. The more they learned about their mother, the more they saw her for the monster she was.

Leonor approached with her arms open. "I am so glad you could make it."

"We're happy to be here," Jade said. "Have you met Declan?"

Leonor extended her hand and shook his. "I don't know if we've been formally introduced. Thank you for coming tonight. We have been working on getting these pieces on loan for months. I am just so excited to share them with everyone."

"Thank you for inviting us," Declan said.

"Please grab a drink and make yourselves comfortable," Leonor said. She gestured to someone entering and excused herself to continue in her role as hostess.

"She seemed in a good mood," Declan said.

"She's in love, engaged, loves her job and no one is trying to kill her," Jade said. A few months ago, the son of Leonor's paternal half brother had hired a hit man to kill her. Leonor was Livia's favorite, and their mother had been keeping a close eye on her. Though Leonor had been hospitalized, she had heard her mother whisper that she *took care of him*. When Barret was found dead, the police had ruled it a suicide. The Colton children suspected Livia was responsible.

"You don't think Livia is sticking around Austin?" Declan asked.

Based on Leonor's relationship with Josh and her openness about hearing Livia in the hospital, Jade didn't believe Leonor would cover for her mother if she showed up. Having the former FBI agent close was another reason for Livia to keep her distance from Leonor, even if Leonor was her favorite child and they had a bond that none of the other children did. "She would be foolish to do so. And Livia is a lot of things, but she isn't a fool."

Jade heard shouting and worry shot through her. She hurried in the direction she had seen Leonor go.

Standing in front of the gallery with pickets and brightly colored signs, The Victims of Livia Colton support group was protesting on the sidewalk. Jade's heart hammered with anxiety and anger. Leonor had been excited about the evening, and this display would be off-putting.

"They came to Austin," Jade said. She had believed the group would stay in Shadow Creek. Seeing them outside the town, Jade questioned their reach and their commitment to their cause. Embarrassing and harassing the Colton children outside their homes and places of business was low.

"Want me to get rid of them?" Declan asked.

Jade set her hand on his arm. His strong, tensed arm. "This is not your battle to fight. My mother was a terrible human being. I live with that knowledge every day. This is another test. To see if I can be okay with being a Colton. You know, I've thought about changing my name and moving far away."

Surprise registered on his face. "That's a big step to take."

"I could take my father's name, Artero, and distance myself from my mother. But that would mean distancing myself from my siblings. I don't want to do that. Things haven't always been great between us, but they've been my lifelines recently. This mess with my mother escaping from prison and showing up in Shadow Creek has brought us closer."

Leonor strode to Jade, frustration plain on her face. "The protesters are making people nervous."

"I'm sorry, Leonor. They are out of control. They've been to my house too," Jade said.

Leonor ran her hand through her red hair. "Josh is trying to make them leave, but the sidewalk is public property." Leonor extended a purple sheet of paper folded in thirds to Jade. "They are giving this to people walking by."

Jade took the pamphlet from Leonor. "The Victims of Livia Colton Support Group." The paperwork listed a website and phone number to call. Below the website was a list of Livia Colton's crimes, including murder, theft, money laundering, sale of controlled substances, human trafficking and then there were moral infractions, like lying, adultery and promiscuity. Having her mother's life summed up in that list hurt. Nothing written was a lie, but Jade wished she had some good memory of her mother, something that would give her a warm feeling about her childhood.

All her good memories were about her father.

"Most of the pamphlets will turn into street litter," Declan said.

Leonor's name was called by a museum staffer over the intercom system. She excused herself and hurried away.

"Do you want to leave? I can find a discreet alternate exit," Declan said.

Jade wouldn't run like a coward. "I'll ignore them. They want me to confront them and make a scene. I'll get my picture posted all over social media and

I'll look as crazy and psychotic as my mother. Let's just try to enjoy tonight."

Declan slipped his arm around Jade's waist and led her to a sculpture of a wave curling into the air.

Declan was relieved no protesters were waiting at the foot of Jade's driveway. They'd left the gallery around 9:00 p.m., but Declan worried they had just relocated to one of the Coltons' other properties.

Jade had asked him to stay out of it, but he was losing his patience with the group. They were showing up everywhere, their signs and their pamphlets being pushed on people. It had been years since Livia Colton had helped run a criminal empire and yet, her victims were still struggling with what she had done. Their scars were deep and Declan understood. He was one of her victims. Her actions had ruined his family. Those hurts still pained him.

Declan turned down the long driveway and to the front of Jade's house.

She had left on her porch light and lights on the barn and stable. In the moonlight, her farm was picture-perfect, a small slice of Texas heaven. Quiet and peaceful.

After the protesters had left, she had pretended to be fine with it. But it was obvious she was shaken and upset.

"Want to come in for a cup of coffee?" Jade asked.

If he went inside with her, he would have a hard time tearing himself away and going home. "I have a meeting in Odessa tomorrow. I have to leave early in the morning to make it in time."

"On a Saturday?" Jade asked.

"Unfortunately," Declan said.

The disappointment in her face was unmistakable. "Another time, then."

Jade stepped out of the car and Declan followed her up the steps to her front door. A gentleman walked his lady to the door, a simple and kind gesture to ensure she was safe.

At the door, Jade faced him.

Declan captured her chin in his hand and kissed her. When their lips met, the world around them seemed to drop away. It was the two of them kissing, the still of the night and the tranquility around them providing a sense of privacy.

"I'll ask again. Want to come in?" Jade asked.

She turned and unlocked her door. Declan followed her inside, pushing the door closed and locking it. He had declined her offer, but he wanted to be with her. He should keep a travel bag with him. It wasn't like the bed-and-breakfast was home. He was living on the road.

The air-conditioning cooled his skin, the humidity of the air disappearing inside the house. In a tangle of arms and legs, they stumbled to the couch. The couch was good. Better than the bedroom. Being in the bedroom would lead to one thing. As it was, this was inviting. Declan pivoted, pulling Jade on top of him.

He was several inches taller than her, but their

bodies lined up, her softness fitting against him. The right friction and pressure made Declan want to peel her clothes away and finish this the right way. But he would wait.

From working on the farm, her body was toned and strong, but curvy in the right places. She leaned over him, bracing a leg on the floor. Her hair swung to one side and he ran his fingers through it. Her blue-and-white dress was spread over his lap and lifting the fabric of the skirt ran through his mind.

Jade sat up. "Did you hear something?"

Declan shook his head. "Nothing." His heart was racing and his breath was fast.

"Like a creak on the porch. Like the wood shifting beneath someone's feet."

Worry speared him. Declan moved Jade off his lap and rolled to his feet. "I'll walk the perimeter and have a look."

Jade's fisted his shirt in her hand, stopping him. "Maybe that's not a good idea. She kidnapped Edith. She killed the man who kidnapped Cody. She killed Leonor's nephew. She has no compunction about killing or hurting people. I could be next. We could be next."

"Call Knox, Thorne and Mac. We'll check the premises together." Though Declan believed he could protect himself from Livia, she had connections to assassins and criminals and if she was armed, all bets were off.

Jade made the calls, and she and Declan waited for help to arrive.

* * *

River stood on Jade's front porch with Edith. Edith looked nervously over her shoulder and then back to River. Declan pulled open the door. "Thanks for coming on short notice."

Edith walked into the house. "Knox called. He said you heard someone creeping around the house?"

Jade was pacing. "I heard a noise. Maybe I'm blowing it out of proportion, but after everything that's happened, I think there's such a thing as underreacting."

"When everyone gets here, we'll look together," River said.

"Coltons stick together," Edith said, touching her engagement ring.

Declan didn't point out that he wasn't a Colton. Edith seemed happy to be marrying into that family and he wouldn't throw a damper on her enthusiasm.

"I haven't heard anything and we've checked out the windows," Declan said.

"You were right to call. Livia and her associates shouldn't be handled alone," River said.

He and his half brother were awkward with each other. Even friendly words and attempts at banter were stiff and unnatural. They needed to get past this, but Declan didn't know how.

"While we wait, why don't you tell us what's going on here?" Edith said, pointing between Declan and Jade.

"We were at Leonor's gallery opening," Jade

said. "The protesters showed up there, which threw a damper on the evening."

"I'm sorry, Jade. That group is going full throttle," River said.

Edith sat on the couch. "Someone needs to talk to them and tell them that lashing out at the Colton children isn't going to make them feel better. They need to direct their energy into therapy and being on the lookout for Livia."

After Thorne, Mac and Knox arrived, they broke into two groups to look for signs of Livia. Declan, Jade and Knox were one search party, River, Edith, Thorne and Mac in the other.

"Are you doing okay? I know you're nervous right now about Livia, but could you have thought you heard something because of everything that's been going on?" Knox asked.

Jade shone the flashlight beam in front of them. "Maybe. Hard to say. It's unsettling to know Mother or the protesters could show up anywhere. I'm on high alert. I could have overreacted to the wind."

"It's okay. Livia can't be underestimated," Knox said. "Doing nothing could give her the opening she needs to do something truly terrible."

After walking around the farm, they didn't see anything. No footprints, no extra tire tracks.

"I'm sorry, everyone. I feel silly," Jade said.

Edith put her arm around Jade. "It's okay. I'm glad you called. We have to be there for each other or we'll never survive."

Chapter 7

After an especially quiet week—no protesters and no Livia sightings—and on the morning of Edith and River's wedding, Jade woke to the sound of her phone ringing. Had she missed the alarm? She had set it an hour early to make sure she could finish her necessary chores before heading to Mac's farm for the afternoon ceremony and reception.

It was Maggie. "Hey, Maggie, everything okay?"

Maggie sounded out of breath. "My bridesmaid's dress doesn't fit. I ordered it two sizes bigger, but I guess I've gained more than I expected. It won't zip. Thorne says I should just leave it unzipped, but he's crazy. I can't walk around half-naked at River's wedding. I tried to call Claudia, but she didn't answer."

Jade tried to think of a solution. Fashion wasn't

her expertise. The pale blue dresses had been suggested by Claudia because they had a high waist, allowing the fabric to flow around Maggie's growing belly. "What about wearing a sweater?"

"A sweater? It's August in Texas and I'm already carrying an extra forty pounds."

"A shawl?" Jade asked.

"Won't cover what needs to be covered," Maggie said.

Jade looked at her dress hanging in the closet. "Maybe we can adjust it somehow. We'll call Evelyn. She's great with a needle and thread."

"Yes, I should have thought of that. I was up early because the baby was kicking me and I've had these terrible leg cramps. Sorry to bother you! I'll head over to Mac's and see if Evelyn can work some magic." Maggie said her goodbyes.

Jade was too awake to go back to sleep. Her alarm would be going off in twenty minutes anyway.

After taking care of her animals and checking the irrigation systems on her crops, she went inside to eat and shower. Glancing at her phone, she had nine missed calls.

Alarm spiked through her. She called Knox, the first on the list.

"What happened?" Jade asked. She rarely received telephone calls and never this many unless something was wrong.

"How'd you know something happened?"

"Nine missed calls in two hours," Jade said.

"There was a problem, and some of the guests flying in for the wedding from Louisiana won't make it in time. One of those was the wedding photographer. Edith is upset. Leonor is calling some artist friends to see if one of them will do the photos. Declan is trying to find a private plane to fly in the stranded guests, but it's going to be tough. Some type of security issue at the airport."

"Declan is involved?" Jade asked. Though he'd spent the night at her place almost every day of the last week, he'd stayed in Odessa after being there all day in meetings.

"Edith called him."

Of course. They were family. "They could postpone the wedding a few hours."

"Nope. Weather report is calling for thunderstorms. The minister is booked for another wedding later in the evening. Mac is okay with letting everyone use the barn and he and Thorne are trying to clean it. But it smells like horses and hay," Knox said.

Jade wished she could offer a solution. Edith didn't need additional stress on her wedding day.

"Josh and Hawk have been assigned Livia duty. They're keeping watch for her or any of her former associates. But we're worried about the protesters. If they start their nonsense again, it will make it worse," Knox said.

"Oh no. Do they know about the wedding?" Jade asked.

"No clue. I can't ask them and tip them off. But if they show up, we need to get rid of them. I've called a couple of my buddies at the Rangers and asked if they could nudge anyone along who shows up. But it wouldn't be an official thing and they can't force people to stay away if they are on public property."

"Wow, this is going to be a tough day," Jade said. The day had barely started and the list of problems was long and growing.

"Cody was up with a fever last night. He's gotten sick twice this morning." Cody was supposed to be the ring bearer. Looked like Edith and River would need a plan B there too.

"Let's try to handle some of these problems without telling Edith. She has enough on her mind."

"I'm trying. Okay, I need to go. Cody's getting sick again," Knox said and hung up on her.

Jade returned the calls: two from Maggie about the dress, one from Evelyn asking if she had any extra fabric from her bridesmaid's dress, one from Declan telling her good morning (that made her smile), one from Leonor and one from River in which Jade could hear Edith crying in the background.

Jade returned the phone calls, mostly listening and trying to reassure her family it would be okay. They needed this wedding for morale, to be together and prove they would find happiness and a good future, despite the horrors of the past inflicted on them by their mother. Getting upset about the problems at the wedding would be letting Livia win.

Jade arrived at Mac's farm three hours before the wedding. She'd had her hair done at Marie's Salon and Spa according to the specifications Edith had laid out. Jade's hair was twisted at the top in loose curls and gathered to the side.

Stepping into the house was chaos.

Men and women in black tuxedoes were working in the kitchen; River was on the phone, one hand on his head, his thumb and forefinger rubbing his temples. Thorne was holding the back of Maggie's dress while Evelyn was adding a white cloth across it.

Jade's eyes landed on Declan. He seemed utterly calm. Speaking on the phone, he disconnected and crossed to Jade. "It's been a wild morning."

"Everything worked out?" she asked.

Declan shrugged. "Edith has accepted that this will not go according to plan. I've called in every favor I can think of to make this right for her, but I can't make any promises."

A passing waiter tripped, dumping a bowl of white dip down the front of Jade's dress. A collective gasp rose up in the room.

The waiter was making apologies. Declan had grabbed some napkins and was wiping at the white dripping down the front of the dress and onto the floor.

River approached. He looked at Jade's stained fabric and frowned. "The van delivering the flowers broke down. Knox is en route to retrieve the flowers."

"I'll try to get some of this off in the bathroom," Jade said.

"Need a hand?" Declan asked.

"Sure." She had agreed more because it would give them a minute to talk alone.

Locating a clean cloth underneath the sink, Jade tried to use some soap and water on the smeared white mess. The dip had soaked through to her skin.

Declan's phone rang and he answered. After listening for a few moments, he closed his eyes. "Of course. Of course they wilted in the van. Does anyone have the phone number for the owner of the Secret Garden? Maybe we can get in touch with her and buy whatever she has in stock."

Jade winced. Edith might be disappointed if her flowers were different than she'd planned.

"I don't know what gardenias look like, but let's just try for a similar color," Declan said. When his call ended, he sighed. "I can't tell Edith about one more problem."

"We have to remind her that the important part of the wedding is getting married to River. The rest of this is just decoration."

Declan rolled his shoulders. "I've never been married, but I know Edith really well and it's going to be hard for her to accept this. Edith is a great person, but she's been handed a lot of crap in her life. People have let her down and she's always wanted a real family and people she can count on."

"Then we'll have to make this as good as we can and keep a happy face while doing it."

"My thoughts exactly. Show her that her new family will be a hundred times better than her parents were to her."

A tap on the door. "Jade? It's Claudia. I have a solution to the dress problem."

What Claudia had brought from her shop to replace Maggie's and Jade's dresses were similar to the ones the bridesmaids had planned to wear. They were shorter, but Claudia had a size that fit Maggie.

Maggie was dressing in the other room and Edith was examining the dresses Claudia had brought over for the bridesmaids. In a sun-filled upstairs bedroom at Mac's house, it was hot and the garment seemed to hang limply on its plastic hanger.

The decor in the room didn't help. Mac had blue-and-red-plaid bedspreads and the walls were wood paneling. The floor was scuffed and dingy.

Edith held up the dress and turned it around. "It doesn't have the same detail on the straps."

No fabric flowers on the straps, but it was beautiful in its simplicity.

Edith sighed. "I guess it will have to do. I don't see other options at this point."

Leonor tapped on the bedroom door. "I'm sorry to interrupt." She was wearing her pristine and well-fitted bridesmaid's dress; seeing it was like rubbing salt in the wound.

She looked at the dress in Jade's hand. "That's gorgeous. Are they the new dresses?"

"Yes," Edith said, sounding distraught.

"Well, I think they'll look great. Not that anyone will be looking at us. All eyes will be on you. I have more good news. I reached out to some photographers to see if they were available today. One got back to me. He is a photojournalist and while he hasn't done weddings before, he has done Fashion Week in New York. He's photographed the supermodel Marissa Walker!"

Edith blinked at Leonor, and Jade thought she might cry.

"He also did some work at the Olympics a few years ago. Several large political events. Some of his prints have been features in international geographic magazines."

Edith handed the dress to Jade. "Please thank your friend and tell him I am grateful. I know it seems like I'm being high maintenance, but I wanted everything to be perfect today. I wanted to have pictures that will hang in our home of our wedding and our family. It feels like that is getting taken away."

Evelyn called to Edith from downstairs. Edith left the room and Leonor followed after her. Jade slipped out of her ruined dress and into the new one.

It was shorter than she would have liked, but she kept her mouth shut. The day had enough problems and her dress being too tight and short wasn't a big deal. Maggie's fit her and that was the important part. Jade sucked in her stomach, the only way the dress wouldn't rip at the seams, and exited the bedroom. She heard River and Edith talking in hushed whispers at the bottom of the stairs.

"I think we should set up inside the barn," River said.

"We planned to have an outside wedding. I don't

want to have it inside a barn. A barn? What about the animals and the smell?"

"We can take care of that," River said.

"Take care of it with what? Fifty gallons of air freshener? Lighting a hundred scented candles? We are having it outside, like we planned."

Thunder rumbled ominously in the distance. Jade stepped onto the stairs. River appeared tired and frustrated. Edith looked upset, her mouth curved down and her arms folded across her chest.

"Don't be like this. Isn't the important part that we'll be married?" River asked.

Edith shook her head and rushed away. River looked after her. "I'll give her a few minutes to calm down. I know she wants this to be picture-perfect. This wedding was supposed to be the first time that Edith had a fairy-tale ending. That's why she's taking it so hard. She can't believe the run of bad luck and she thinks someone is sabotaging our wedding."

Jade didn't think it was any one source causing the problems. "We have a couple of hours to get it together." Never having planned a wedding, she didn't know what went into the details, but she could understand how Edith would feel strongly about having a good day.

"I hate to ask this of you, but do you think you and Declan can find flowers for the bouquets and centerpieces?"

Jade mentally cataloged her garden. "I can come up with something."

"We're trying to get in touch with the owner of

the Secret Garden, but she's not answering. If Edith doesn't have a bouquet, it might send her over the edge."

"I'm on it." Jade saluted him and went in search of Declan.

He was setting up chairs for the ceremony. The clouds overhead were ominous, but stating it didn't help.

The area Edith and River had picked at Mac's farm was quiet and picturesque. Gray clouds rumbled overhead, and a stone pathway led from the back of the house to the barn toward the well-tended, tidy gardens. Mac's fruit and vegetable plot was elaborate, with tomatoes, lettuce, radishes, green beans, squash, cucumbers and several types of berries. Evelyn had taken an interest in the garden and was helping Mac with its care.

The string quartet was setting up and every time the thunder rumbled, they looked toward the sky.

"I need your help," Jade said.

Declan set out the white wood chair he had been carrying. "With?"

"I need to go to my farm and gather enough flowers to make bouquets and centerpieces for the wedding."

Declan looked at her skeptically. "Do you have enough flowers to accomplish that?"

Jade wasn't sure. She didn't invest a lot of time growing flowers; they were beautiful but didn't serve a purpose. "We have to try."

Twenty minutes later, she and Declan were doing their best to gather enough blooms.

"This isn't going to work," Declan said. "The stems are wrong."

They weren't long and sturdy. She had more flowers that grew in tufts. "What are our choices? We can't let Edith down."

Declan picked up his phone. He started typing. "I'll find a florist and pay them triple to be here by the start of the wedding."

Four calls later, Declan had located one who answered the phone and who had the requested flowers on hand.

Jade pulled at her dress. "This is going to squeeze the life out of me."

Declan walked around her. "Looks amazing on you."

"The last-minute swap-out meant I couldn't get my size. These were the only dresses Claudia had that would work that she had enough of for everyone. Leonor's fit well." She should have changed into more comfortable clothes, but she hadn't realized she'd be hunting for flowers.

"Claudia has an eye for design. Thank you all for trying to make this day special for Edith. I want her to be happy."

"I care about both her and River," Jade said.

Declan kissed her. His sweet words settled over her, but his lips delivered passion and heat. Jade dropped the blooms she had gathered and pulled Declan toward the house.

"We have an hour before we need to be back at Mac's," Jade said.

"I can do a lot with an hour," Declan said.

Once inside her house, he proved it to her.

Not even ten thousand dollars in flowers from Flowers on the Hour removed the ominous feeling from the day. Declan was a firm believer in positive thinking and mentioning to Edith that something about the day felt wrong wouldn't help her. She was superstitious and he didn't want her overreacting and thinking that the wedding and marriage were doomed.

Edith had planned this wedding under a tight deadline. With all that had gone not according to their plans, Declan hoped the rest of the day would run smoother.

Declan was walking Edith down the aisle. He didn't think of it as if he was giving her away. Edith had an independent streak a mile wide and she wasn't his to give. But he viewed it as a change in their relationship. She was his family, and now she would be River's.

Edith was in Mac's guest bedroom getting ready. Tapping on the door, Declan announced himself.

"Come in." Edith was inside, standing at the window. Her face seemed pensive and worried, a contrast to the beauty and lightness in her dress. The dress was elegant and simple and suited Edith. Her veil fell to her shoulders and had pearls sewn through it.

"Ready to do this?" Declan asked.

Edith smoothed her dress. "Do I look okay?"

"You look beautiful. Your dress is perfect." He had more to say and couldn't find the words.

Edith's hands fisted in the fabric of her dress. "What about the wedding? Do you think the problems are a sign it shouldn't happen?"

Declan wasn't a believer in signs. "Life tosses problems at us and we handle them."

"I like the flowers you sent over better than the ones I picked," Edith said.

"I can't take responsibility for that. I put the responsibility on the florist."

Edith hugged him. "Thank you for doing what you did today. I know you are not a hundred percent excited about this wedding."

"Sure I am. I want you to be happy. If marrying River makes you happy, then I'm behind your decision."

Edith shot him a look as if she still didn't believe him. "One day soon, you'll see what I see in River. I think you already see some of it in Jade."

Jade was becoming more special to him. He had fun when he was with her and he admired her dedication and passion for her work. "Getting to know Jade has been great."

Edith looked in the mirror again and pulled on the edge of her veil. "Days like this make me think about the family I never had."

"Me too," Declan said. That vulnerability wasn't news to Edith. Over the years, he and Edith had shared the loss that children in the foster system had: never really being part of a family and carrying around that rejection. "Being in Shadow Creek, I think of Livia Colton and then I think of my father."

Edith nodded in understanding. "Have you told Jade the whole story about your father and Livia? About how you felt?"

"Not yet. I want to tell her. I know she's heard some of it from River."

"Knox, Leonor, River, Claudia, Thorne and Jade are nothing like their mother. I've gotten to know them more over the past couple of months and I know that they are good people."

Declan trusted Edith's instincts. They were spot-on in most of her life decisions. Her experiences had taught her to look out for herself and to be careful in whom she trusted. Anyone else marrying a man she had known a month would have made Declan laugh and predict divorce in a year. But not Edith. She knew what she wanted and she had found it in River.

Leonor poked her head into the room, her red curls swinging around her shoulder. "The quartet is ready when you are."

Edith took a deep breath and shook out her hands as if getting rid of nerves. "I'm ready."

Declan handed her the bouquet and extended his arm and Edith took it. Together, they walked out of the house and into the garden. His anxiety had nothing to do with River. He had seen the way the man looked at Edith. The affection and warmth between them was inspiring. This wedding was the start of a new chapter in Edith's life and Declan hoped that chapter included him.

Though the flowers were festive and the white chairs filled with their guests, the dark sky and crows circling were ominous. Declan kept his expression pleasant as he walked toward the officiant. He wouldn't show Edith that anything was wrong. The day would be great and she would go to sleep tonight as Mrs. River Colton.

River stood to the right of a white archway decorated with flowers. Jade was standing to the left, holding a bouquet of pink and yellow flowers. He winked at her and her smile broadened. Declan kissed Edith's cheek and hugged her.

"All the luck in the world," he said.

"Thank you, Declan. For everything."

Then he stepped behind her and sat in the front row on the end.

As the officiant spoke, the wind picked up. Even sitting close, it was hard to hear. Thunder boomed in the sky and lightning flashed in the clouds.

The quartet looked nervous. The rain could hold. The minister continued speaking, and while he wasn't rushing, he was speaking quickly.

A fat plop of rain hit Declan's cheek. Then another.

"Do you want me to continue?" the officiant asked Edith and River.

Edith said yes and then the skies opened up. The rain poured so hard, it was impossible to hear. The crowd ran for Mac's house, gathering on the covered porch.

Evelyn was passing around hand towels for guests to dry themselves. Edith looked devastated and River was speaking to her, perhaps trying to reassure her it would be fine.

Declan strode to Edith. Though this matter was between River and her, he wanted to help.

Edith's dress was wet, sticking to her, and muddy at the bottom. Her makeup was smeared and her veil hung down the side of her head. Leonor, Claudia, Jade and Maggie had the same idea about comforting Edith. Though their dresses were wet, their shoes muddy and their hair drenched, they appeared more concerned about the bride.

"Tell me what you want and I'll make it happen," Declan said.

"I want you to go back in time and when River asks me if we should rent tents, I want to say yes. Or, in the immediate, I want you to stop the rain," Edith said, pushing wet hair away from her face. She laughed, but he heard the strain in her voice. Close to tears, she was doing everything she could to hold it together.

"Do you want to postpone for a few hours? Maybe the minister can come back later. You could get married in the barn? Get married beneath an umbrella? I'll stand in the rain and hold it over your heads."

Edith looked out at the rain slamming to the ground. Mud was washing over the pathway. "I want to marry River. Today. Now. It doesn't matter where."

She looked at her future husband adoringly, and Declan was jealous. Jealous that Edith had found someone who mattered so much to her and that she was ready and willing to love with all her heart. It didn't matter to her who River's mother was and she didn't seem to care about his physical scars.

"Let me talk to Mac. We'll organize what we can," Declan said.

"Edith? We'll fix your hair and makeup and we'll try this again," Jade said.

Edith went with her bridesmaids into the house. Declan approached Mac, who was speaking with the minister. "She says she'll marry him anywhere as long as it's today."

"We can use the barn, but that will involve running out in the rain again," Mac said.

"Why not the porch?" Declan asked.

Mac pointed to the line of windows. "Folks can sit at the windows. We can open them so they can hear the vows. We can make it work. Standing room only, I'm afraid."

As Declan, Mac, Knox and River went to work setting up the porch, Declan's thoughts wandered to Jade. Beautiful, strong and caring Jade. Though her family life saw to it that she was not naive, she had a gentle innocence about her. She hoped for the best and she anticipated goodness in people. Declan needed that in his life.

He had learned long ago that listening and stewing on the negative brought him down too. Hopes and dreams and positive energy got him through the day and had helped him build his empire.

Though today would be one of the most unconventional weddings he had been to, he vowed he would do what he could to make it right for Edith and River.

The summer storm didn't blow through Shadow Creek. It raced in and lingered. Though it had lightened to a drizzle, allowing guests, the musicians and caterer to move around without being soaked to the skin, it was dreary and hot. Most men had removed their suit jackets and ties and the women were barefoot.

After the ceremony, with River and Edith married, the festivities were held in Mac's barn. Jade didn't mind the smell. Even with the doors open, the horses and hay scented the air. The thick humidity did nothing to dissipate the smell, either.

Leonor's photographer friend was snapping pictures, though Jade noticed him taking more pictures of things than people. He was circling the cake and the centerpieces. Perhaps everyone looked like a disaster, hair flattened or frizzy from the rain, makeup running and clothing clinging from dampness.

Curious about what her family was doing, Jade searched for them. Since she was on the outskirts of her family dynamic in most situations, the busyness of the reception gave her a chance to observe.

Maggie was eating and Thorne sat beside her. They talked and laughed and looked at each other with love and affection. Rubbing her hand over her pregnant belly, Maggie giggled at something Thorne whispered in her ear.

Edith and River were mingling and speaking with their guests, stopping to pose for pictures every few minutes.

Knox was dancing with Allison. As Allison looked up at her child's father, Jade saw no hint of the drama they had endured, in part due to Livia's manipulation of their relationship.

Leonor and Joshua were standing away from the group, looking out of the barn at Mac's farm. When they met, Joshua had been undercover pretending to be a billionaire interested in donating to the museum where Leonor worked. Leonor's close relationship with Livia made her the Colton most likely to have assisted Livia with her escape and to be assisting her now. Piecing together what Jade knew about Leonor's father, she believed their mother's affection had everything to do with the weighty trust left to Leonor. Now that Joshua was no longer working for the FBI, he and Leonor seemed closer than ever. They'd be planning their wedding soon. Leonor's huge engagement ring sparkled on her finger and even from this distance, Jade admired it.

Claudia was looking as glamourous and city-chic as usual. Though the sisters were all wearing the same bridesmaid's dress, on Claudia, it looked taken straight from the runway. Her private investigator boyfriend had helped Claudia answer questions from her childhood. Having reunited Claudia with her biological family, Hawk had done his job, but the connection he had with Claudia was still strong.

Mac and Evelyn danced, locked in each other's embrace, their bright smiles catching.

Jade tried to imagine what her family saw when they looked at her. Her passion was her farm and her horses. Educating children in the community about off-track Thoroughbreds and caring for horses took most of her time. She loved her animals and took pride in her garden and farm. And now she had a man in her life who sparked an even deeper passion. Her feelings might be written on her face, the way her siblings' feelings about their significant others were written on theirs.

She and Declan hadn't made declarations about their intentions. They didn't know what would happen when Declan finished with his business at La Bonne Vie.

Declan came up behind her, casually running his hand along her hip. A brush of his fingers and she was totally tuned into him. She had been lonely before she'd met him, a fact she hadn't recognized until he was traveling. "I used to live on this farm. It was Mac who taught me the most about caring for horses."

"I hadn't realized that," Declan said.

"Most people don't know why Mac took us in. He did it to help Knox and because Mac loved us like his own. Knox was too young to be a responsible guardian for the rest of us and saddling him with that burden was too much. But Mac made arrangements and cared for us. I owe him a great deal."

"He seems like a good guy," Declan said.

"He is. The best," Jade said. "After my mother was taken to prison, I struggled. Mac's farm was a great place to ride and run and blow off stress. He didn't place restrictions on me when I fought my grief."

"He must have seen your hurt and wanted to help you," Declan said. "Do you still feel upset when you think about the past?"

"In some ways, I'll never get over who my mother is. But in others, it seems like part of another life. A life I have no interest in returning to," Jade said.

"The rain has let up," Declan said.

The drizzle had turned into a sprinkle, a fine mist that spread across the property, giving the night a dark feeling. "Are you mentioning it because you want to move the party outside?"

Declan shook his head. "I like being in the well-lit barn. Easier to see someone coming at us. But I mention the weather because I'd like for you to take a walk with me." He extended his hand and Jade took it.

They walked out of the barn and they were alone in the quiet of the night.

"I am so tired. I would ask you to take me home, but I think Edith would be upset."

"Not River?" Declan asked.

"Nah. He'd understand."

"Would you think less of me if I asked you to come with me to the car?" Jade asked.

"What's in the car?"

"A quiet place to be alone for a few minutes," Jade said. "The bugs will start biting if we don't find shelter."

Declan laughed. But he pressed the unlock button on his car.

They climbed in the back seat of his sporty car and Jade kissed Declan. No point in pretending she wanted to be alone with him for any other reason. Seeing her siblings as parts of couples had highlighted what she was missing in her life. It hadn't bothered her until she had a man who could help her loneliness, who she actually wanted to be with and share her life with.

Share her life. Her crazy, busy, in-over-her-head life. A mother on the run from the law, a business that was floundering and barely making ends meet, and a family with which all relationships were underscored with past drama and hurts. Adding Declan to that wasn't the right fit, except she wanted him so much, it pulsed through her.

"Declan, I don't want to wait anymore." She reached for his belt buckle and unfastened it.

He didn't argue. Lifting her skirt, he slid her thong down her legs. It got caught on her shoes. Shifting in the car, she pulled them off, letting them hit the carpet in the car.

Then Declan was rolling on protection and positioning himself. They were both breathing heavily. Every other time they had been together, she had felt as if it was foreplay leading to something. This was the something.

He surged inside her and her body exploded in excitement, desire spiraling in her veins. Shifting her hips and moving one of the seat buckles away, she brought Declan fully inside her. He fit her, filled her, made her feel like her life had been building to this moment of pleasure and contentment.

That fled as Declan started to move. The steady rhythm of his hips and his hands on her body, brushing her oversensitized skin, drove her need higher. Chasing completion, she lifted her hips. He moved harder, insistently, inside her. She squeezed hard, wanting to feel him come apart and watching his face while he found ecstasy with her.

She got her wish. But Declan didn't stop moving. His thumb brushed her sensitive skin at the apex of her thighs, rolling, sliding, and then she was following him, spasms rocking her body.

He gathered her against him and held her as their breathing returned to normal.

"Ready to return to the party?" he asked.

Jade would have slept in the back of the car with him. Being apart felt wildly unappealing. But it was her brother's wedding. She wasn't certain what to say in the aftermath. Instead she kissed him, a quick press of her lips to his, and straightened her clothes. "Sure. Can't miss the cake."

Except cake was unimportant. What she had done with Declan had touched her deeply and she wondered if it meant their relationship was leading somewhere. Or if it was just leading to an ending.

Leonor called to her siblings. With a wineglass in her hand and in such a jovial mood, something about her outgoingness reminded Jade of Livia. "I want to get one picture of just us. There won't be many of these around soon, with husbands and wives and babies."

Jade looked at Thorne and Maggie, River and Edith, Claudia and Hawk, Leonor and Josh, and Knox and Allison. She felt like the odd man out, even if she had just had sex with Declan. The decision had been impulsive, but she wasn't going to analyze it too deeply.

Feeling like she needed to tell someone, she pulled Claudia over. "I slept with Declan."

Claudia's eyes grew wide and her mouth broke into a big smile. "Hot. When?"

"In his car. An hour ago."

Claudia hugged Jade. "I saw something between you two. Go with it. Don't fight it so much."

"Claudia! Jade! Come on!" Leonor called.

A quick squeeze of their hands and Jade and Claudia jogged over to the haystack where the Coltons were gathering. Leonor's photographer friend stood in front of them. Snapping several pictures, he changed the angles and the Coltons changed their positions.

"You guys really came through for me today," River said. "I can't tell you how much today meant.

To marry the woman of my dreams and start a new life with her. Not that I want to lose everything from my old life. But I feel like tonight, we're setting off down a new path. A more joyful path."

River had gone through a lot of changes in the last year. After leaving the marines and struggling with his career, he was getting his life together. He seemed happier and lighter than he had since returning to Shadow Creek. Edith had unburdened his soul.

A high-pitched shriek sounded through the air and then a boom, followed by another whine and more explosions.

River flinched. Knox ran out of the barn, Hawk and Josh on his heels. Jade looked around and found Declan. He was moving in her direction. His arms going around her was the safest she had felt.

"I think it's fireworks," Declan said.

No one had said anything about fireworks when planning the wedding. Jade wasn't looped into every decision though, so perhaps this was a surprise River and Edith had arranged for their guests. It was an unusual choice; the fireworks would spook the horses and other animals.

Declan led her outside. The air exploded in red, green, blue and white fireworks. They filled the sky, launching high and showering down sparks.

Edith and River came to stand next to Declan and Jade.

"Did you do this?" Edith asked Declan.

Declan shook his head. "I had nothing to do with this."

Edith and River exchanged confused glances.

"Maybe someone from town?" Jade asked. Heaviness hung on her heart. As the wedding guests gathered outside the barn and watched the fireworks, Jade wondered.

Her siblings had all seemed confused about the fireworks. Could Livia be sending them a message? Usually, Livia was more direct and more aggressive. Fireworks were a nice ending to a beautiful, happy wedding. Livia wouldn't celebrate their successes in life, especially when she wasn't around to take credit for them.

Jade had to be paranoid. If Livia wanted to send them a message, she would do it more directly and it would be something hurtful or contain a warning or threat.

When the fireworks ended, the guests returned to the barn.

Edith's screams split the air.

Declan ran to Edith, the fear in her voice shaking him. Her hands were clasped over her mouth, muffling her cries.

"What's wrong?" River had his arm around his new wife.

She pointed to the place setting in front of her. Her champagne glass was half-empty; her cake sat untouched. Next to the plate was a pink handkerchief, embroidered around the edges with black and brown. Declan looked at it.

A note was scrawled on it.

I always threw the best parties. Hope you enjoyed the fireworks. Will be seeing you all
soon.

"Did anyone see who put this here?" Declan asked.

Josh and Hawk approached. Hawk lifted the handkerchief with his pen. "How could Livia be here?
She couldn't have gotten this close without someone seeing her."

"Livia loved antique handkerchiefs," Leonor said,
her voice robotic.

"We were watching the fireworks. I didn't see
anyone," River said. He looked miserable, worry
etching lines into his face.

"I'll call my buddies from the Rangers and ask if
they saw anything. They're still standing post at the
driveway," Knox said.

Livia was slicker than that. She was far more careful. Waltzing up to Mac's farm with two off-duty
Rangers on the premises wasn't her style. Her connections to the town and the people would give her
a way to find out about River's wedding, and she
would have planned the details of her message carefully. Not a single scrap of evidence would have been
left behind.

As murmurs rose around the barn, Declan looked
for Jade. She needed him. Law enforcement would
respond to this event. Any place Livia Colton showed
up or left a clue to her presence reignited the manhunt for her.

Instead of a night of celebration and joy, they were
in for a long night of questions and searching.

Chapter 8

Jade's nerves were frayed. On top of the long day was the knowledge that her mother was lurking around Shadow Creek, watching them, keeping her finger on the pulse of everything they were doing, having the power to get into Mac's barn and leave Edith a creepy note—and Jade had no doubt the message was from Livia—meant Livia was still slick and careful.

She could be at Hill Country. Showing up anywhere to do anything because she had power. Prison hadn't taken away her strength. Loyalty to the criminals in her organization had earned her their respect in return. Favors could be called in.

"I'm spending the night. I'll sleep in the guest

room if you prefer, but I'm staying with you," Declan said.

He had caught on to her frame of mind and she was grateful that he hadn't needed her to ask. Her desperation to not be alone had to be clear. "Please come inside."

Jade had left the light on in the kitchen. Now she turned on the ones leading to the bedrooms. Every light on in the house didn't seem like enough. "My room." Having him close felt important.

She kicked off her shoes, her feet grateful to be free. Then she took off her dress. It was still damp from the rain. Declan removed his coat, dress shirt, tie and pants.

"I need a shower," Jade said.

"Me too."

"Save water. Shower with a friend?" she asked.

He laughed and followed her into the bathroom.

A quick twist of the handle and the water spurted on. As steam billowed from the stall, she stepped in. Declan was close behind her. Unlike their rendezvous in the car, which had been passionate and intense, this felt lighthearted and easy.

Declan helped her remove the bobby pins from her hair and wash out the hairspray. When they were clean and dry, Jade felt more like herself. "I am glad to be out of that dress. I was afraid the seams were going to give out!"

"You looked great. Thank you for doing this for Edith and River," Declan said.

Finding clean T-shirts and shorts, Jade gave Declan a shirt and an oversize pair of cotton shorts.

They crawled onto the mattress, the sheets cool on her body, and lay at the center of the bed. Declan took her foot into his hands and rubbed the arches and her aching toes. It was great to be out of the rain and humidity and crowd. The day wouldn't have a perfect ending; Jade continued to think about her mother.

"It will be okay," Declan said.

"When Livia is caught, it will be better. For now, I have to hope that she's fixated on other things. Edith and River are leaving for their honeymoon tomorrow and getting out of town will be good for them. Every Colton has their guard up. She went after each of them, so she could go after them again."

"Livia seems to have an ax to grind with her children. That's incomprehensible to me. You're her *children*. What could she possibly think you've done to deserve punishment?" Could Livia know Jade had told the authorities about the password book?

Jade took a deep, shuddering breath. "There are reasons. My mother did many bad things. She broke the law. She lied and hurt people without any remorse. Even during her trial, she didn't apologize to her victims. When she was sentenced, she had the opportunity to express remorse for what she had done, both to the community and to her victims. She said her only regret was being caught. After she went to prison, she knew I'd betrayed her. And now, I'm afraid she's figured out what I know."

"Figured what out?" Declan asked. He stopped rubbing her foot and his face was filled with concern.

Their eyes connected. "I saw my mother kill my father."

Declan set her foot on the mattress and drew her to him. "Jade, I'm so sorry."

Jade nestled against him, enjoying the comfort of his touch. "I'm not sure how much she knows. But she might have known that I saw her bludgeon my father. I never said anything to her. I never asked her why. But I told the authorities her passwords to her bank and investment accounts, and the information gathered from that was a huge part of the case against her. If she's put that together, that I was the one who revealed her passwords, she'll want revenge. Me being her daughter has no meaning to her and after what I did to her, I expect only retaliation." She had been waiting for that backlash for ten years. Until she spoke the words, she didn't realize how burdened she had become.

Declan and Jade settled back on the pillows and Declan pulled the sheet over them. It was cool and crisp and tucked against Declan, she felt cozy and warm.

Declan kissed the top of her head. "She won't come tonight. You'll be safe with me."

Jade was becoming accustomed to the protesters following her around town and showing up at the places where she did business. She'd seen the flyers and pamphlets, the long looks when she passed by someone in the group who recognized her, but they weren't always confrontational enough to sling angry words at her. Between them and her mother lurking around Shadow Creek, almost nowhere felt safe. The only safe place in Jade's world was with Declan.

He had been spending the night at Hill Country since Edith and River's wedding the week before. They'd fallen into an easy pattern of work, dinner and early bed. Sometimes they read, sometimes they talked, sometimes they watched a movie, but it was developing into an intimate relationship that was shedding light on the more lonely parts of her life. With Declan in her life, she felt like she had more than her work, and that was good, because the protesters were having an impact on her business, scaring off donations and possibly making potential buyers change their minds about her horses.

Jade hadn't realized how much she enjoyed Declan's company until he was working in Austin and messaged her that he'd be late. They hadn't made official plans and he hadn't promised to meet her at any given time, but the disappointment was real and palpable. It put her in a low mood. He said he would call if he could make it by that night.

Her phone rang at nine. Reading in bed, she set her book on her bedside table and answered the phone. Declan's number on the display made her heart flip-flop. "Hey, you."

"Hey. Am I calling too late?" Declan asked.

"No, you're fine. I was up." Her eyes were heavy though. She had been up since four in the morning and she was ready for sleep. One of her horses had mistakenly pushed her against a fence, and her calf was bruised and aching.

"I'm twenty minutes out from Shadow Creek, but the FBI has a roadblock up. They're stopping cars, and it's either a drunk driving checkpoint or they're looking for Livia."

Jade shivered and rose to her feet. Though she had checked the locks on the doors and windows before bed, she wanted to check them again. "I'd love for you to stop by. Call when you're outside." Though being woken to answer the door wasn't ideal, she wouldn't be able to sleep with her door unlocked. This could be the unlucky night that Livia came after her.

A memory split into her brain and Jade winced as it rolled over her. "Oh my God."

"What's wrong?" Declan asked, alarm in his voice.

"I just remembered something. Something about Livia." The memory was so disturbing, she wanted to purge it from her mind.

"Do you want to talk about it?" Declan asked. "I wish I could be there right now." He swore under his breath.

The memory was filling in, little details coming to mind. "When I was little, I remember waking one night to hear voices in the house. It didn't sound like my father or brothers, but it was a male voice. I was worried that something was wrong, that maybe someone needed to go to the hospital. I got out of my bed." She had been scared and had tried to listen harder to hear what was going on. The floor had been cold beneath her feet and she had moved to the railing of the grand entrance and looked down. Only two lights by the front window were lit and she couldn't see anyone. Checking her brothers' and sisters' rooms, she found they were sleeping quietly. Claudia was her first pick of someone to wake, but if it was nothing, she didn't want to get in trouble.

Hearing the voices again, Jade had crept down the stairs, praying they didn't creak.

Standing by the French doors leading to the back-yard was a man and Livia. The man had his hand on Livia's throat. He was speaking to her and she was hissing words back at him. Jade knew she should call the police, except her mother had been strange about the police. Even when they had learned in school about calling for assistance in an emergency, Livia had told Jade to never call for help without asking Livia first. It had struck her as odd and not what the teacher had explained, but Jade knew better than to question her mother.

Jade thought about getting her father and then had remembered that he was traveling to look into the purchase of another horse. She could get her siblings to help. Would it be too late? She peered around the corner again and saw her mother kissing the other man.

Livia wasn't fighting him. He had her on top of the giant kitchen island, her legs wrapped around his waist and they were kissing. Not her father. Her mother was doing something she shouldn't. Jade knew it and she was in no position to confront her mother over it. Worry and confusion had tightened around her, making her feel dizzy and sick.

She had slinked back to her room, got into bed, closed her eyes and waited for morning. "My mother was cheating on my father. And after my father returned from a trip, I saw the man my mother had kissed around the house. He worked for my mother, but in what regard, I didn't know. I avoided him. I never made eye contact and I never told my father what I had seen."

"That's a terrible burden for you to have carried," Declan said.

"It was another moment that made me hate my mother. Hate her. When I had the opportunity to lash out at her years later when the police questioned me, I took it. My desire for justice was second only to my need for revenge. That's why I feel guilty. My motives were not pure in confessing to the police about my mother's secret accounts and her book of passwords. I wanted to hurt her. I wanted to make her suffer like I had." Jade waited for the judgment in Declan's voice, for him to tell her that she shouldn't have betrayed her family.

"You did the right thing helping to bring down your mother. That's all that matters. Reasons aside, you did what was needed."

His acceptance was healing salve on her soul. "I wish you were here," Jade said.

"I know, me too, and I'll be there soon."

* * *

Declan had brought Jade dinner every day for the last week, including cooking for her twice in her home with groceries he had bought. She appreciated his company and his dining choices hit the spot every time. Tonight, she had told him she'd arrange dinner. Ticking through the list of possible meals she could serve—slow-cooker beef, lasagna, microwave dinner—she settled on El Torero's. The location of their first sort-of date, and this time, she would pull out all the stops.

She had remembered what he ordered and she arranged for takeout of the same items, adding extra chips and salsa and a double order of flan. After picking up the meal from the hostess and paying, she exited the restaurant. At six thirty, Main Street was crowded, and she'd needed to park a couple of blocks away.

She heard shuffle of feet behind her and then a quiet, raspy voice. "You have a black heart like your mother."

Jade froze. *Keep walking. Don't take the bait.* If it was another of her mother's victims, their anger blinded them. They wanted revenge and they didn't care if that meant lashing out at the Colton children. Their anger needed a release.

"Black heart. Dead inside."

Jade whirled and met the eyes of an elderly woman wearing a calf-length, button-down, burnt-orange dress. She had a yellow scarf over her head and she was supporting herself on a knobby wood cane. Despite the weather, she was wearing black leather calf-high boots.

Jade struggled for calm and peace in her words. Getting into a throw-down on the street wasn't helpful to anyone. "I am not dead inside. What my mother did to me, my family and this town is inexcusable. But I won't answer for her crimes."

"You know where she is. She hides in your home." The woman's voice was low and scratchy and she pointed an accusatory finger.

Passersby stared as they walked by.

"I do not know where she is. If I see her, I will call the sheriff," Jade said.

The woman poked at Jade with her cane. "Lies. Lies! A Colton mouth only speaks lies."

Tears burned behind her eyes. Her mother was evil. She didn't defend her or deny it. But to carry the blame of her mother's choices was a burden she didn't deserve. "Good day, ma'am." She turned and stalked away, clutching the bag of food in her arms. She got into her car and set it on the passenger seat.

Her legs felt weak and her hands were shaking. Deep breathing. The old woman wasn't wrong. Livia Colton was somewhere in Shadow Creek, lurking around, waiting to do God-knew-what to her and her siblings. People walked by on the sidewalks, oblivious to Jade's distress. A young couple strolled past, laughing and holding hands. A family of four hurried down the sidewalk. She had never felt more alone. Rejected by the town where she had grown up and an outsider in her own family.

Jade set her arm on the steering wheel and laid her head on top of it. After several minutes, she was composed. If nothing else, through being Livia's daughter, she had learned to mask her feelings and shut down parts of her emotions she didn't want to confront.

She turned the key in the ignition and then checked her mirrors. A dark sedan was parked behind her. A man with a mustache sat in the driver's seat.

He looked out of place, though Jade couldn't pinpoint why. Perhaps an FBI agent following her, waiting to see if she was going to visit her mother. Jade sighed and decided after her encounter with the elderly woman on the street, she wasn't up for another confrontation. Instead, she pulled out of her spot and drove to Hill Country. The mustached man in the dark sedan didn't follow her. Perhaps she was being paranoid.

When she arrived home, Declan was seated on her porch in the wooden rocking chair she had bought at a yard sale a few months ago and had spray painted aqua. Even after a long day at work, he managed to look unbearably handsome. His gray pants and white shirt were still crisp and his posture was relaxed and inviting. Success in business probably had something to do with how he carried himself. Confident and calm, the type of man who was unwavering and firm, even in the worst storms.

"Sorry I'm late," she said, getting out of the car and holding up the bags for dinner.

"No problem. I was enjoying the view. It's so peaceful and after the day I had, I need some quiet."

Sounded like a rough day. Ups and downs with her horses were the norm, but she liked that she worked with animals and not people. People created complicated problems.

Unlocking her front door, they entered the house. Twenty minutes later, they were eating. Jade debated telling him about the run-in with the woman and the strange man parked behind her just off Main Street.

"When I was leaving the restaurant, I had another person tell me I was a liar. Among other things." The words were harder to speak than she would have guessed and the emotion she had tamped down rose in her throat.

Declan's eyes creased in concern. "That sounds bad. Are you okay?"

"I was upset. Am upset. But I'm okay."

"You should have told me right away."

"It's not something I like thinking about. Will my mother's legacy ever be forgotten?"

"Eventually. Because she escaped prison, the news ran those stories again and rehashed the past and everything they print is sordid and dark. It refreshed things in people's minds, and even newcomers to town or people who didn't know about what had happened with Livia now know the story."

"Do you think I'm destined to become like her? Or one of my siblings?"

"You are nothing like her. I see goodness in you. You're creating your own legacy. Running this farm, caring for the animals the way you do. It's incredible. Giving and warm."

Jade blushed at his compliment. "Thank you. This farm means a lot to me. I've invested everything I have in it. But when people scream at me in the street, I wonder if I shouldn't move. Go where no one knows me. Take my father's last name. It was strange that my mother insisted her children's last names be hers. But I like the sound of Jade Artero."

"Do it. Change your name. Give yourself a fresh start. Take it from me. No good can come from dwelling on the past or letting it define who you are."

He sounded almost angry. Though he had never spoken about it to her, Edith had told Jade that she and Declan had met in foster care and that their experiences had not been great.

"But if I'm not a Colton, I lose that connection to my siblings," Jade said.

"That might be healthy for all of you. Maybe you should all break ties with Shadow Creek and the mess your mother made. From what Edith tells me, Mac was a better parent than Livia. Take his last name."

Jade heard open hostility in his tone and she wasn't sure how to react. Declan had never been like this with her, usually a sympathetic ear and kindness all around, but tonight, something was bothering him. His anger felt personal. "Did I say something that upset you?"

Declan forked his fingers through his hair. "I'm sorry, Jade. You hit a nerve."

"Can you explain what nerve I hit?" Jade asked.

Declan shook his head. "I need to get some sleep. I need to think." He stood and pushed away from the table. "I'll call you tomorrow."

"You're leaving?" She couldn't keep the hurt from her voice.

"I need to pack and be in Odessa tomorrow to deal with a legal matter. I'll be there a few days."

"Then you're planning to leave in the middle of this discussion and not even tell me what's on your mind?" Jade asked.

"Jade, just let it be," Declan said. His voice was uncharacteristically irritated.

"I can't!" He was the most stable and warm part of her life. In the span of a few weeks' time, he had come to mean a lot to her. "Tell me what I said that upset you this much. Are you upset at me? Are you upset at what my mother did in a personal way?" He certainly had reasons to be.

Declan forked his fingers through his hair. "I can't get into it right now. I have a lot on my mind. I'll call you tomorrow."

With that, he left, locking the door behind him.

Jade stared after him. Something about her mother had infuriated him. Again, her mother was causing problems in her life. But Jade wished she knew what exactly she had said to make him so upset.

When Jade had spoken of her mother and father, Declan thought of his own. From that point, thinking of Livia having an affair with his father and the turmoil and heartbreak that had followed brought up fresh wells of pain.

In purchasing La Bonne Vie, Declan had realized that he wasn't over what Livia had done to his family. He wanted to see her burn for ruining his parents' lives and destroying his.

Being in Shadow Creek, and spending time with the Coltons talking about Livia, was causing him to relive those dark moments from his childhood. His parents fighting, arguing, his mom throwing dishes, and pots and pans slamming to the ground. It had been so loud and violent, Declan had hid in his closet. When his father had died, his mother had lost it. There had been no one to help Declan. Alone and scared, he had done the best he could.

He sometimes wondered if living with his angry, depressed mother would have been better than being in the foster system. He had known his mother loved him. It was a strange, push-and-pull kind of love, never knowing what mood she would be in, walking on eggshells. But she had loved him. If Declan had been older, he might have been able to take care of the two of them enough that he wasn't a burden. In his mother's degraded mental state, she hadn't been able to care for herself or him. The choices she had made were selfish, and yet she had loved Declan enough to know she could not care for him.

Declan tried not to think of his mother. That hurt was too sharp even after so many years. He did not know where she was or what she was doing. In many ways, he didn't care.

The best thing about having a ravaged childhood was that, having lived through the ordeal of his parents' marriage falling apart and being tossed out onto the street, Declan feared nothing in business. Whatever his company threw at him, it would be easier than what he had faced as a child. He had thick skin and he rarely let anyone or anything get to him.

A former employee stealing from him had been another obstacle. It hadn't rattled him. He had handled the financial fallout, contacted his lawyers and went after the thief to the fullest extent of the law.

His business was where he put all his time and effort when his personal life was a mess. Turning his attention to work, Declan relaxed. Work was in his control.

Edith had found a lead for an interesting property in Odessa. She couldn't come with him today, though when she returned from her honeymoon with River, she would start looking for a new place for them to live. Declan would have liked to help her find a great place at a good price, but he knew Edith had superb house-hunting skills and it seemed like an activity better suited for the couple. It was another way Declan felt nudged out.

The property Edith had found in Odessa was in an up-and-coming neighborhood; house prices were on the rise and local shopping centers were beginning to fill in with high-end retailers and restaurants. Declan sought those signs of progress when moving into an area.

Declan was fifteen minutes early for the meeting.

He checked his paperwork and the address and then entered the building. The area was in need of renovation, but that was what Declan liked. The more opportunity for upgrading properties, the higher the income potential.

He opened the metal door to the office marked Sky Realty.

Tim DeVega, the employee who had stolen from him, was waiting inside. Shock struck him, rendering him momentarily speechless. The police had been looking for DeVega and he was here. Before Declan could say anything or understand how DeVega came to be in this office, DeVega lifted his right arm, aiming a gun at Declan. He had no time to react, and the sound of the explosion echoed around him and pain pierced him. Everything went dark.

Something was wrong with Declan's eyes. The left one was twitching and wouldn't focus. His eyelids felt weighted down with concrete. Something was wrong with his right side too. His entire arm was asleep. His hand was heavy, too heavy, like it was being crushed by a car.

"It's okay. You're okay."

Pressure on his left side and Jade's voice. Steady beeping from a machine.

Forcing his eyes open wider, he stared into the open, warm, beautiful face of Jade Colton.

Opening his mouth, he tried to speak, but his throat was dry.

Jade handed him a cup with a straw and he took a long sip.

"You were shot. You're at the hospital now."

He took a minute to process that. "Shot."

Her eyes were filled with concern. "Someone in the neighborhood called the police. They got a description of the man who shot you. The police are looking for a man named Tim DeVega. The police found my number in the call log on your phone and contacted me."

Declan closed his eyes and the memory of DeVega shooting him, at least part of it, popped to mind. His body felt numb, but anger and fear made his chest tight. How easily DeVega had gotten to him. Looking at Jade, another sensation washed over him: warmth and happiness. She had come from Shadow Creek, disrupting her busy schedule to be with him. He had been a priority to her.

"Edith is looking for a flight to come home from her honeymoon. She feels terrible."

Edith had no reason to feel bad. "Why?" Declan asked.

"She set up the meeting and she didn't realize it was a trap," Jade said.

Declan should have seen it. It was rare for him to travel alone and he was glad Edith hadn't accompanied him, or she might have been shot too. "Tell her to stay on her honeymoon. I'm fine," Declan said.

"I don't understand what you're saying. You're slurring. Can you speak slower?" Jade asked.

He repeated himself, feeling like his head was

being held underwater. Drugs from the surgery? What had happened when he'd arrived at the hospital? "What about my arm?"

"You were hit in the shoulder." Emotion choked her and Jade took a few seconds to compose herself. "The surgeon saved your arm. But you need to rest."

He was exhausted, but it was daylight. The drugs in his system and the numbness of his arm were indications he was not himself. "Will you stay?" The unexpected surge of neediness surprised him. He wasn't used to needing anyone. He liked having Edith around, but he made it a point to never make anyone in his life essential. But he hated the thought of Jade leaving and him waking alone in this stark cold hospital room.

"Yes, I'll stay."

Unable to hold open his eyelids, he closed them and quiet surrounded him.

Jade hadn't taken a day off of work in over a year. Finding the right farm, buying the land, building the right structures and then getting her business off the ground was a struggle. But Declan needed someone to help him while he recovered at home in Louisiana. Edith was making arrangements for a nurse and his regular housekeeper and chef to be on duty, but leaving him to the care of strangers felt cold and impersonal.

Declan was a strong man, a force to be reckoned with, and seeing him pale and still in a hospital bed had been knives to her stomach. She was staying with him until he was better, until she could see for herself that he was going to be fine.

When Edith had offered to stay with Declan in Louisiana, Jade had heard the hesitation in her voice. Edith didn't want to cut short her honeymoon. Jade had not thought through the details when she had volunteered to stay with Declan. She had just known she had to be with him.

Then Mac, Thorne, Evelyn, Knox, Allison and Cody had offered to step in and run Hill Country for a few days. Jade had composed lists of to-dos and who to call for various problems, and hoped she hadn't missed anything. Being available by phone, she knew her family could call with questions. It wasn't her intention to be a burden, but she appreciated everyone taking on some of her responsibilities so she could stay with Declan. Being with him was something she needed to do, more than caring for her horses or worrying about the problems with her mother. Declan came first and that spoke volumes about how she felt about him.

Mac had made some calls and a local 4-H club was willing to pitch in too. Though being away made Jade nervous, she planned to stay with Declan for four days.

Jade picked up Declan from the hospital. She listened as the doctor carefully described the medications, what symptoms necessitated an emergency call for an ambulance. Declan couldn't fly on an airplane, so he and Jade were making the long drive to Louisiana from the hospital in Odessa.

The five-hour drive took closer to nine and Jade was exhausted. They had stopped several times to eat, take the needed medications and to check Declan's bandages. Pulling up to his home, Jade sucked in her breath. His house put La Bonne Vie to shame. Even at its most beautiful, Livia's home lacked the style and architecture of Declan's.

The two-story house had wraparound porches on both the main and upper levels. The pristine white of the house glinted in the afternoon sun. White pillars jutted from the front of the house and a dual, grand curving staircase extended from the top floor to a long walkway constructed of paving stones. The landscaping was green and lush and trimmed neatly.

Following the long driveway, Jade pulled around the back of the house and parked in a garage that was tucked under it. A valet took her keys as she stepped out.

"It's a rental. See that it gets returned, please," Declan said.

"Yes, sir," the valet said, nodding and bowing slightly.

"You have your own chauffeur?"

"Nick isn't a chauffeur. He takes care of my cars, making sure they get maintenance and are detailed on a strict schedule. Edith called to let him know I was coming home." He started to get out of the car without waiting for her.

Jade rushed to his side. "You promised you would wait for me to help you. You might get dizzy and if you fall and hit your head, we have to go back to the hospital."

She ducked under his good arm and tried to support him.

"I'm all right. I've managed this far," Declan said.

Taking his key from his pocket, Declan opened the door from the garage. The house was elegant and detailed, the crown molding, wainscoting and ceiling beams a gleaming cherry wood. The far wall was lined with glass French doors leading to a courtyard.

"Welcome home, sir," a man in a suit with perfect posture said.

"Thanks, Albert," Declan said.

"Will you and your lady be needing anything?"

"No, we're fine, thanks."

Albert bowed and hurried away.

"You have a manservant?" Jade asked.

Declan scoffed. "Albert is not a servant. He's a butler and a historian and a friend. He worked for the family who previously owned this house and when they sold it to me, he asked to be kept on to help maintain it."

"That was nice of you."

"It was a sound business decision. Albert does a good job. Lets me know when something needs repairs and then oversees the repair to maintain the house's historic value."

Exploring the house interested her, but Declan needed rest. "We need to change your bandage. Edith said a nurse is coming at 6:00 p.m. That's in an hour. I want to have all the medication laid out so she can check them and we can go over what needs to be done."

Declan squeezed her hand lightly. "Relax. I'm okay."

Jade leaned into him, wanting his strength, but feeling guilty because she was supposed to be supporting him. She had known being with him was the most important thing in her life, but it was surprising to realize he had come to mean this much to her. Tears threatened and she held them back. Declan would recover from this. She needed him to be okay. "It was the most terrifying call I have ever received, hearing from the police that you had been shot and were headed to the hospital. They wouldn't even tell me if you were alive."

"I'm sorry you went through that. Thank you for coming and staying and taking care of me," Declan said, kissing her temple.

"Lead the way to your bedroom," Jade said.

Declan pointed and they headed toward stairs tucked away in the corner of the house. "I'll give you a tour later. But my bedroom is on the top floor and takes up most of the south-facing part of the house."

They took the stairs slowly. Though Declan didn't lean on her, she noticed he gripped the bannister with white knuckles. He wouldn't tell her if he was in pain, but from the set of his mouth and narrowed eyes, he was. She would not break down. He needed her to be strong, and weeping over every bump in his recovery would slow him down. But wow, it was hard to see him this way. In every other instance, he was composed and larger than life. This was a side of him she had not seen and his vulnerability made her feel closer to him and protective of him. She would do what was needed to make this right.

His bedroom suited him. It was what she would have selected for him if she'd been asked to design a room for Declan. It was tidy and orderly and the hardwood floors were made of three distinct shades of dark brown. The four-poster king bed had pineapples carved into it and the bedding was navy and gold. On the walls were pictures of sailboats.

"I didn't realize you liked being on the water," Jade said. She removed the pile of pillows from the bed one by one, setting them on the settee in the corner of the room.

"Everyone likes the water. I sold my boat recently, but I have my eye on another one," Declan said.

"Where will you keep it?" Jade asked.

"A boat slip at a nearby marina," Declan said.

His words accented a harsh truth. His life was based in Louisiana. Hers was rooted in Texas. Operating under the assumption they had a future was a huge leap.

Declan flopped on the bed. "This feels good. I know I'm tired when I'm falling asleep in the evening."

"It's good for you. The doctor said you needed rest, hydration and good nutrition."

Declan's eyes were closed and Jade watched the steady rise and fall of his chest. She kicked off her shoes and crawled into bed next to him, wanting to be close if he needed anything. He had been through terrible times in his life, sometimes alone, sometimes with Edith, but now, he had Jade and she would be there for him. In every way that he needed her, she would be strong and at his side.

The pain was bad, close to the time he was supposed to take his pills, but Declan was substituting what the doctor had prescribed for over-the-counter meds five days after his discharge. He didn't want to risk getting hooked on prescription painkillers.

Having Jade with him those first days was healing in its own right. Attentive and sweet, Jade had pushed him to eat when his appetite flagged, kept track of his medications and changed his bandages. That quick, he was used to having her around and while his staff kept the house running and another associate was keeping the business running, Jade kept him going. But he couldn't start thinking he had to have her in his life. Wanted her; that was obvious. But need crossed the line.

Her horses needed her and he understood when she'd had to leave. He had insisted on it and hidden the pain, telling her that he was healed. The physical pain was tolerable, but he missed her. She'd come to mean a lot to him and without her in his house, it felt empty and he was decidedly lonely. The house was too big and empty without her in it.

Now two women he cared about were living in Texas. It was tempting to move close to them, but Declan couldn't live with those ghosts.

Livia Colton was haunting that town. Even if she was caught and returned to prison, her victims would continue to share what she had done to them. The reminders would be daily and ever present. Declan didn't want to think about Livia for the rest of his life. Once he sold La Bonne Vie, he was finished with her and his dark, painful past.

Chapter 9

Jade felt as if her brain was fogged.

She missed Declan. Texting and calling constantly would interrupt his rest, so she checked in with his nurse and Albert. It had been four days without him and she was planning a return trip soon. Her family had done wonderfully, taking care of her farm, but it had been difficult for them to make time in their busy lives and she hated to burden them again.

But Declan needed her. Or maybe it was she who needed him.

Focusing on her horses was a problem when her thoughts veered to Louisiana often.

"Jade!" Knox's voice. Jade spun.

Knox was wearing blue jeans and a T-shirt with

a band logo on the front. His hair was poking up at the top; his son was with him.

She had been standing in the stable with a rake in her hand, planning to clean the stalls, lost in thought. "Hey, Knox."

"I called your name like five times," Knox said. "You okay?" He glanced over at Cody.

"I'm sorry. I didn't hear you. Hi, Cody, so glad to see you. I heard you were a big help while I was in Louisiana."

Cody was speaking to Tots. At the age of nine, Cody knew not to stick his hand in the stall or open the door without Jade. His sneakers were muddy and his red shirt spattered with paint. "Yeah, I helped."

Jade turned her attention to her oldest brother. "I'm fine. Just tired." Not sleeping as well at night because she wasn't with Declan and was worried about him and his health.

"I wanted to come by and make sure you understood the notes we left." Her family had kept careful track of what they had fed her animals, how often they watered her vegetable garden and any behavior that was out of sorts for the horses. Which, for her horses at this stage, could run the gamut.

"Thank you. Those were great. You were all so generous with your time. I was so touched that you added my work to your overcrowded schedules," Jade said.

"Allison and I were talking last night. We had no idea how much work you put into this place and with so little help."

"I'm a new business. Things will get easier." Eventually, she hoped. Being on the farm fifteen hours a day, it was hard to find the time to fund-raise. Without more money, she couldn't hire help and it continued in a vicious cycle. When she had some free time, lately, she had been spending it with Declan.

"Don't be a hero. Ask for help if you need it more."

Jade wasn't used to relying on people. Her mother had taught her a vicious lesson. Few could be trusted. "There are times when I think I've bitten off more than I can chew. But I think about the horses that I've helped and I want to stand by this mission."

"What about Declan? What does he think about all this?"

Jade looked around her stable. "He's not involved in the farm and I wouldn't expect him to be. He's busy with his real estate company."

"Which is based in Louisiana," Knox said.

Jade knew the complications of the distance and their demanding work schedules. "Edith works for Declan. She's planning to live with River."

"Edith's work can be done from anywhere. Harder to say the same about a relationship."

Jade shifted. The fragility of her relationship with Declan made her feel self-conscious and she didn't know what to say exactly. "We could make it work."

"How would you have time to travel? You can't expect Declan to come to Shadow Creek every time you see each other, and you can't leave the farm."

Jade felt a headache coming on. She wasn't a pie-in-the-sky daydreamer, but this was too new for her to make decisions. "If it gets to that point, if Edith can work from anywhere, then Declan can too."

"You want him to move to Shadow Creek? I doubt that would happen."

His pessimistic words surprised her. "Why doubt?"

"River told you about his father and Livia. How does Declan feel about all that now? Is he ready to put it behind him?"

A sense of unease crept over her. Declan had mentioned a few things, but nothing in detail. She had sensed it was a delicate topic and he would tell her when he was ready. "He still seems angry at Livia."

Knox set his hand on his hip. "What about Declan's mother? Where is she?"

"Declan hasn't said." Knox's tone was making her feel defensive. "I don't know. We've only been out together a few times and this is new. I don't have the answers today."

"I just don't want to see you hurt," Knox said.

After what had happened with Allison, Knox might have been projecting some of his feelings about Livia and her uncanny ability to destroy lives. Knox had missed out on years of Cody's life because Allison had lied about her son's father. It had been a careful manipulation from Livia, seeing that her children did what she wanted, regardless of who was hurt. "I know that. But this conversation is bumming me out. Why don't you tell me about your plans for being sheriff? How is the campaign going?"

"I don't know how it's going. I get the general

anti-Bud sentiments in town because the guy is just incompetent. But the protesters are making it hard to be a Colton."

"It's always been hard to be a Colton," Jade said.

Knox laughed. "True. But when it's being screamed in your face at every turn, it's worse."

"What are you going to do?" Jade asked.

"I need supporters. Maybe I'll try a fund-raiser. Mac and Thorne have both offered to hold it at their place."

"That's a good idea. You could also ask Declan."

Knox inclined his head. "Declan?"

"He and Edith are close, and she is family now. Declan will be selling the La Bonne Vie estate, so he has a vested interest in the community. You as sheriff makes more sense than Bud as sheriff. That guy is a joke."

"Who is a joke?"

Declan walked into the barn, his walk slow but even. Her heart took flight. He was wearing a sling and he still seemed tired, dark circles under his eyes. Jade ran to him and wrapped him in a hug.

He groaned. "That hurts a little."

She released him. "What are you doing here? You should be resting."

"I'm doing fine. My doctor said it was okay to travel. I needed to check on the progress with La Bonne Vie. Knox, how are you? Cody, good to see you."

Cody waved politely.

"I'm okay. Just checking in on Jade. I was telling

her about my bid for sheriff. Isn't going as easy as I would like. Not with the protesters around town stirring up trouble," Knox said.

"I drove past a couple of them on my way here. They were outside Claudia's shop holding up their signs," Declan said.

"That must be bad for business," Jade said.

"I keep thinking the group will lose interest or find something more constructive to do with their time. But they are fixated on protesting the Coltons," Declan said.

"If they ruin my chances of being sheriff, we'll have to live with Bud Jeffries for another term in office."

"So Bud is who you were referring to," Declan said. "I have to say, he is not my favorite person in Shadow Creek. I've been working on the zoning of La Bonne Vie. He's on the local council and the guy is slow and lazy. Lost paperwork Edith gave him twice."

"Then maybe you should put your support behind Knox," Jade said.

Declan looked at Knox and nodded. "Wouldn't be the first time I played politics to get my way."

"Have you seen Cody?" Knox asked with alarm in his voice.

The three adults turned around. Cody wasn't in front of Tots's stall.

"Cody!" Knox and Jade shouted.

The boy poked his head out of an empty stall. "What?"

Knox hurried to his son and slid an arm over his shoulder. He hugged him. "I lost sight of you. I was worried."

"I'm okay, Dad," Cody said.

Since Cody had been kidnapped, Allison and Knox were often worried about their son, his mental health and his coping mechanisms, and they feared Livia or one of her former associates would strike again and try to take him.

"Stay where I can see you, okay?" Knox said, his voice calmer.

"Can I look at the other animals?" Cody asked.

"I need to talk to your aunt about something," Knox said.

"I'll take him," Declan offered.

"Go ahead. I'll be there in a few minutes," Knox said.

Declan and Cody walked off to the barn.

"The other reason I'm here, aside from being worried about you, is to ask about Tots. Allison and I think Cody is ready for his own horse for his tenth birthday and we'd like one of your rehabbed ones," Knox said.

Jade felt warmth and pride spreading through her. Her family believed in what she was doing. They wanted to be part in their own way. Knox could have asked Thorne or Mac, but he'd come to her. "Most emphatically yes," Jade said. "I love that horse and I love Cody. This is wonderful."

They discussed the details of the arrangement and then Knox hugged her.

"I'll go check on Cody," Knox said.

Five minutes later, Declan sauntered into the barn. "I'd love to assist with whatever you are doing, but I've only got one arm."

"Keep me company? Then I'll go in and shower and we can talk."

"Do we have something to talk about?" Declan asked.

Jade hadn't been planning to bring up her feelings for him, not when she had only just realized herself how much she wanted him in her life. But she wanted to revisit their conversation from the night she had bought dinner and he had left abruptly. "Just haven't seen you in a while." She hoped she sounded casual. Four days. Four long, heartrending days.

Declan jerked his head. "Come here. Please."

She walked to him and he put his good arm around her and delivered the softest, sweetest kiss. Her toes curled in her shoes and her body arched toward him.

"I've wanted to kiss you that way as soon as I saw you, but I didn't want to upset your brother," Declan said, brushing his nose against hers.

"It was worth the wait," Jade said.

After she finished her chores, they turned and walked toward the house.

"Let me check your bandage," Jade said.

Declan touched it lightly. "It feels good. My nurse changed it before I left."

Declan hadn't mentioned coming to Shadow Creek before showing up. He could have told her over the phone first. "Why are you here? Just worried about La Bonne Vie?"

"Isn't it obvious? I missed you," Declan said.

"Then welcome and please stay awhile," Jade said, taking his hand and leading him to her bedroom.

"I'm glad you offered. Edith packed my things from the bed-and-breakfast where I had been staying. Suitcases are in my car. What are the chances I could crash with you?" Declan asked.

Though he wasn't asking to move in with her in the traditional, let's-live-together way, her heart fluttered with anticipation. "I'd love to have you. Let me get your suitcases and we'll get you settled."

Jade was hosting her weekly 4-H club meeting. She had long been a part of the program, but since opening Hill Country, she had become more involved, holding club meetings and teaching what she could. Inspiring another generation to care for horses was one of her top goals. Her father and Mac had done a good job with her in that regard.

Eight girls from the local high school were due to arrive. They usually carpooled with each other's parents. After waiting twenty minutes, Jade called one of the girls, worried. No answer on her cell phone. She tried two others with the same result. A sinking feeling struck her. Calling the local 4-H office, she found they were closed for the day.

Finally, she called one of the girl's mothers from the roster she kept for emergencies.

The woman answered sounding out of breath.

No, the girls would not be coming back. Ever. They had changed their mind about working with horses. The 4-H program was trying to find a better fit for them. Livia had helped fund the program years before, but they had been quick to put distance between themselves and her. Now they didn't want anything to do with Jade, either.

Jade hung up, shocked and trying to think if she had done something to cause this turnabout. She had missed last week, but Thorne had stepped in and run the session. Everyone in town knew she was Livia Colton's daughter and that hadn't stopped them from visiting the farm before.

Three more awkward phone calls and one of the moms finally told her, bluntly and to the point, that the protests against Jade and her family made them profoundly uncomfortable and that they felt it best to stay away from the Coltons. The girls were getting made fun of at school for spending time with a Colton.

Jade's throat was tight and she was barely able to say goodbye before she burst into tears. She stifled them, not wanting to wake Declan. He had spent the night at her place and was resting. Tossing and turning all night, he hadn't looked well in the morning and Jade had encouraged him to go back to bed after a quick breakfast.

She took a shower and changed into clean clothes. The shower was as much for the sweat and mud as the therapeutic value of hot water.

Declan was sitting up in bed with his laptop on

his lap. "What's wrong?" He set the laptop to the side and straightened. Her face must have made it plain she was upset.

The mothers' words echoed through her thoughts. *Black Heart Colton. Get out of town. Bad influence.* "The girls from the 4-H didn't come today."

"Are they okay?" Declan asked. Something in his expression read of worry.

"They're fine. They won't be coming anymore. The protesters have scared them away. Their parents don't want them to be near me. They are getting made fun of at school for coming to my farm." Tears she had tried to hold inside bubbled up and spilled over. She crawled into bed next to Declan, curling her body against his.

"That's ridiculous. You've been working with them and all of a sudden they don't want their girls near you?" Declan asked.

"I guess so. Maybe they're worried that my mother will come here. I don't know. It was all I could do not to hang up the phone when we were talking."

"I'm so sorry. That's awful," Declan said.

"I have to get used to it," Jade said. "This is the reality. For a few years, it was more peaceful around here. My mother wasn't in the news every week and people started getting to know me as Jade Colton. Now I feel like her escape has brought up bad feelings again and the town is turning on us. The Victims of Livia Colton group is stirring up so much anger."

"It will pass. It will get better and easier with

time. They can't run you out of town unless you let them."

Except the longer she stayed in Shadow Creek, the less she felt she belonged there.

Tinker was more skittish than usual. Jade had advanced her training, giving her long periods of relaxation time and trying to give her purpose and meaning. Some horses did better when they were taught new skills. Others never lost the instinct to run.

Jade had to calm Tinker and then make sure all the horses were fed and their stalls clean. Declan was with Edith at La Bonne Vie and he wasn't sure how late he would be. Jade wished he wouldn't push himself, but he said lying in bed and resting was making him batty.

Suddenly, she heard a metallic click and turned to see a gun, the cold metal pressed against her head, which sent fear jolting through her.

"Where is Livia Colton?"

This was a strange way for the FBI to question her. But this couldn't be the FBI. They wouldn't hold a gun to her head to get information about her mother, especially when she truly did not know where Livia was hiding out.

"I don't know," Jade said. She started to turn around and the man set a hand on her shoulder. She caught a quick glimpse of his face. He had dark eyes and a mustache, but she couldn't place him. Someone from her mother's past?

"Face the wall. Do not turn around. Tell me the truth and maybe you'll live through this," the man said.

Jade's heart pounded harder. Speaking the truth hadn't worked. If she did continue to admit she didn't know where Livia Colton was, would this man kill her? "I am telling you the truth."

"Livia wouldn't care if you were dead. But she might care if *I* killed you. She seems to be oddly affected when someone messes with her family. More because she believes you all belong to her. Only *she* can kill you or give the order for your deaths." The man chuckled.

"I do not belong to her or anyone," Jade said.

"You are as stupid as the rest," the man said. "If you don't tell me where she is, I will cut out your tongue."

Jade pressed her lips together. How would she get out of this? "I don't know. If you think I'm protecting her, you're wrong. She was a terrible mother and she's a bad person. She ruined my childhood and she's still ruining my life." She felt the gun move away from her head.

Jade waited. She was too scared to move, afraid he would make good on killing her. Her heart was racing and sweat covered her body. After several moments of silence, she turned around. Alone in the barn, she let herself process what just happened. The man might come back. Her hands were trembling and her legs felt weak. He could harm her horses. It took her three tries to lock the stable, and then she ran into the house to call the sheriff. Her second call was to Declan and her third to Knox.

When Declan arrived, he wrapped her in a hug. "I'm sorry I wasn't home yet." He kissed her temple. "Are you okay?"

She was still jittery. "I was terrified. But as quickly as it started, it was over."

"I'm going to hire a security guard to stay with you," Declan said.

"Don't be silly. I don't need someone following me around all day," Jade said.

Declan hugged her again, holding her tight to him. "This was a close call. It could have been worse. I don't know what I would do if something happened to you. At least let me have one of my security experts come out here and install some better locks and some alarms and video monitoring."

Jade was shaken and upset enough to agree. While the prospect of strangers watching her on video cameras made her nervous, being trapped by Livia or one of her cohorts was worse.

Jade's phone rang. "It might be Knox or the sheriff."

She looked at the display. "It's Thorne." She answered.

"Maggie's in labor. It's too soon. I don't know what to do," Thorne said.

"Did you call the midwife?" Jade asked.

"Yes and she's on her way. Maggie won't go to the hospital. She thinks she's prepared for this. But I'm scared."

"I'll be there soon. Maybe I can help."

* * *

Declan didn't sleep well on the couch at Mac's house. Maggie was in labor and progressing slowly. The midwife was encouraging her to go to the hospital, but Maggie wanted a home birth. They had a doctor on call, but Jade was worried. And because Jade was worried, Declan was concerned too.

Declan was at Mac's house with Knox, Allison, River and Edith. Jade, Thorne and the midwife were at his house. The whole family was keeping their phones close. There was little they could do but offer their prayers and support.

As the hours ticked by, Declan's anxiety grew. He had read that labor, especially with a firstborn, could take hours. Trying to be useful, he made runs for food and drinks and delivered meals to Thorne's house.

Jade always answered the door, took the delivery, kissed his cheek and returned to what she had been doing.

After eighteen hours, the family was exhausted and worried. Declan could only imagine how Maggie had to be feeling. He hadn't wanted to bother them, but he called Jade.

"Maggie is doing great. She's getting to the hard part and the midwife is concerned she'll be too weak. Thorne is trying to convince her to go to the hospital, but she's refusing."

"Why?" Declan asked. If he were in her position, he'd want to be drugged up in a medical facility with doctors and nurses to care for him and the baby.

"She hasn't fully explained it, but I think it's something about Livia having built the hospital. She thinks it's cursed or that Livia has influence over what happens there. I can't blame her entirely. Too much of our lives have been wasted dealing with my mother. If this means a lot to Maggie, she should have the delivery she wants."

Except medical complications could mean needing other plans. "I'll let everyone know," Declan said.

"Are you still at Mac's?" Jade asked, sounding surprised.

"Yes."

"You're a good man. I'll let you know when I know something."

Declan relayed Jade's message to the family. Then more waiting.

When he woke next, he was seated on a plush chair in Mac's living room. He moved his shoulder; it was stiff and tight and still ached. His phone buzzed with Jade's number.

"Good news?" he asked.

"Great news. Maggie and Thorne have a healthy baby boy. Five pounds, ten ounces. They're naming him Joseph." After Thorne's father, Mac.

"Maggie is resting, but she said it's fine for everyone to meet baby Joseph."

Declan's announcement to the Colton clan was met with cheers. They clicked their coffee mugs together to Joseph Colton and his happiness.

A dozen different times during Maggie's labor, Jade swore she would never have a baby. The sweating and screaming and crying. It looked painful and scary, and though the midwife and Thorne seemed calm and in control, Maggie had seemed scared and angry during the delivery.

The family had stopped by, staying only for thirty minutes before heading home to rest.

The pediatrician had made a house call to check the baby. Though underweight, Joseph was healthy. Upon hearing that, Thorne and Maggie went to sleep. Jade had been able to take a few power naps over the course of the last twenty-seven hours and now she was holding Joseph.

Jade wrapped Joseph in the pale blue swaddling blanket and held him against her chest. He was small and seemed to fall asleep as soon as she put him against her. Following the instructions the midwife and Maggie had given, Jade fixed Joseph a bottle, taking care to measure the powder and check the temperature of the water. Feeding the nipple into his little mouth, he instinctively sucked, draining the fluid quickly. Jade burped him and then changed his diaper. Then another swaddle around his small frame. The labor had been horrible, but this was amazing.

A quiet knock at the door and Declan entered. He had hung back while the rest of the family had visited and had gone to get the new family of three a meal.

Maggie had wanted a burger with extra fries from Big Jim's. The smells of beef and fries filled the room. Declan set the bag on the kitchen table. "Everything Maggie and Thorne asked for and some extra. And this package was on the front porch."

A generic brown box with no return address. "Someone must have dropped off a gift."

The lack of addresses made Jade nervous, but she held Joseph close, confident she would keep him safe no matter what.

"This is the man of the hour?" Declan asked, taking a look at Joseph. "I'll wash my hands, and then can I hold him?"

The question surprised her. Declan didn't seem like the baby type. "Sure. He's practically weightless. Won't bother your shoulder."

Declan cleaned his hands and then Jade handed him the baby. Her heart melted into a puddle on the floor. Businessman Declan was strong and powerful…and sexy. Lover Declan was sweet and fun… and sexy. Declan with a baby was overwhelming. Like fall-head-over-heels-in-love-with-him overwhelming, her heart was lost in the moment to him completely. If she hadn't been half in love with him before, she would have fallen at that moment. He was gentle and warm, talking to Joseph in a soft voice.

"Where did you learn to do that?" Jade asked.

"Do what?" Declan asked. He was so attractive with his shirtsleeves rolled to the elbows and the baby tucked in the crook of his arms, he knocked the breath out of her.

"Hold a baby."

Declan frowned. "I guess foster care. I helped with some of the kids sometimes."

"That's amazing."

"I think it's biological," Declan said, returning his attention to Joseph.

Thorne came into the kitchen looking tired, but proud. "How is my son?"

"He's great," Declan said, extending the baby to Thorne.

Thorne snuggled the baby against his chest with one arm and reached for the bag of food with the other. "Thanks for picking up food. I really appreciate it."

"Someone dropped off a package," Jade said.

"Probably one of the guys," Thorne said. The ranchers and cattlemen who worked for him knew Maggie had been in labor. Thorne had asked them to work away from the house and not bother him while Maggie was giving birth. "Could you open the box and take the gift into Maggie?"

"Sure," Jade said. She should have looked at the item before mentioning it to Thorne, but her paranoia about Livia's presence in their lives shouldn't ruin everything, especially happy moments like this one.

Taking a pair of scissors from the knife block, Jade slit the packing tape and opened the flaps of the box. Inside was a green baby outfit with dark green pants and a light green onesie. Across the front of the onesie were the words I Love Grandmom.

Jade stared at it. "Have Maggie's parents been by?" Her voice cracked and she cleared her throat.

"No, they're on their way," Thorne said.

Jade shoved the outfit into the box, feeling anger and fear rising inside her.

"What's wrong?" Thorne asked.

"Nothing," Jade said, but the word came out on a choked whisper.

"Jade?" Declan asked.

"The clothes are from Livia. I'm calling the sheriff and I'm calling Knox." The second time she had spoken to the sheriff this week. He had driven to her farm after the incident with the mustached man. He had not seemed particularly interested in helping her or looking further into it. Maybe a second incident would convince him the Coltons were in danger, but she doubted it would convince him to care.

Thorne took the box and lifted the outfit from it. "No one says anything to Maggie. I'll tell her eventually, but not today. Please put this on the back porch for the sheriff."

Jade took the box and walked to the back door. Declan followed her. "Let's keep a buddy policy, okay?"

Jade was so shaken she had forgotten that Livia could still be lurking around the house. Fear wrapped around her and doubled when she thought of little Joseph. They couldn't know what Livia was thinking or if she was thinking about kidnapping him.

The family would need to protect the baby with their lives.

Jade's mother was queen of ruining everything. Most recently, her fireworks at Edith and River's wedding and the outfit at Joseph's birth. Why was Livia staying in Shadow Creek? If she was smart, she would go far away where the authorities would be less likely to find her. Except Livia Colton was no one's fool and if she was in Shadow Creek, it was for a reason. Like settling a score with her youngest daughter.

Jade didn't know much about her siblings and their parentages, because many of Livia's claims were lies or attempts to manipulate the situation to her benefit. Claudia wasn't even her sister by blood. That craziness, the constant flow of men into their lives, had made Jade never want a family of her own. Now that her mother wasn't in her life, she wanted to rebuild her family. She wanted stability, like Knox and Allison had, like Leonor and Josh, like Thorne and Maggie, like Claudia and Hawk, and like River and Edith. She could have that with someone. With the right man who was willing to accept her past and who liked her business and who wanted the same things. A home and the horse farm and a baby. Or several babies.

Jade didn't want her children to have the broken family she had. Her mother never kept one man around for long and her romantic relationships were volatile. Though Jade had been told that her father had loved her mother, she didn't see how he could have tolerated her cruelty. Unless he was utterly clueless, he had to know that Livia was breaking the law, using her house and her status in the town to smuggle illegal goods in and out of Texas.

Declan had asked her to come to La Bonne Vie, if she was up for it, to take a look at a box of items Rafferty Construction had unearthed. Jade almost told him to throw it all away, but then thought better of it. Maybe there was something that could give her insight into her mother. Memories she may have locked away. Anything that would explain how a person like Livia could fool so many people for so long. People must have seen something good in Livia once, aside from her charitable giving. Small comfort now, but at least she could then believe that she had inherited something good from her mother.

When La Bonne Vie came into view, Jade wasn't afraid. The roof had been torn off, giving the house an exposed, fragile look. The windows were gone and the right side was broken and crumbling. Jade parked next to Declan's car and walked around to the back of the house.

Declan was waiting for her. He strode to her and greeted her with a kiss on her cheek. A kiss that lingered. When he pulled away, his eyes were filled with concern.

"Let me show you what the team found. If there's anything you don't want, I'll pass it to your siblings to look at."

"What kinds of things?" Jade asked, wanting to steel herself against an emotional punch.

"Some pictures, costume jewelry, pottery and Christmas ornaments," Declan said.

Jade walked to the cardboard box. The outside

was covered in dust from the construction site. Peering inside, she saw the items stacked neatly.

Declan grabbed a blue tarp that appeared reasonably clean and spread it across the ground. Jade sat and took the first item from the box.

A Christmas ornament that someone had made of beads and pipe cleaners. Didn't ring a bell. Jade set it on the tarp.

The next item was a family photo album. Flipping through the pictures, Jade was disgusted. Every one was of the Colton family posing with their mother. Livia had her arms around her children as if she was the most warm and loving mother. Not a single picture was of them doing anything together. No picnics or goofy pictures of laughter. Every photo was of them posing. Looking closely at her siblings, they all seemed tense and nervous, their smiles fake. The only genuine-looking smile was Livia's, the consummate liar, who was used to pretending. Pretending to love people, pretending to want her children, pretending she was a devoted wife and mother and a pillar in the community. A wealthy philanthropist who shared her good fortune with the town. No one had thought to question Livia about where her wealth had come from.

Jade set the album down, feeling anger rumbling through her.

A few vases that Jade remembered holding flowers on the kitchen island brought no good memories. Her father had asked her mother about the flowers and her mother had claimed she'd bought them herself. But Jade knew they were from one of Livia's lovers. Just like she knew that her mother didn't love her father. The way she knew that her mother hadn't loved her. Her father had tried to control her mother, tried to soften her and make her be kind. But Livia would not allow anyone to influence her, even for the better. That pervasive feeling that nothing about their family was whole and good persisted in Jade's life. Family was a charade and they'd all played their parts.

"I wasn't sure if I should even show you these things," Declan said. He had been kneeling quietly next to her.

It took Jade a couple moments to compose her thoughts. "Nothing about my childhood with my mother has meaning to me. I'll take these to Knox, Thorne, Leonor, Claudia and River. If they want them, they can have them."

She set the items back in the box and stood, dusting off her jeans.

"I can take them if you'd prefer," Declan said.

Jade set her hand on Declan's elbow. "No, it's okay. You're sweet to offer."

"I'll be home late tonight," Declan said. "I have some things to wrap up here and then I have a conference call."

"No problem. Don't forget we have Cody's party tomorrow," Jade said. Cody's tenth birthday was the following day. She had dropped Tots at Mac's earlier in the day, and Allison and Knox were presenting the horse to him at the party. It would be a great day if Livia didn't show up to ruin it.

Chapter 10

Mac had taken over decorating the barn for Cody's
birthday. He had been helping around Thorne's house
as much as possible since baby Joseph slept all day
and stayed awake through the night. Thorne and
Maggie were exhausted, but they hadn't wanted to
cancel the party for Cody.

Blue and green streamers, balloons and tablecloths set the tone. The entire family was thrilled for
Cody to be getting his first horse. Jade had bought
Cody a book on caring for rehabbed horses. River
and Edith were providing a month's worth of feed.
Leonor and Josh were giving him a saddle. Claudia
and Hawk were supplying grooming tools.

"What did you get Cody?" Jade asked Declan,

nodding to the small box in his hands. "Looks like jewelry."

Declan shot her an are-you-kidding-me? look. "I would not buy your elementary school–aged nephew jewelry. It's a gift certificate to the local vet. I figure the horse will eventually need something and this way, Cody can deal with it himself."

Jade threw her arms around Declan's neck. "That is a really sweet present."

"Just trying to go along with the family."

"Yes, but it's my family. You could have just signed the card on my present."

"Nah, this is a big day for Cody. A boy's first horse is the start of a great love and many exciting adventures. I'm happy for Cody."

"What about your first horse?" Jade asked, hearing the whimsy in his voice and wondering.

"I've never owned a horse," Declan said.

"Then when we get home, you'll have to take ownership of one of mine."

Declan's hand tightened and Jade checked her words. The casual use of the word *home*, the implication that they were living together? Or that she was giving him a horse, which was no small matter? She retracted the words. "I'm only half-serious. I couldn't expect you to take care of a horse."

"I travel," he said. His posture was tight.

This was about more than his traveling for his work. He didn't want ties to Shadow Creek. Knox had warned her that whatever had happened between Livia and his father could still be painful. Could be the reason he was tearing down La Bonne Vie instead of living there. Except he never wanted to talk about the specifics and Jade wasn't sure how to bring it up.

Mac called to them, beckoning them over. Jade let the conversation with Declan drop. He didn't want to discuss that part of his past and she wouldn't push. When he was ready, he would tell her.

Allison and Knox had gone all out for the party. Though it was being hosted at Thorne's, Cody's parents had done the planning. Trays of chicken nuggets, a dozen pizzas, containers of fresh fruit, juice and water bottles, popcorn, chips and pretzels were among the buffet of food for Cody's family and friends gathered to celebrate his birthday.

Cody was having a great time. He and his friends were kicking around a soccer ball and running around the farm. When it was time, he opened his gift from his parents and he seemed confused.

"A picture of Tots?" Cody looked at Jade. "Are you selling him?" The little boy's face filled with concern.

Jade pointed to the barn where Mac was leading the horse toward Cody.

"The horse is for you, Cody," Knox said.

Cody threw his arms around his father and hugged him tight. Allison joined in and the three wrapped their arms around each other. Seeing the joy on their faces, Jade felt a hollow sensation of loneliness. Between Maggie holding baby Joseph in a wrap against her as she bounced slightly to keep him soothed,

Cody's affection for his parents, and Mac's look of pride and pleasure, Jade knew something was missing from her life.

She glanced at Declan and he was watching her, his expression thoughtful.

This might not be the time to have a serious conversation, but the sense of urgency pushed her to her feet and she strode to where he stood against the split rail fence.

"Cody is happy. I'm sad to see Tots go, but I know he'll be with a loving family in a great home."

"Special day for you all."

Jade set her hand over his. "For all of us."

Their eyes met for a charged moment and then Declan looked away. "Jade, I don't really belong here. I'm not a Colton."

Jade hadn't expected him to say that. He had been staying with her to keep her safe from Livia. He had attended this big family function. Not feeling like part of the group didn't make sense. "You're not a Colton, but you're important to me. That means you belong. I was thinking about the stuff you salvaged from La Bonne Vie. Livia's crap was a farce, but you know what was real? How I feel for my siblings. We looked out for each other when we were young and even though we drifted apart, we're coming back together. I like that we're almost building a new family minus Livia."

"That's great for you." Declan glanced at Edith, who was standing close to River, her head on his shoulder, and Jade read hurt on Declan's face.

"You won't lose Edith. She's part of this family, but she'll always have a special bond with you."

Declan met her gaze. "Edith is all I have. I don't have other family. Not a single person."

"That's not true. You have me." And River. But Jade didn't think saying that would be helpful. There was still an unfinished conversation between them about their parents, but now wasn't the right time to broach that.

Declan wouldn't look at her and she would give a million dollars to know what he was thinking. "It's complicated, Jade."

Life always was. "You can tell me."

"I've told you everything I can. I've done everything I can. You can't ask more of me," Declan said.

"I'm just asking for you to let me in," Jade said. She hated the desperation in her voice. They'd grown closer and she wanted to have that connection with him, that same closeness she saw in her siblings and their significant others. She felt it when she and Declan were alone, when she woke in the morning in his arms, but now, in the light of day, surrounded by her family, she felt distant from him.

Before he could respond, a shriek of fear cut into the air. Claudia had her hands over her mouth. "I saw her. I saw Livia." She was pointing to the woods on the far side of the barn. Knox was already on the phone calling the sheriff and the family moved together as if forming a protective barrier around the children from whoever was lurking.

"I know she's around. I can feel the evil," Claudia said. "She wants to get us back. All of us."

Knox organized search parties, with three of his armed friends from the Texas Rangers each leading one. They had attended the party as guests, and Jade was glad they were there. The rest of the family and their friends went inside the house.

Jade and Declan went with Knox. Finding Livia and closing that part of her life would be liberating. The emptiness in her soul might be filled if she knew she could let another person inside without fear of Livia hurting them or trying to take them away. After looking for several minutes, the search felt hopeless.

If Livia had been in the woods, she was gone. Underground tunnels like the one she had built in La Bonne Vie?

When the sheriff arrived with sirens screaming and lights blazing, they circled the perimeter.

A day that had been joyful had turned to sadness.

Since Claudia's Livia sighting at Cody's party earlier that day, Jade expected Livia to appear everywhere. In her car. On her driveway. On her porch. The sense of unease wouldn't dissipate. Having Declan with her helped.

"You can head inside," Jade said. "I want to make my rounds."

Declan turned toward the stable. "I'll keep you company. I'd say I'll help, but my shoulder is still beat."

They hadn't finished their discussion about how

close they had gotten and why Declan needed limits between them. Jade didn't know if it was a conversation that would play out in actions, if she needed to press the issue or if making it a big deal would drive Declan away. It was hard to be with him, spend time with him and still feel that hollow distance at times.

Jade opened the stable and went inside. She'd had one of her part-time employees fill in for her that afternoon. He had seen to it that the horses were fed and stabled before dark. After checking their water was filled for the night and their bedding was clean and dry, she relocked the stable. Locking the stable was new for her in the last couple of months.

Her pigs, goats and sheep were also in their pens, which had been mucked out, and fresh food and water were set out. It was a relief, after so many days of taking care of task after task, to have another person handle it.

"I'm exhausted and I'm really glad that I don't have to deal with cleaning and feeding the animals tonight. Not that I don't love my work. But working seven days a week is starting to wear on me," Jade said.

"When I started my real estate company, for the first three years, all I did was work. I had no social life. Weekends and holidays meant nothing because I didn't acknowledge them. I just went to the office every day without fail."

"That sounds tough," Jade said. Is that what her life would be like until she had more donations to make the farm profitable and had the means to hire more help?

"It was. I don't wish that on anyone," Declan said.

"Mac told me that it would be tough on me to start this business. The mortgage alone is prohibitive, but I have animals and the food and everything I need to care for them. It's harder than I realized."

"Don't give up. You have a good thing going here. It will get easier," Declan said.

"The girls from the 4-H club were just getting to the point that I was teaching them less and they were doing more. In a few more months, they would have been amazing assets to have. But I've lost that now. All because of my mother."

"You have to keep going even when you hit obstacles. I know it's hard, but stay the course. You believe in this place. I believe in this place. Eventually, the whole town will believe in this place and it will become like a town landmark. You'll have waiting lists for volunteers."

"Thanks, Declan. I need some encouragement," Jade said.

"The security expert is coming next week. I wanted her here sooner, but she's wrapping up another job. She agreed to do an assessment of the farm and she's going to work with you to make you feel safe. No forcing anything you aren't comfortable with. When I'm traveling, I need to know you're okay."

Because he asked in that way, she had to agree.

* * *

Declan lay in Jade's bed next to her. His shoulder was aching. It had been hurting since that morning before the birthday party, but he didn't want to cause a problem for Jade and her family. They were dealing with enough and they didn't need for him to make excuses about needing to be home early to rest. Jade would have felt compelled to accompany him and she had needed time with her family.

At this point of his recovery, Declan had expected to be doing better. The police hadn't caught Tim De-Vega. He was as elusive as Livia Colton.

Insomnia kept Declan awake, his spinning thoughts that grew darker closer to dawn. When the green digital numbers on the clock switched to 5:00, Declan got out of bed, showered, changed his bandage and brewed coffee.

Jade seemed to wake as the smell of coffee drifted through the house. She joined him in the kitchen.

"Eggs?" he asked.

"Yes, please." She walked to the fridge and pulled out some sliced melon and set it on the table.

"I'd like to ask you about La Bonne Vie," Declan said.

Her shoulders tensed. "What about it? I've been there more times in the last month than I have in the last ten years. No interest in going back. That place is all bad memories."

Declan chose his words carefully. The town council wanted to keep the land argricultural, and they'd implied he would be taxed heavily for rezoning. "I need to make plans for the house and barn. I'm thinking about tearing them down and trying to sell it as one large plot, maybe two, depending on interest. Prospective buyers have expressed concerns about La Bonne Vie, the tunnels and the history of the property. Without the barn and the house to remind them of what Livia did, it may sell better."

Jade flinched when he mentioned the barn. She took a sip of her coffee, thinking it over. "I knew about the house. No one wants that place. It's a disgrace to the town. I guess it's a logical next step for you to take down my father's barn."

Usually, he and Edith did a thorough investigation into everything about a purchase. This one had gotten away from him. The personal nature of this deal had put blinders on him and it would cost him. "This was a screwup. I let my emotions get in the way." His father's affair with Livia Colton still messed with his head.

"I'm surprised to hear you say that," Jade said. She took a sip of her coffee.

"I want to be honest with you. The only good thing is that La Bonne Vie brought me to Shadow Creek, and I met you."

Jade's cup trembled against the tabletop as she set it down. "That's nice of you to say. I'm glad you're in my life too."

It was the closest he had come to telling her how he felt about her. It was as if he hadn't resolved it in his mind and until he did, he couldn't talk to her openly. In the space of a few weeks' time, they had been through more than he'd been through in any other relationship. The stress hadn't broken them and that surprised him. Turning toward each other instead of against each other was a novel concept.

"Do you have other ideas about what could be done with the land?" Declan asked.

Jade slid her coffee cup between her hands. "If you offered the land to Mac and Thorne at a fair price, they could expand their ranch. I doubt the history of the property will bother them. They couldn't afford it when the state auctioned it. La Bonne Vie was appraised at a high value. Without it, maybe they could afford the land."

"I can pitch the idea to them," Declan said. The town council would be happy with a local sale.

"Would you really sell to Thorne or Mac?" Jade asked.

Declan knew he'd take a loss. At this point, with the zoning restrictions, getting rid of the land was the quickest way to deal with the problem. He wasn't planning to work the land, and paying taxes and insurance on it added to the expenses. The construction costs in tearing the main house down had added to the overall cash outlay. It hadn't been a total waste to buy the property. Destroying La Bonne Vie had done something positive for his psyche. Seeing the house ripped apart and disappear provided closure.

More than the financial reasons, Declan was willing to sell the land to Mac or Thorne if it meant something to Jade. "If they're interested."

Jade beamed at him. He slid the eggs onto two

plates and set the plates onto the table. Taking a seat, he watched Jade, curious about what she was thinking.

"What's on your agenda for today?" Jade asked.

"Edith and I are looking at a few properties. I'll be home late."

They finished their eggs and were out the door. The setup was decidedly domestic and Declan rather enjoyed it.

Declan rarely spoke about his family. Aside from River being his half brother, Jade didn't know how Declan's father had gotten involved with Livia or where the two had met or why he had chosen her over his wife and son. After their conversation that morning, Jade had wondered about it and it played on her mind.

It was seven when Jade finished her chores. She had an hour until the town library closed. She wanted to know more about Livia Colton. Livia loved being in the spotlight and welcomed reporters to her social functions. Jade might be able to find out something about Declan and River's father, put another piece of the twisted puzzle together.

Driving to the local library, she accessed the archive machine where old newspapers had been scanned. Though the library planned to add them to a digital database soon, at present, they had to be read locally. Jade sat at the computer and typed her mother's name. Thousands of search results. Clicking on the first link, Jade cringed. The article had nothing nice to say about her mother.

Typing in a more specific search, she added Declan's last name. No results. Disappointment tightened in her stomach. Livia and Matthew's affair wouldn't necessarily have been publicized in the newspaper. Where else could she find the information?

Declan had met Edith in foster care. How had he landed in foster care in Louisiana when his father lived in Texas?

Jade opened another article about her own mother. This article had to do with Livia's crimes, specifically, that she had used her house and her vast network of smugglers to move drugs between Mexico and Texas. Another article mentioned Matthew Colton, Livia's half brother, who was a convicted serial killer. Dark family history.

When someone set a hand on her shoulder, Jade nearly jumped out of her skin.

"I'm sorry, dear, but we're closing in four minutes," the librarian said. She adjusted her narrow glasses on her nose, the ball chain connected to the frames swinging. Her white hair was nearly blinding.

"No problem." She closed the windows on the computer. Reading about her mother was depressing her. Jade didn't know everything about Livia's life; in fact, she knew very little, and discovering it crime by crime was hard.

On the drive home, Jade couldn't get her mother

off her mind. A fog was setting in, casting shadows and reflections from her car lights.

Jade took her foot off the accelerator, letting the car slow. When she pulled into Hill Country, it was pitch-black. The lights were out in the barn and stable and she had forgotten to leave her porch light on.

With her mother's crimes fresh on her mind, Jade felt her skin prickle. She hurried up the steps to the porch and unlocked her door. Darting inside, she shut the door behind her and locked it. Then she threw the bolt. As she walked to the back of the house, she turned on every light she passed.

Buying the farm had been her dream. But she hadn't thought through the details of how it would feel to be alone there. Declan wouldn't be by that night.

Jade turned on her computer, planning to send Declan a quick email about her day. Instead, she typed into the internet search engine: Victims of Livia Colton. The first result was the official website of the group, based in Shadow Creek, Texas. According to the site, it had members from fourteen states.

Going to bed would be a good idea. Shutting off the computer and waiting for another day. Or ignoring the site and group completely was an option. Like a glutton for punishment, Jade clicked the menu option for the discussion board.

Every story was worse than the last. Her mother was a cruel, evil monster. Even if the stories were exaggerated, they depicted a woman whose only intent in life was to make herself rich by using others. Her road to wealth was littered with bodies.

One of Livia's first victims was Tad Whitman, the oldest son of a wealthy family. When she became pregnant, Tad had married her and she gave birth to Knox. There was some question as to whether Tad or his father were the true father. However Livia arranged to walk away from the Whitmans with a divorce from Tad, a name change for Knox from Whitman to Colton and a hefty settlement.

When Knox was two, Livia moved to Austin and seduced and married Richard Hartman, an elderly CEO. Leonor was born six months after their wedding. When Richard died a short time later, he left half his fortune to Leonor with Livia as the executor. Richard's grown son, RJ, protested, but a judge ruled that Leonor was a rightful heir and the will stood. RJ's son Barret had later tried to have Leonor killed because her existence disgusted him.

Money or not, Livia had a hard time getting along in Austin. She had two young children and society didn't accept her. It was like they sensed she wasn't from a wealthy family. Even when she had pretended to be high-class, she couldn't quite hide her viciousness. Livia invested Leonor's fortune into a large ranch outside the city in Shadow Creek. She met and married Wes Kingston. She had a son, River, and for several years, the family of five was the center of the county. But when Thorne was born, that all changed. Everyone suspected Livia had had an affair with the ranch's foreman, Mac. Before Livia's adultery was uncovered, she smeared Wes's reputation, distracting the town and media from the fact that she'd had an affair on her husband.

When Wes divorced her, he left Livia additional land and custody of both younger boys, whose last names Livia changed to Colton. Livia wanted control of everything, including her children's names, and she wanted to pretend like they were the perfect, cohesive family. Curiously, Mac stayed on as foreman at the ranch, but he didn't stay involved with Livia. It was a part of Mac's life he rarely discussed. His love for Thorne was obvious and while Mac had done the right thing stepping in caring for Claudia and Jade after their mother went to prison, he seemed to carry deep hurts from that time in his life.

The discussion board mentioned Claudia and her biological mom and dad, too. Claudia had recently learned that she wasn't Livia's daughter. Claudia had believed her father to be a Frenchman named Claude. The lie had been manufactured by Livia to cover up that she had kidnapped Claudia's biological mother from her parents, who had never stopped looking for her, and then stolen Claudia from her mother.

Livia's victims were shamed into silence. In Shadow Creek, she was wealthy and in control. Funding the building of a hospital, local agricultural and children's programs, allowing ranchers to use her water supply, and providing entertainment for the town at elaborate barbecues had made heads look the other way when questions arose.

The discussion board also mentioned Jade's father. Livia married Fabrizio Artero, an Argentine horse breeder. When Jade was born, she had become the light of her father's life. Though Jade sometimes had a hard time remembering her father, she thought sometimes she could recall his booming laugh and the warmth in his hugs.

Losing him had been the darkest day of her life. Jade had never forgiven her mother and she never would.

Jade paused over the name on the discussion board who had posted about Fabrizio. Ana Artero. She could be related to her father. Though Livia had made sure to sever ties with the Artero family and forced Fabrizio to isolate himself from his relatives, Jade had wondered about her family in Argentina. Fabrizio had hurt them and the name Colton brought out their hatred. She could not reach out to them without expecting rejection.

She fell asleep thinking about horses and her long-lost family in Argentina.

Declan wanted to see Jade. Though he had spent one night in a five-star hotel in Killeen, Shadow Creek called to him. Except the latest problem at La Bonne Vie called the loudest due to the disturbing nature.

Allison had phoned that morning around 6:00 a.m., reporting that items had been moved around the house. She had spoken to her crew and they were certain their tools had been shifted to other rooms. Trash from the Dumpsters had been thrown onto the ground, as if those had been searched. The construction site was easily accessible with the windows and doors missing, but it was also dangerous to be inside. The state of the floors and walls was questionable and they were close to bringing in the heavy-duty equipment to start tearing the house apart.

Declan heard a car and walked to the front of the house. A dark sedan was parked, watching them. The FBI? Someone else?

Irritated about this recent development and tired of feeling watched and stalked, Declan strode toward the car. The engine roared and the driver pulled away before Declan could see who it was.

That type of response led Declan to believe it was unlikely to be the FBI. They wouldn't need to turn tail and run from him. Special Agents Monroe and Fielder had been open to talking with him at the B and B. Someone was watching him and Jade. The build was decidedly masculine, so not likely Livia. But she could have hired someone to watch.

Declan would reach out to the local authorities and FBI. Maybe finding whoever was driving that sedan would lead them to Livia Colton.

Chapter 11

Nothing could take the smile off Mac's face, not even the wailing of his namesake, baby Joseph. The child wanted to be held by his mother or be nursed around the clock. Maggie was exhausted, but Mac had invited everyone over and the family had promised to help with the newborn.

Mac had added the leaves to his kitchen table and had a second table with matching white lace tablecloths. Two centerpieces on each table were made of sand, shells and a blue candle. The kitchen smelled of basil, cilantro and oregano. The tables were set for sixteen people.

"Can I assume this is Evelyn's doing?" Jade asked. Mac's taste was more simple, salt of the earth. He wasn't a candle-in-the-sand type.

Mac had updated the curtains on the windows to white with bold blue geometric prints. Everything was clean and shiny, the counters wiped down and clear, the floors and the windows gleaming.

"She's been coming by after work to help me get ready the last couple of days," Mac said.

"Ready for what? Is everything okay?" Jade asked. Jade usually cleaned when she had something on her mind.

Mac's eyes seemed to sparkle. Whatever the reason he had called the family to come for dinner, he had good news to share. They needed to hear good news. Since going on her research expedition about their mother, Jade was feeling down. It had been three days since she had read those articles at the library about her mother and it was hard to shake. She hadn't learned anything new, but seeing everything in black and white had been utterly demoralizing. Not even having Declan back in town fully lifted the sense of gloom and doom.

"We're great," Evelyn said. She swept into the room.

Mac's eyes swerved to her. He strode to her, with Joseph in one arm, and scooped her into his free arm and kissed her.

"He's just been so happy since Joseph was born," Evelyn said, smiling at the baby.

As the Coltons arrived, Mac and Evelyn served drinks, beers for the guys, wine for the ladies and soda for Cody.

"How's Tots?" Mac asked.

Cody looked at Jade and flashed a huge smile. "Awesome! I rode her today."

"He's doing great taking care of her," Allison said. "Thank you again, Jade, and thank you, Thorne."

"I have some news," River said, setting an envelope on the table. "I managed to track down Tim DeVega at a hotel outside Dallas. He's in police custody."

Declan stared at River for a long moment, the expression on his face unreadable. "You were looking for Tim DeVega?"

River nodded. "Hawk helped me. But DeVega shot you. It was a matter of time before one of us took him down."

"One of us," as if it was a foregone conclusion that Declan was part of the Coltons. Something happened in that moment between River and Declan, like a wall coming down between them. They didn't rush to each other and hug, but the mutual respect in their expressions warmed Jade's heart.

Mac cleared his throat. "That's excellent, River. I'm glad to hear your job is working out and you're watching out for the family. I appreciate you all coming tonight. I know you're busy and it's hard to make time. Evelyn and I want you to be the first to know that we're engaged."

The family erupted in exclamations of joy.

"This was all my idea," Claudia said, hugging Evelyn tight.

"We're planning to have a big wedding in the spring," Evelyn said.

"Whatever she wants," Mac said.

Thorne clapped his father on the shoulder. "Congratulations, Dad." Thorne lifted a toast to his father and the Coltons clinked their glasses together.

Perhaps this was the start of something good. It might be too much to hope that Livia would leave town and let them live their lives, but Jade hoped whatever business Livia believed remained that she would move on. Sticking around Shadow Creek would bring the authorities out in full. Someone would find her.

After they hugged and congratulated Evelyn and Mac, Knox tapped his glass with his fork. "I want to say something to all of you. I'm glad we could be here together. Allison and Cody are the family I never thought I would have. They are my world and despite what Livia tried to do, she couldn't tear us apart. Having us all together like this means everything. Welcome to the family, Evelyn."

Leonor stood. "Welcome, Evelyn. I am so glad Mac has found the happiness he so deserves."

Thorne had his arm around his father's shoulders. "Dad, you showed me unconditional love and despite what Livia did to you and to all of us, we've managed to still be happy. I know you'll love Evelyn too and you will have a happy life together."

Claudia leaned into Hawk. "Here's to new memories."

River kissed the back of Edith's hand. "I came home to Shadow Creek lost and looking for something that had always managed to elude me. And now with Edith, I feel like everything is complete. When Evelyn and Mac look at each other, I see that same love I feel for Edith, and I know they'll be stronger together."

Jade looked at Declan and wondered where his thoughts had gone. He was part of the family. They accepted him. She cared deeply for him. Would they ever be a couple announcing their engagement? Or even their intentions to spend their lives together?

"Here's to family sticking together, staying together and growing stronger," Jade said.

Without each other, they wouldn't have survived the last months.

Chanting, almost like a television had been left on in another room, floated through the kitchen. The Coltons went quiet. Only Maggie, who was bouncing Joseph and shushing him, made noise.

"Get out of town! Get out of town!"

The protesters were outside Mac's house. Jade's heart sank. Had they been followed or had the protesters noticed the cars and known they'd struck Colton gold?

Mac looked furious. "This is private property. I'm calling Bud."

Bud sent one of his deputies to drive away the protesters, but it had put a damper on the night. When Declan and Jade left around nine in the evening, they drove back to Hill Country in silence. Declan was in a dark mood. The thundercloud of his emotions whirled around him.

None of Jade's efforts to put him in a better mood

were helping, and Declan hated that he was stewing. She sat on the couch next to him, drawing her legs into her chest. She pointed to the tea on the coffee table. "Drink that. It will calm you."

"What is it?" Declan asked.

"Lavender tea," Jade said.

He didn't usually care for tea, but she had made the effort and he took a sip. "Not bad."

"Now tell me what's on your mind," Jade said.

"The protesters," Declan said. Between them and Livia, every Colton event took a downturn.

"I know they're hard to deal with, but let's focus on the best part of the night. Evelyn and Mac are engaged!"

He was happy Mac had been able to move on from his past with Livia, but he couldn't shake the heaviness hanging over him. If he could share his past with Jade and then put it behind him, he could move forward. "I've been struggling with talking with you about something important."

Jade nodded and sipped her tea.

"River and I have the same father. My father's affair with Livia is the reason my parents divorced. Livia is the reason my dad killed himself. Livia Colton is the reason that my mother had a break with reality and dropped me off on the streets of Louisiana. My mother knew it was too far for me to walk back to Texas and since I had no money, I would be stuck there. She hated me because I looked like my father. She left me to fend for myself with nothing except my clothing and shoes. Not even a dollar so

I could buy anything from a vending machine." Declan swallowed hard, memories from those long-ago nights cutting him to the quick. He had been terrified and alone.

Jade's eyes were dark with emotion. "Declan, I had no idea."

"I don't like to talk about it. I'm not sure that anyone aside from Edith and River knows that part of the story. Those first nights on the street were terrifying. But a police officer noticed me and took me to family and protective services. Without his kindness, I don't know what would have happened to me." He had been so thirsty he had drunk water from a puddle. He had eaten food from a garbage can.

Jade wrapped her arms around herself. "My mother was an abysmal person and knowing you were one of her victims, I don't know what to say to you."

"I didn't tell you so that you could feel terrible. I told you so that you'd know. We're involved and keeping it from you felt like a lie."

She reached for his hand, taking it in her own. "Thank you for telling me. I know it wasn't easy for you."

She leaned against him and put her arms around him. "I'm sorry, Declan."

Declan felt the weight of his anger and grief and sadness rushing through him, but this time, it didn't stay and linger. It evaporated, leaving him feeling lighter and refreshed.

Somehow, falling in love with Jade Colton had

brought him healing and closure. Admitting it to himself was powerful and Declan was overcome with emotion. "I want to be alone for a bit." He stood and Jade released him.

He had fallen in love with Jade Colton. It was as plain as day to him. Now he just needed a way to tell her.

Jade had no trouble rolling out of bed when the sun rose. Declan preferred to take his time and wake around seven. After their difficult conversation, he had slept in the guest bedroom. Declan didn't know how to bridge the gap. Telling Jade about his past had been hard for him. It felt like a weakness, admitting that Livia had easily pulled his family apart.

He wouldn't entertain the fantasy that Livia had cared about his father, even after getting pregnant by him. Livia had used his father and then discarded him, sending Matthew into a tailspin from which he couldn't recover. Unable to sleep Declan went outside. The morning was chilly and Declan strolled around the house, admiring Jade's garden, and thinking.

The sight of the black sedan parked across from Jade's stable filled Declan with anger. This nonsense ended today. Except he was wearing a T-shirt and sweatpants and he had no weapon. What would stop the driver from peeling out of Country Hill? He couldn't read the license plate from this distance.

Declan returned to the house and called Bud.

"I've seen a man in a dark sedan watching the

Colton family. He's parked outside Hill Country Farm now."

Bud sighed. "Those Coltons. Always making trouble. First, it's their mother. The FBI agents in town, asking questions and bothering me. Then the protesters and now this."

Declan tamped down his irritation. "Bud, you need to get down here or I'm going over your head. You might be unaware that the governor is a poker buddy."

Bud sighed heavily and dramatically into the phone. "Fine. I'll be there shortly."

Declan didn't want the car to leave. He took several photos and watched from a distance.

Bud must have put his foot on the accelerator, because he turned into Hill Country Farm with two other deputy cars closing off the driveway in under fifteen minutes. They had the sedan blocked in.

Bud and his deputies approached and the man got out of the car.

He said something to Bud. Hands gesturing and pointing. Then the man took a swing at Bud, catching him across the chin. Bud stumbled back, holding his face. His deputies moved in to arrest the man.

If they only had him on trespassing, now they could add assault charges. If Bud would have let the man slither away out of sheer laziness, now he would throw the book at him for the landed punch.

Jade came out of the stable. "What's going on?"

"The man who's been watching you showed up again. I called Bud."

Jade's jaw dropped. "I've seen that guy! He was parked behind me in town. At a certain angle, he looks like the man who held a gun to my head in the stable."

"I'm calling Knox. We're going to find out who he is and why he's stalking you."

The man who had been watching Jade's house admitted he was Roman Blackwell, a former associate of Livia's, and according to the FBI, a suspected general in Livia's crime organization.

Knox, Jade and Declan were observing the interview between Blackwell and the FBI agents investigating Livia Colton's jailbreak.

Bud was pacing in his office, phone pressed to his ear. He was speaking on a tan landline, the curling wire attached to the base whipping back and forth as he moved around the room. His face was red and the middle button on his shirt had popped open.

Agent Monroe was seated at the head of the table, taking notes with a red pen. Agent Fielder questioned Blackwell from the corner of the room. His arms were folded and he tapped his foot every few seconds.

"Come on, Blackwell. You've got a dozen outstanding warrants for your arrest. You added more charges today. Level with me about Livia Colton and I'll see about getting some of the lesser charges dropped."

Blackwell's mouth was drawn into a thin line. His

dark hair matched his pencil-thin mustache. "I don't know where Livia Colton is."

The agents exchanged looks. "Too bad. Because that piece of information would be highly valuable. Like the biggest get-out-of-jail card possible."

Blackwell tapped his handcuffs against the table. "You're not the only ones looking for her."

"Who else is looking for her?" Monroe asked.

Blackwell forced a cruel bark of laughter. "She hurt many people. She kept her mouth shut in prison, which kept her from meeting her end. But there are those waiting for their due."

"What does Livia owe you?" Fielder asked, leaning on the table.

"Livia had contingency plans for everything. And contingency plans if those went wrong. Escaping prison was bound to happen. Sticking around this area must mean she has resources hidden. She had stash houses all over the country. No way they've all been found," Blackwell said.

"What do you think she has hidden in Shadow Creek?" Monroe asked.

"I heard about a rare set of gold coins that went missing twenty years ago. Then I heard that Livia had been overseeing the transaction. The coins didn't go missing. She had them. She couldn't have fenced them back then without being found out. I heard from a friend in the district attorney's office that they were not listed in the inventory of the items confiscated from the house."

Jade set her hand on Declan's elbow. "He believes she's sticking around for those coins."

Declan didn't think Blackwell knew the whole story. If Livia wanted the coins and knew where they were, she would grab them and go. "Could be part of her reason for staying."

"What's the other part?" Jade asked.

"To terrorize us," Knox said. "What else?"

Idling in her pickup truck outside the small blue clapboard house, Jade had no idea how to move forward. The house had a narrow porch and bare gardens. A cross was hung on the front door and the gravel driveway had an old beige sedan parked in it.

Declan's mother, Beatrice, was still alive. He had not spoken to her since she had abandoned him, on the street to fend for himself. After speaking to Declan the other night about his trials with his father's death and his mother, he needed to speak with her and find closure to the situation. Though it was incomprehensible to imagine how Beatrice could have left him, she must have had her reasons.

Arguing with herself about it, Jade was hesitant to get involved, except she could see how much it hurt Declan. A man of Declan's means could hire a PI to find his mother and he hadn't.

With Hawk's help, Jade found a lead on Beatrice Sinclair. She had changed her name to Beatrice Lake. Armed with that information, Jade was surprised how much of Hawk's guidance had to do with using the right online resources. Beatrice had volunteered information about herself in the form of a publicly accessible social media account. Though she didn't have many pictures, Jade wondered about the woman who said nothing about her late husband, Matthew, or her son. Only posted were pictures of Beatrice's second husband and what looked like her teenaged daughter. More surprising, Beatrice was living twenty minutes outside Shadow Creek.

When Jade had presented him with the information, Declan had been willing to come to the house. Jade was having second thoughts. Declan might not want his mother in his life. He could have hired a PI to find her. It could have been a step he was afraid to make, or it could have been a step he did not want to make, and now she had pushed the issue.

"What if she isn't the same Beatrice Sinclair?" Declan asked.

Jade touched his shirtsleeve. He was normally so confident and yet she could feel the self-consciousness and worry pulsing from him. "Then tell her that you're sorry for bothering her and leave."

"What will I say if she is?" Declan asked.

Jade shifted in her seat, adjusting her seat belt to be able to look at Declan. "She might recognize you. You'll have to stay calm. That will be hard in an emotionally charged situation."

"Will you come with me?"

She would be by his side, though her mere presence presented a complication. "She might recognize me as a Colton, which could understandably anger her."

"That's okay. After what she did, I'm not sure that she has the right to judge."

Jade recognized Beatrice Lake when she stepped out of her house. Jade slid lower in her seat, hoping the glare of the morning sun hid her. Beatrice was one of the members of The Victims of Livia Colton who had protested outside of her house. But now, it blew her mind to think about how close Declan had been living to his mother and yet they hadn't connected.

The same way that Livia Colton was in Shadow Creek and she remained elusive.

Declan was halfway out of the car before Jade realized his intentions. She scrambled to follow him, wanting to be close without crowding him. He stood at the end of the sidewalk, silent and unmoving.

His mother started when she saw him. "Oh, you surprised me." Beatrice looked at Jade and her eyes narrowed. "What are you doing at my home?"

Declan folded his arms across his chest. "You've been to her home. At least she isn't shouting and holding a sign. You know we could. I have a lot to say about a woman who protests a Colton, but threw away a child."

Beatrice's mouth fell open. "How did you know that?" The words escaped on a choked whisper. "I never told anyone."

Then her hand clamped over her mouth and she started to cry. "You're Declan. You're the little boy I gave away."

She fell to her knees and covered her face. Declan

said nothing. He wasn't moving. Perhaps her display of emotion was enough to prove she felt bad. She was speaking, but it was impossible to hear through her sobs.

A man came out of the house, alarm written on his face. "Bea! Beatrice? What did you do to her? Who are you?"

Beatrice's daughter came to the screen door, but she didn't come outside.

Beatrice's husband was yelling now, confused. "Who are you people? Wait, I recognize you. You're the daughter of Livia Colton. The youngest one."

The words didn't upset Jade the way they usually did.

Declan stepped in front of Jade protectively. "I'm Declan Sinclair. Beatrice is my mother."

Declan felt no obligation to stay, but he had come this far and he had questions to ask his mother. Jade sat quietly on Beatrice's back porch. Her husband was fixing them iced tea and her daughter was watching from the window.

"I've thought of you every day since I left you," Beatrice said.

Small comfort. "Why? Why did you leave?" Declan was keeping a lid on his anger. His mother didn't look the way he remembered. She had deep lines around her eyes and mouth and across her forehead. Of slender build, she seemed almost frail.

"I couldn't take care of you," Beatrice said.

"You felt the only option was to drive me across state lines and leave me on the street?"

Beatrice flinched but Declan didn't feel he had to temper his words. It was the truth of what had happened. "I wasn't thinking clearly."

"Why Louisiana? Do you know how scared I was? I had never been there."

Though his volume was low, the sharpness in his tone was brutal. If Beatrice started to cry again, Declan would leave. His mother had disappointed him then and she was a disappointment now.

Instead of breaking down, Beatrice straightened. "You had been to Louisiana before."

Declan stared. Not that he could recall.

"When you were a little boy, your father and I took you there for Mardi Gras. You loved it. It was exciting and fun. You danced and clapped along to the music and you gathered so many beads. When your father killed himself, all I could think about was that happy time and how much you liked Mardi Gras. I thought about Livia Colton coming for you. You don't know how evil she was, Declan. She controlled this town. She made people disappear. I didn't know what danger your father had put us in getting involved with her. I felt I had to protect you. If I went to the authorities and asked for help, they would have taken you, but then she could have gotten to you."

Declan heard the fear and desperation in his mother's voice. "You could have run and stayed with me."

"That would have been the right thing to do. But

your father committed suicide and I was going out of my mind with fear and worry. I made a terrible mistake. By the time I realized that and tried to find you, I'd learned you were in the foster system. I didn't have money for a lawyer to get you back and I knew my mistake would cost me," Beatrice said.

Declan heard her love for him. She had cared. She had been sick and panicked, but she had cared. That realization opened a part of his heart he had closed off.

"How are you involved with The Victims of Livia Colton support group?" Declan asked.

Beatrice glanced at Jade.

"Please, tell him. It's okay," Jade said.

"I needed to be part of a group who understood my anger. After our family broke down, I lost everything. I had nothing. Your father had spent our savings on gifts for her. He took out a loan against the house for her. He ran up our credit card bills. Without him and being upside down on the house and in debt, I fell apart. What I did to you was wrong and under other circumstance, incomprehensible. But at the time, I did what I could to protect you. I admitted myself to a mental hospital. When I was better and I started my life over, I kept tabs on you. I never told anyone you were my son. I felt like I would be taking credit for something I didn't do. But I have never stopped loving you, Declan. Do you want to meet your sister, Sarah?"

She had been lingering in the doorway. At the mention of her name, she came outside.

Declan extended his hand. "Hi, I'm Declan."

Sarah ignored his hand and hugged him instead.

Jade caught a glimpse of Declan through the window. He was standing behind her house with wood between two sawhorses to create a makeshift table. In front of him were unrolled scrolls of paper, held open with gray rocks on each corner. At the sight of him, her heart beat faster. He had mentioned earlier that day he had something special planned for the night. It had been on her mind for hours; she'd been wondering.

It was two-dollar margarita night at El Torero's, but she had the feeling it was something more than that. In the last few days, since talking to his mother, he had been acting differently. Not in a bad way. The conversation with Beatrice and Sarah had changed him.

Beatrice had spoken to The Victims of Livia Colton group and they had toned down their protests. They were still running their website and dedicating themselves to bringing Livia to justice, but the Colton siblings hadn't reported any protests at their homes.

Jade tapped on the window and Declan looked over his shoulder at her. He waved her outside. Jade was barefoot and she slid on a pair of sneakers she had lying by the back door.

"What are you doing out here?" she asked. The

weather was warm, but the occasional breeze felt great. It made her happy to have a job working outdoors.

"Making plans," Declan said.

He was looking across her land, the fenced pasture where she grazed her horses and beyond that, the untouched land she hadn't yet made plans for. More room for her horses and maybe an expansion of her stables. "Plans for what?"

He stepped to the side and showed her the drawing he was looking at. White paper with blue sketches. It almost looked like her father's barn and it took her a minute to follow.

"You want to move my father's barn here?"

He nodded. "I spoke with Allison and she has a specialist in mind for the job. You'll have a piece of your father with you at Hill Country."

Tears of happiness filled her eyes, blurring her vision. "That's incredibly nice of you. What made you think of it?"

"I saw the look on your face when I spoke of the barn. When you were looking around inside it, I could see the happiness on your face. I want you to have it."

Jade hugged him.

He was trembling slightly.

"Are you cold?" Jade asked.

Declan released her. "I'm not cold. I have something important I want to talk to you about." Then he dropped to one knee and took a ring from his pocket. Holding it out to her between his thumb and index finger, he knelt before her. "Jade, I need you in my life. I love coming home to you each night and I love our conversations. Most of all, I love you. Will you be my wife?"

Jade couldn't take her eyes off Declan's. "Yes, I'll marry you. I love you too, Declan." She threw herself against him, knocking him to the ground.

They laughed and Declan slid the ring on her finger. "I also have one more piece of news."

Jade's heart already felt so full, she didn't know if she could take anymore.

"I called your father's family in Argentina. After I move the barn, they will deliver a foal that is a descendant of one of your father's favorite horses. Your grandparents would very much like to meet you and get to know you."

Jade and Declan sat in the grass. Jade laid her head on Declan's shoulder. "For so long, I felt like I didn't belong anywhere. That I was an outsider in my family and since I had lost my father, I didn't belong anywhere. But now I feel like I'm part of something more."

They sat outside as the sunset and the moon rose higher in the sky, the shiny lights from the stars twinkling above them, like good luck wishes for the future.

Jade couldn't take her eyes off her engagement ring. It had only been four days and every time it caught her eye, she felt butterflies all over again.

Declan was at physical therapy for his shoulder and she had time to think about their wedding.

Funny, she had never considered herself the type of woman who wanted a big wedding, but now, she couldn't stop thinking about flowers and dresses and menu ideas. Obviously, she would invite her whole family and their significant others and Declan's mother, stepfather and half sister. They would move on from the hurts of the past and build something real together.

She heard a noise behind her and turned to welcome Declan home. His shoulder was doing much better and his physical therapist expected he would regain full use of it.

When she turned, she came face-to-face with her mother holding a gun. Livia looked tired and ragged. Jade had last seen her mother appearing put-together and in control. Now she was wearing ill-fitting clothing, the roots of her hair were dark. Jade felt physically ill. Fear and horror rolled over her.

"Hello, Jade. It's been a long time. Where's your boyfriend?" Livia asked.

The protesters hadn't been around in a few days and now Jade wished they would come by. Or that anyone would. "He's not here."

Livia sneered. "Obviously. He has something I need. Take out your phone, very slowly, and call him."

Jade reached into her back pocket and withdrew her phone. With quaking hands, she called Declan.

"Hey, just finishing up here, about to drive back to the farm," Declan said.

"Declan. I have a problem. Livia is here. She wants something that only you have."

A key. Livia was holding Jade at gunpoint demanding a key.

As he drove, Declan called Knox. Knox said he would alert the authorities, the local sheriff and the FBI, and meet Declan at La Bonne Vie. Declan's heart was racing and he felt almost light-headed, but he had to stay focused and get to Jade. Livia could kill her and finally have the revenge she craved. She wanted the key, but Declan trusted nothing Livia said or did.

Livia's instructions were to bring the key from La Bonne Vie to Hill Country in twenty-five minutes. Drive time alone would take him most of that. Four minutes had passed. His heart was racing and the adrenaline firing through his body was making him simultaneously tuned up and dizzy. To think clearly, he had to stay calm. With Jade's life in Livia's hands, that was impossible.

Declan got out of his car, leaving his high beams on to illuminate the house. A key. Something so small in the house. If it wasn't exactly where Livia said it would be, if it had been moved during construction, he wouldn't find it. Jade would die.

Headlights turned down the long driveway. Declan didn't wait. He entered, knowing the tear-down process had left the house unstable. The floors seemed to shake under his feet. He located a flash-light. The electricity had been turned off in the house and he didn't have time, nor did he know if it was safe, to turn it back on to help aid his search.

He took the stairs to the bathroom where Jade had showed him the hidden cabinet behind the bath-room vanity.

The last time they had looked, it had been empty.

"Declan? Are you here?"

Knox's voice. "Upstairs."

Declan pulled off the door to the secret compart-ment and felt inside. He couldn't find the key. His arm wasn't long enough to reach to the back.

Knox entered the bathroom. "How can I help?"

"We need to move the vanity. Livia believes there's a key in this cabinet, but I can't find it."

Together, they tore the vanity from the wall, throwing it out into the hallway. Then they resumed the search.

With better access, Declan patted around inside the enclosure. The key wasn't there. Using the flash-light to illuminate the space, Declan caught a flash of metal glinting back at him.

Nailed to the top of the compartment was a key. He pulled down on the head of the nail, but it wouldn't budge. "I need a hammer!"

The construction site had a few lying around. Declan maneuvered inside the small space with the hammer and pulled down on the nail, freeing the key. He caught it in his palm.

"This better be it," he said.

The clock was ticking and Knox and Declan raced to their cars. Declan would need to drive like a madman to reach Hill Country in time.

Livia had instructed Declan to come alone. With Jade's life on the line, he wouldn't risk angering Livia. She had asked him to leave his car keys in the ignition with the car running. Once she had the key from La Bonne Vie, she would take off.

Livia was waiting for him in the barn. When he entered, Jade was sitting on the floor by her goat pen. The goats were bleating and pigs were moving around their pen, obviously agitated.

When Jade lifted her eyes to meet his, terror shone in them.

"I have the key," Declan said, holding it up. "Let Jade leave and you can have it."

Livia didn't look well. Her face was gaunt, her hair stringy and greasy. Gray hair streaked through her once blond locks. Her clothing was torn and dirty. "You are not in a place to negotiate. Toss me the key."

Declan threw the key high and to the right. Livia reached for it, taking her attention off Jade. Jade rolled away and Declan launched forward, tackling Livia. His shoulder burned where he had been injured, but he ignored it. He had to protect Jade.

Declan reached for the gun, forcing Livia's arm away. The gun went off.

Adrenaline fired through him. Knox, Mac, River, and Thorne had been waiting outside. They rushed into the barn.

Livia was shrieking and fighting to get free of Declan's grasp, but he wasn't letting her get away. She had to be stopped. Her reign of terror ended tonight.

Knox, River and Declan subdued Livia, tying her hands behind her back.

"I will never go back to prison," Livia said. "Be smart. I have allies. Rich allies. Let me go and I'll make it worth your while. This key is important. It's the only way to open a security box I have with priceless treasures. One of these coins, and you'll be rich beyond your wildest dreams."

Then Roman Blackwell had been right about the coins. Livia did have them hidden away.

"You killed my father. You are a liar and a cheat. Why would any of us let you go?" Jade asked. Her voice was calm and Declan was thrilled she had this opportunity to speak her mind.

Livia narrowed her eyes. "You. It was you who turned me over to the authorities."

Declan hugged Jade and ignored Livia's ranting. No one was interested in a bribe from Livia. "I am so glad you're safe."

"Isn't this interesting? Matthew Sinclair's little boy falling for my daughter," Livia said.

Declan heard manipulation and calculation in her voice. She was likely already thinking of ways to hurt them and pull them apart. The trouble with Livia's plan was that he and Jade were stronger than ever before. Nothing could tear them apart. They had truth and trust between them.

"You betrayed your family, your own mother, and

for what? So you could go live in a run-down ranch house with Mac?" Livia's voice was shrill and shrieking. The more Declan and Jade ignored her, the more panicked she seemed to become.

Mac glanced over, but said nothing.

"Mac was a better parent to me than you ever were," Jade said.

Livia snorted. "One of you will let me go. This isn't how family treats each other."

The Coltons exchanged glances. They weren't releasing Livia. They had their own definition of family now: the people who kept each other safe, the people who loved each other. Livia wasn't part of either of those.

Special Agents Monroe and Fielder arrived on the scene. They handcuffed and leg cuffed Livia. She shuffled to their car and they pushed her inside. As they watched her drive away, a sense of relief washed over Declan.

He wrapped his arms around Jade. "I was terrified she would kill you."

"I thought she would kill me too," Jade said. "While I was waiting for you, she ranted about the problems she had with my brothers and sisters. How none of us helped her in prison and how she would make us pay by killing us."

"She can't hurt you now or ever again. She's out of our lives forever and I'll be at your side for the rest of your life, making sure of it," Declan said.

"And now we can have a fresh start and a new life together."

Epilogue

La Bonne Vie had been torn to the ground, the tunnels leading to it blasted shut and the plans for Fabrizio's barn being transported to Hill Country were in the works. Declan was pleased with the progress that had been made in a few short weeks. The Coltons and their closest friends were gathering for a potluck picnic to celebrate the good things in their lives. After spending time in county lockup, Livia was en route to prison, escorted by Special Agents Fielder and Monroe.

Beatrice, her husband and Sarah had come to the picnic. Sarah seemed to look up to Declan and she was excited to talk to Jade about her horses.

The next phase of their lives would be leaps and bounds better than their past. Now each would have marriages, babies and career success. Thorne and Mac were in the process of securing a loan to purchase the La Bonne Vie land from Declan and were expanding their ranch. Edith and Declan were relocating their company's headquarters to Shadow Creek. Declan was selling his estate in Louisiana and Albert was handling prospective buyers. Business was booming for River and Joshua, and River was opening an office in Shadow Creek. Hawk and Leonor were talking about having a destination wedding in Venice. Evelyn and Mac were planning to marry the following spring at Mac's ranch. Allison and Knox were talking about having another baby, to make Cody a big brother.

Jade and Declan's engagement had been wonderful news for the family.

Jade couldn't remember the last time she had been this happy.

She had even noticed a gentleness and genuine warmth between River and Declan when River had offered his congratulations on their engagement. Jade hoped she and Edith could be good friends and help bring the brothers closer.

Jade's greatest strength was her family and that would continue with every new member, by birth or by marriage or by love.

Declan's phone buzzed and he stepped away to answer. Jade watched him, admiring how handsome he was, the seriousness of his face and his perfect mouth. He would be her husband. Unlike her mother, Jade would be a good wife, loyal and true and when they had a family, they would come first always, not just in pictures.

Except now Declan was frowning. Putting the phone back in his pocket.

"That was Agent Fielder. He and Monroe were in a car accident driving from county lockup to the prison. During a storm, their car went off the road and into Stony Bend River. They are okay, but they can't find Livia or her body."

The area around Stony Bend wasn't well populated and that made the terrain treacherous, with no available food or water.

"If she wasn't killed in the crash," River said.

"She's still handcuffed and in leg irons," Mac said.

"That river is filled with gators," Knox said.

"And water moccasins, rattlesnakes and copperheads," Leonor said.

"Cougars," Mac said.

"Coyotes," Edith said.

"Wolves," Evelyn said.

"Scorpions," Allison said.

Declan put his arm around Jade. "Even if she did survive, she can't hurt us. We'll stay together like we've done, and Livia won't stand a chance of hurting any of us again."

* * * * *

Love pulse-spiking romance and
spine-tingling suspense?
Don't miss this exclusive excerpt from
FATAL THREAT
The latest FATAL *book from* New York Times
bestselling author Marie Force!

A JOGGER SPOTTED the body floating in the Anacostia River just south of the John Philip Sousa Bridge.

"I hate these kinds of calls," Lieutenant Sam Holland said to her partner, Detective Freddie Cruz, as she battled District traffic on their way to the city's southeastern quadrant. "No one knows if this is a homicide, but they call us in anyway. We get to stand around and sweat our balls off while the ME does her thing."

"I hesitate to point out, Lieutenant, that you don't actually *have* balls to sweat off."

"You know what I mean!"

"Yeah, I do," he said with a sigh. "It's going to be a long, hot, smelly Friday down at the river waiting to find out if we're needed."

"I gotta have a talk with Dispatch about when we're to be called and when we are *not* to be called."

"Let me know how that goes."

"To make this day even better, after work I have to go to a fitting for my freaking bridesmaid dress. I'm too damned old to be a damned bridesmaid."

His snort of laughter only served to further irritate her, which of course made him laugh harder.

"It's not funny!"

"Yeah, it really is." With dark brown hair, an always-tan complexion and the perfect amount of stubble on his jaw, he really was too cute for words, not that she'd *ever* tell him that. Everywhere they went together, women took notice of him. For all he cared. He was madly in love with Elin Svendsen and looking forward to their autumn wedding. Wiping laughter tears from his brown eyes, he said, "I won't make you wear a dress when you're my best-man woman."

"Thank God for that. I need to stop making friends. That was my first mistake."

"Poor Jeannie," he said of their colleague, Detective Jeannie McBride, who was getting married next weekend. "Does she have any idea that she has a hostile bridesmaid in her wedding party?"

"Of course she does. Her sisters left me completely out of the planning of the shower, no doubt at her request. I'll be forever grateful for that small favor." Sam shuddered recalling an afternoon of horrifyingly stupid "shower games," paper plates full of ribbons and bows, and dirty jokes about the wedding night for two people who'd been living together for more than a year. The whole thing had given her hives.

But Jeannie… She'd loved every second of it, and seeing her face lit up with joy had gone a long way toward alleviating Sam's hives. After everything Jeannie had been through to get to her big day, no one was happier for her—or happier to stand up for her—than Sam. Not that she'd ever tell anyone that, either. She had a reputation to maintain, after all.

She'd been in an unusually cranky mood since her husband, Nick, left for Iran two weeks ago for what should've been a five-day trip but had twice been extended. If he didn't get home soon, she wouldn't be responsible for her actions. In addition to worrying about his safety in a country known for being less than friendly toward Americans, she'd also discovered how entirely reliant upon him she'd become over the last year and a half. It was ridiculous, really. She was a strong, independent woman who'd taken care of herself for years before he'd come back into her life. So how had he turned her into a simpering, whimpering, cranky mess simply by leaving her for two damned weeks?

Naturally, the people around her had noticed that she was out of sorts. Their adopted thirteen-year-old son, Scotty, asked every morning before he left for baseball camp when Dad would be home, probably because he was tired of dealing with her by himself. Freddie and the others at work had been giving her a wide berth, and even the reporters who hounded her mercilessly had backed off after she'd bitten their heads off a few too many times.

During infrequent calls from Nick, he'd been rushed and annoyed and equally out of sorts, which didn't do much to help her bad mood. Two more days. Two more long, boring, joyless days and then he'd be home and things could get back to normal.

What did it say about her that she was actually *glad* to have a floater to deal with to keep her brain occupied during the last two days of Nick's trip? *It means you have it bad for your husband, and you've become far too dependent on him if two weeks without him turns you into a cranky cow.* Sam despised her voice of reason almost as much as she despised Nick being so far away from her for so long.

Twenty minutes after receiving the call from Dispatch, Sam and Freddie made it to M Street Southeast, which was lined with emergency vehicles of all sorts—police, fire, EMS, medical examiner.

"Major overkill for a floater," Sam said as they got out of the car she'd parked illegally to join the party on the riverbank. "What the hell is EMS doing here?"

"Probably for the guy who found the body. Word is he was shook up."

Dense humidity hit her at the same time as the funk of the rank-smelling river. "God, it's hotter than the devil's dick today."

"Honestly, Sam. That's disgusting."

"Well, you gotta figure the devil's dick is pretty hot due to the neighborhood he hangs in, right?"

He rolled his eyes and held up the yellow crime-scene tape for her. Patrol had taped off the Anacostia Riverwalk Trail to keep the gawkers away.

The closer they got to the river's edge, the more Sam began to regret the open-toe sandals she'd worn in deference to the oppressive July heat. The squish of Anacostia River mud between her toes was almost as gross as the smell of the river itself. She had her shoulder-length hair up in a clip that left her neck exposed to the merciless sun.

Tactical Response teams had boats on the scene, and from her vantage point on the riverbank, Sam could see the red ponytail belonging to the Chief Medical Examiner, Dr. Lindsey McNamara. She was too far out for Sam to yell to her for an update.

"Let's talk to the guy who called it in," she said to Freddie.

They traipsed back the way they'd come, with Sam trying to ignore the disgusting mud between her toes. Officer Beckett worked the tapeline at the northern end of the area they'd cordoned off. He nodded at them. "Afternoon, Lieutenant. Lovely day to spend by the river."

"Indeed. I would've packed a picnic had I known we were coming. Where's the guy who called it in?"

"Over there with EMS." Beckett pointed to a cluster of people taking advantage of the shade under a huge oak tree. "He was hysterical when he realized the blob was a body."

"Did you get a name?"

Beckett consulted his notebook. "Mike Lonergan. He works at the Navy Yard and runs out here every day at noon." He tore out the page that had Lonergan's full name, address and cell phone number written on it and gave it to Sam.

"Good work, Beckett. Thanks. Keep everyone out of here until we know whether or not this is a crime scene."

"Yes, ma'am. Will do."

"Why would anyone run out here during the hottest part of the day?" Sam asked Freddie as they made their way to where Lonergan was being seen to by the paramedics.

"For something called exercise, I'd imagine."

"When did you become such a smart-ass? You used to be such a nice Christian boy."

"Things began to go south for me when I got assigned to a smart-ass lieutenant who's been a terrible influence on my sweet, young mind."

"Right." Amused by him as always, Sam drew out the single word for effect. "You were easily led." She approached the paramedics who were hovering over Lonergan. "We'd like a word with Mr. Lonergan," she said to the one who seemed to be in charge.

He used a hand motion to tell his team to allow her and Freddie in. The witness wore a tank top, running shorts and high-tech running shoes. Sam put him at midthirties.

"Mr. Lonergan, I'm Lieutenant Holland—"

"I know who you are." His shoulders were wrapped in one of those foil thingies that runners used to keep from dehydrating or overheating or something like that. What did she know about such things? She got most of her exercise having wild sex with her husband. Except for recently, thus her foul mood.

Lonergan's dark blond hair was wet with perspiration. His brown eyes were big and haunted as he looked up at them.

"Can you tell us what you saw?" Ever since she'd taken down a killer at the inaugural parade, she was recognized everywhere she went. She hated that and yearned for the days when no one recognized her. But that ship had sailed the minute her sexy young husband became the nation's vice president late last year. Her blown cover was entirely his fault, and she liked to remind him of that every chance she got.

"I was running on the trail like I do every day, and when I came around that bend there, I saw something in the water." He took a drink from a bottle of water, and Sam took note of the slight tremble in his hand. "At first I thought it was a garbage bag, but when I looked closer, I saw a hand." He shuddered. "That's when I called 911."

"How far out was it?" Sam asked.

"About twenty feet from the bank of the river."

"Was there anything else you could tell us about the body?"

"I think it's a woman."

"Why do you say that?" Freddie asked.

"There was hair." Lonergan took another drink of water. "Once I realized what I was looking at, I could see long hair fanned out around the head." He looked up at them. "Do you think it's that student who went missing?"

Sam made sure her expression gave nothing away. "We'd have no way to know that at this point." The entire Metro PD had been searching for nineteen-year-old Ruby Denton for more than two weeks. She'd come to the District to take summer classes at Capitol University and hadn't been seen since her first night on campus. The story had garnered national attention thanks in large part to the efforts of her family in Kentucky.

"I bet it's her," Lonergan said.

"Do me a favor and keep that thought to yourself for now. No sense upsetting the family before we know anything for certain."

"That's true."

Sam handed him her card. "If you think of anything else, let me know."

"I will." After a pause, he said, "I was out here yesterday, and she wasn't there. I would've noticed if she'd been there."

"That's good to know. Thanks for your help."

"It's sad, you know? For someone to end up like that."

"Yes, it is." She stepped away from him to confer with the paramedic in charge. "Is he okay?"

"Yeah, he's in shock. He'll be fine. You think it's Ruby Denton?"

"I'll tell you the same thing I just told him—we have no way to know until Dr. McNamara gets the body back to the lab. Until then, we'd be speculating, and that sort of thing only makes a hellish situation worse for a family looking for their daughter. Ask your people to keep their mouths shut."

"Yes, ma'am. No one will hear anything from my team."

"Thank you."

"What's going on over there?" Freddie asked, drawing Sam's attention to the tapeline, where Beckett was arguing with a bunch of suits.

"Let's go find out."

They walked back the way they'd come, along the trail to where Beckett held his own against four men in suits with reflective glasses and attitudes that immediately identified them as federal agents.

"What's the problem, gentlemen?" Sam asked.

"There she is," one of them said in a low growl that immediately raised Sam's hackles.

"Let us in," another one said. "Right now."

"I'm not letting you in until you tell me what you want," Beckett said. "This is a potential crime scene—"

"We need to speak to Mrs. Cappuano." The one who seemed to be in charge of the Fed squad took another step forward. "It's urgent."

Sam's heart dropped to her belly and for a brief, horrifying second she feared her legs would give out under her. *Nick...* Why would federal agents have tracked her down at a crime scene in the middle of her workday unless something had happened to him?

Please no.

Sam immediately began bargaining with a higher

power she didn't believe in. She'd give up anything, anything in this world except Scotty, if it would keep the man in front of her from saying words that could never be unsaid or unheard.

Only Freddie's arm around her shoulders kept her from buckling in the few seconds it took for Sam to recover herself enough to speak. "What do you want with me?"

"We need you to come with us, ma'am."

"That's not happening until you tell us who you are and what you want," Freddie said.

In unison they flashed four federal badges.

"United States Secret Service," the one in charge said. "We need you to come with us, ma'am."

Sam didn't recognize any of them. Why would she? Nick's detail was in Iran, and Scotty's was with him. "I… I'm working here. I can't…" Bile burned her throat as her lunch threatened to reappear. With her heart beating so hard she could hear the echo of it strumming in her ears, she somehow managed to choke back the nausea. Later she'd be thankful she hadn't puked on the agents' shoes. Right now, however, she couldn't think about anything other than Nick. "Has something happened to my husband?"

Freddie tightened his grip on her shoulder, letting her know his thoughts mirrored hers. That didn't do much to comfort her.

Looking down at her with a stone-faced glare, the agent said, "We're under orders to bring you in. We're not at liberty to discuss the particulars with you at this time."

"What the hell does that mean?" Freddie asked. "You can't just take her. She's not under Secret Service protection, and she's working."

"I'm afraid we *can* take her, and we will, by force if necessary."

"What the fuck?" Beckett spoke for all of them. At some point he'd moved to the other side of her.

Like someone flipped a switch, they moved with military precision, busting through the tapeline, grabbing hold of her arms and quickly extracting her before her stunned colleagues could react. Sam fought them, but she was no match for four huge, muscled, well-dressed men who whisked her away with frightening efficiency.

In the background, she could hear Freddie and Beckett screaming, swearing—at least Beckett was—and giving chase, but they, too, were no match for this group. Before she knew what hit her, she was inside the cool darkness of one in the Secret Service's endless fleet of black SUVs, the doors locking with a sound that echoed like a shotgun blast.

"Move," the agent in charge ordered.

The car lurched forward just as Freddie and Beckett reached it. Freddie pounded once against the side window with a closed fist before the car pulled out of his reach.

Sam watched the scene unfold around her with a detached feeling of shock and fear. Something awful must've happened. That was the only possible reason for this dramatic scene. She was far too afraid for Nick to work up the fury she'd normally feel at being kidnapped by federal agents. Her hands were shaking, and her entire body was covered in cold chills.

If Nick had been harmed in some way or if he was… *No, no, no, not going there.* If he was hurt, what did it matter if Secret Service agents had grabbed her? What would anything matter?

She bit back the overwhelming fear and forced herself to focus. "Would someone please tell me what's going on here?"

Don't miss the explosive new book in
New York Times *bestselling author*
Marie Force's FATAL *series*

FATAL THREAT

Available August 2017 wherever
Harlequin HQN titles are sold.

Get 2 Free Books,
Plus 2 Free Gifts—
just for trying the Reader Service!

ROMANTIC suspense

*After befriending Mandy Wright in a snowstorm,
Brody Booth is certain they'll stay "just friends." That
is, until a killer forces Brody into a protector role that
brings all his worst fears about himself to bear.*

Read on for a sneak preview of
SHELTERED BY THE COWBOY
by New York Times bestselling author Carla Cassidy,
the next thrilling installment of
THE COWBOYS OF HOLIDAY RANCH.

Most people gave him a wide berth, but not Mandy. He shoved those thoughts away. She was nothing more to him than a woman in trouble, and he just happened to be in a position to help her. It was nothing more than that and nothing less.

He left the bathroom and blinked in surprise. All the lights were off except a nightstand lamp next to Mandy's bed and the glow of two lit candles on the same stand. The room now smelled of apples and cinnamon.

"I hope you don't mind the candles. I always light a couple before I go to sleep."

"I don't mind," he replied. Hell yes, he minded the candles that painted her face in beautiful shadows and light. Hell yes, he minded the candles that made the room feel so much smaller and much more intimate.

He walked over to the sofa and found a bed pillow and a soft, hot pink blanket. He placed his gun on the coffee table, unfolded the blanket and then stretched out.

HRSEXP0817

"All settled?" she asked.

"I'm good," he replied.

She turned off the lamp, leaving only the candlelight radiance to create a small illumination. Too much illumination. From his vantage point he could see her snuggled beneath the covers. He closed his eyes.

"Brody?"

"Yeah?" he answered without opening his eyes.

"Somehow, some way I'll make all this up to you."

Visions instantly exploded in his head, erotic visions of the two of them making love. He jerked his head to halt them. "You don't have to make anything up to me," he said gruffly. "Now let's get some sleep."

"Okay. Good night, Brody."

"Good night," he replied.

Seconds ticked by and then minutes. When he finally opened his eyes again she appeared to be sleeping. Candlelight danced across her features, highlighting her brows, her cheekbones and her lips.

He couldn't be her friend. She was too much of a temptation and he couldn't be friends with a woman he wanted. He didn't want to be friends with anyone.

He'd see her through this threat, and then he had to walk away from her and never look back.

Don't miss
SHELTERED BY THE COWBOY by Carla Cassidy,
available September 2017 wherever
Harlequin® Romantic Suspense books
and ebooks are sold.

www.Harlequin.com

HRSEXP0817

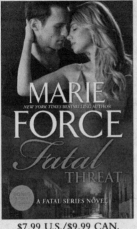

Turn your love of reading into rewards you'll love with

Harlequin My Rewards

**Join for FREE today at
www.HarlequinMyRewards.com**

Earn **FREE BOOKS** of your choice.

Experience **EXCLUSIVE OFFERS** and contests.

Enjoy **BOOK RECOMMENDATIONS**
selected just for you.

PLUS! Sign up now
and get **500** points
right away!

Earn
FREE
REWARDS
HarlequinMyRewards.com
Join
Today!

MYR16R